## The Zero Trap

Paula Gosling, an American by birth and education, came to England in 1964. She worked in several advertising agencies as a copywriter and married an Englishman in 1968.

She has two daughters who she says are patient and pragmatic and have learnt to make their own sandwiches. They live in Bath with a cat who, she claims, 'knows considerably more about everything than we do, but won't explain any of it'.

Also by Paula Gosling
in Pan Books
**A Running Duck**

Paula Gosling

# The Zero Trap

Pan Books in association with
Macmillan London

First published 1979 by Macmillan London Ltd
This edition published 1980 by Pan Books Ltd,
Cavaye Place, London SW10 9PG
in association with Macmillan London Ltd
© Paula Gosling 1979
ISBN 0 330 26174 6
Printed and bound in Great Britain by
Richard Clay (The Chaucer Press) Ltd, Bungay, Suffolk

**for Tony** – another incarnation

It was a white telephone beneath a vase of hothouse roses.
It rang once.

The man's hand was carefully manicured, emerging from
immaculate linen and the shot silk sleeve of a dinner jacket.

'Well ?'

'It is on the runway now.'

'And she *is* on it ?'

'Yes.'

'And our friend ?'

'Also.'

'Very well. Proceed.'

And the phone went down.

# One

All the engines were running, their low roar felt as much as heard through the metal fabric of the plane. Laura fastened her seatbelt in dutiful response to the light on the bulkhead, and leaned back against the seat. Outside, the glare of the setting sun bounced back from the concrete of the runway and hammered at her eyes until she closed them. The interior of the plane was still filled with the heat of the afternoon, and she hoped they would take off soon. Cool distant air, she yearned for it.

The past six weeks had baked all the energy from her, left her numbed by the luxury, pomp and circumstances of her mother's life. It was obvious her mother was happy, revelling in the society of which she was automatic queen by virtue of her new husband's position in the hierarchy of the oil company. But to Laura the brittle chatter, laughter and competition for meaningless social ascendance had been terrifying. Everyone seemed to be all flashing white teeth in tanned faces, their gold and diamonds worn like cheap beads, their eyes never still.

'My daughter, everyone, come and meet my daughter,' her mother had summoned. 'Little Laura – not so little anymore.' (Much supportive laughter required here.) 'Her Daddy finally let her out of his sight to visit her dreadful, dreadful mother. Afraid I'll seduce her to the rich life . . . I'm an *evil* influence, you see!'

Oh, mother, Laura thought, you aren't, you never were. Just afraid of dying unseen on that other desert air of Army life.

'Hello.'

She had prayed no one would sit near her. She had seen

9

the long hours of flight in the near-empty plane as an opportunity to get back to herself again. She opened her eyes, prepared to be polite, and found herself staring directly into the face of a small boy. He was about eight, dressed in a white shirt and dark shorts, with a sweetly rounded face and large grey eyes. Around his neck hung an enormous pair of binoculars, and he was leaning against the armrest ready to run down the aisle if she looked the least bit cross at being disturbed.

'Hello,' Laura said, relieved. 'What's your name?'

'Timothy Andrew Morgan. What's yours?'

'Laura Amanda Louise Ainslie.'

He thought about that for a moment, then pronounced. 'La-la.'

She laughed, she couldn't help it, he looked so serious. 'What?'

'Your initials – they make La-la. Mine make Tam.'

'So they do. I never thought about that before.'

He settled himself on the armrest, encouraged. 'You can find lots of words in other words if you look for them, you know.'

'Tell me one.'

'Well . . . there's a rat in separate – and a ring in staring.'

'So there are. How about a cat in vacate?'

'What's vacate?'

'To leave . . . to get out of a place.'

'Oh.' He fiddled with the binoculars which nearly covered the whole of his narrow chest, then slid down into the seat next to hers. 'Then the plane will vacate the airport, won't it?'

'Yes, I suppose it will. Sort of.'

Movement caught her eye and she looked up. An attractive, freshly made-up but harassed looking woman stood in the aisle, her handbag held tightly. 'Timmy, you'd better come back with me to your seat. I hope he wasn't annoying you.' She was slightly plump and about thirty-five, with large grey eyes like her son's.

'No, of course he wasn't. We were discussing semantics,

as a matter of fact, weren't we, Tim?' His eyes widened at the introduction of yet another new word. She spoke to him as if he were a grown-up person. He decided he liked Laura *very* much, even if she did jump like a rabbit whenever anyone spoke to her.

'I want to stay here,' he told his mother, firmly.

'No . . . come on, Timmy. You can visit later on, if Miss . . .'

'Ainslie, Laura Ainslie. You come back after the plane has gotten right up in the air, Tim. I'll try to think of some other words by then, okay?' Laura could see the woman wanted the boy with her, seemed to need him. Were they travelling alone? She was almost certain she had seen a man enter the plane with them earlier.

'Oh, all right,' Timmy muttered, standing up with enormously exaggerated resignation.

'And *where* did you get those binoculars?' his mother demanded.

'The man said I could look through them. I won't hurt them.' The woman shepherded the boy up the aisle, and Laura saw them stop and speak to someone several rows ahead of her. His mother was telling Timmy to give back the binoculars, they were expensive and he mustn't . . .

The man interrupted gently in a quiet British voice tinged with amusement. 'I know Timothy will be careful. And I do assure you they're very old and not very good . . . perhaps they'll help to pass the time. It will be a long flight, after all.'

'He said he'd tell me the names of the stars when it gets dark,' Timmy wheedled.

'Well . . .'

'It's all right,' the quiet voice murmured. Laura could just see the top of his head over the seats, light brown hair touched with grey. She thought she remembered him getting on, too. A man who kept his eyes down and carried a bulging briefcase close to his chest as he went down the aisle.

'Thank you, Mr . . . ?'

'Skinner. It's a pleasure. Really.'

The woman glanced nervously at the darkfaced steward who was scowling at them. The engines were really very noisy now, and there was a slight lurch as the plane began to taxi toward the runway. With a brief smile Timmy's mother pushed the boy ahead of her and they took their seats. Laura heard a set of clicks, and another male voice that was quickly lost in the tumult of take-off. She closed her eyes and gripped the armrests, annoyed at herself for being frightened by the rush and lift of the plane as it surged into the sky. She'd flown all over the world with her father, she should have been used to it by now. It was just . . . the power of it, and the excitement, too. That's what frightened her. That's what always frightened her, every time.

When the sign winked off, Laura unfastened her seatbelt and sighed. Soon it would begin to be all right. She took out her compact and pretended to powder her nose, staring all the time into the mirror and trying to recognise something, anything, that was familiar. The new 'face' her mother had supervised at the salon sat oddly on her small features. It might be the latest fashion in make-up, but to her it was ugly. And so was the hair style. Closing the gold circle with a snap she got up and made her way to the toilet at the rear of the plane. When she returned Timmy was standing in the aisle next to the man . . . Skinner? . . . and Laura could see one tweed-clad arm extended as he demonstrated how to adjust and use the binoculars. Another glance in the compact assured her that the water *had* taken most of the silly curl out of her hair. Her face felt natural for the first time in weeks, and when she wriggled her nose she could actually feel her skin again.

'You look like a rabbit when you do that.' Timmy had returned.

'Do I?' She put the compact away.

'Mmmm. You've unfastened your hair, too.'

'Unfastened it?'

'Undone it?'

'I just put it back the way I usually wear it, that's all.'

'Ah.' He nodded, fifty-five going on nine. 'A defnit improvement.'

'I'm glad you think so.'

'Yes. I know how to work these now.' He held up the binoculars. 'This way they magnify . . .' he reversed them. 'And this way . . .'

'They smallify?'

He looked at her in disgust. 'That's not a word. Smallify.'

'Well, it should be,' Laura said emphatically. 'Smallify – to make small. It should be a word.'

He plunked himself down and pressed his feet against the back of the empty seat in front. 'Do you like me?'

'Yes. Do you like me?'

'Yes. You're not so old as you were.' He glanced at her sideways. 'I'm going to be an engineer when I'm old.'

'A train engineer?'

He looked disgusted again. 'No . . . a civil engineer, like my dad.'

'Oh. Sorry.'

'I'm not a *baby*, you know.'

'I said I was sorry.'

The steward went down the aisle toward the back of the plane, still scowling, his eyes flicking impatiently over the child. It seemed to Laura he wasn't the most delightful steward she'd ever seen, even on a military flight. He had shown her to her seat without a smile, and had conducted his other duties with a minimum of grace. Obviously the fact that the few passengers had spread themselves widely throughout the cabin annoyed him.

'What are *you* going to be?' Timmy asked.

'When I grow up, you mean?' Laura smiled. 'I'm going to be a wife and have a little boy just like you, I expect. I'd like that.'

He leaned over to inspect her hands. 'But you're not married now, that's only an engagement ring like my Mom has. What does your fi-nance do?'

13

Laura's mouth twitched. 'Oh, he's in the Army. He works with my father.'

'Is your father a soldier?'

'Yes, he is. A general.'

'A *general*?' This was obviously an impressive piece of information. 'A real general with stars and everything?'

'Oh, yes. Three stars, actually.'

'Three?' Timmy breathed. 'Here?' He gestured vaguely toward his own small shoulders, bumping the binoculars against the armrest.

'Yes . . . he . . .'

'Ladies and gentlemen, this is the Captain speaking.' The metallic voice from the loudspeaker interrupted.

'You sure jump around a lot,' Timmy admonished her.

'We're turning out over the Gulf now, and will be ascending to a level of 30,000 feet.' Laura had noticed the slight incline and the movement of the squares of sunlight across the folds of her skirt as the plane banked into its new course. 'We have helpful tail winds and we'll be arriving in Rome slightly ahead of schedule. The weather looks good all the way, so we should have a pleasant flight. Thank you.'

'We're going to London, are you?' Timmy asked when the speaker clicked off.

'No – I'm going on to Oslo to join my father.'

'Why, has he come apart?' Timmy shook hugely with his joke.

'My goodness, I hope not,' Laura said, wide-eyed. 'I glued him together *very* carefully before I left.' Timmy guffawed appreciatively and Laura chuckled at his whole-hearted reaction. Children were so satisfactory. Why couldn't she ever talk this easily to adults? They usually froze her mouth and her mind into total immobility. She heard a voice somewhere behind her, a perfect example of the kind of voice that stopped her cold.

'Well, all right, then give me something to go *with* it. Or is *that* too much to ask?' It was a too-loud voice, with too many expectations in it. A god-dammit voice, her father

14

would call it. He used one himself, when things got out of hand.

She heard the steward's conciliatory murmur and the too-loud voice descended into a mutter of resentment. There was a clink of metal on glass and the steward returned to the front of the plane, his face a carving in sallow anger. She only caught the profile, but it was enough.

She asked Timmy to show her how to use the binoculars, and spent the next ten minutes being carefully, if inaccurately, instructed. She was peering out of the window to her right with Timmy leaning breathily over her shoulder (he refused to take the binoculars off) trying to spot a 'whale' when there was a sudden shriek. It sounded like Timmy's mother, and Laura turned quickly, nearly striking Timmy's ear with the binoculars. He, too, had turned toward the unexpected sound and was now staring at the front of the plane. Everyone was staring at the front of the plane.

At first Laura thought it was the steward, but after a second realised that the man standing by the door to the cockpit was much bulkier than the steward, and much taller. The fact that he had a gas-mask over his features was almost more frightening than the large revolver he held in one hand and the equally large gas cannister he held in the other. His voice was muffled by the mask but his words were clear enough.

'You stay in your seats, please. Not to move, anyone, please.'

Now the steward appeared, also wearing the ugly snouted covering. For a long moment there was utter silence in the plane, and then the too-loud voice came from the rear.

'Oh, for crying out sideways . . . wouldn't you just know it?'

The larger of the two masked men said nothing, simply depressed the valve on the cannister. A sharp hissing sound filled the plane, and Laura put her arms around Timmy, pulling him closer to her. His small body was rigid with either anger, fear, or excitement – she couldn't tell which because he was facing away from her. And then she couldn't tell anything at all, because she was slipping away into unconsciousness, blurring, drifting, going, gone. She never even felt Timmy slump across her lap, his head coming to rest against the sharp edge of the binoculars that lay beneath his rosy cheek.

# Two

Larry Carter stared at the telephone as if it had bitten a piece out of his lip, but there was no sign of blood. Just the dull reflection of the overhead lights curving snake-like around the receiver.

'Will you repeat that, please?'

Again the phone rattled its message of danger, possible death. He reached a long thin hand for pad and pencil, began jotting down relevancies, trying at the same time to word the things he'd say to the General. Accustomed to tracking two or even three things simultaneously, his brain fed facts into one channel, emotions into another. When he put the receiver down he had both categories more or less organised, but it didn't seem to help.

Pushing back his chair he took the pad and walked across the outer office, knocking on the panel and turning the handle of the General's door at the same time. Ainslie looked up from his daily reports and raised an eyebrow at the interruption. He was a large, ungainly man whose aggressive nose dominated an otherwise kindly face. Strangers noticed his nose, but remembered his eyes.

'Sir . . . I've just had a phone call.'

'And?'

Carter came all the way into the large luxurious office and closed the door gently behind him, leaning back against it. 'Flight 816 is missing. The last message they had from it was picked up by Beirut, a standard status transmission, no indication of anything out of the ordinary. Since that time there's been nothing.'

Ainslie dropped the folder he'd been holding onto the desk blotter, his face paling except for two circles of red high on the cheekbones. 'That's Laura's flight, isn't it?'

'Yes, sir, I'm afraid it is.' Larry swallowed hard. 'That's all they have at the moment. The plane was not picked up on Italian radar, nor on Cyprus, nor on Crete. To all appearances it dropped out of airspace less than twenty minutes after take-off. No ship in the area has reported seeing anything, nor have any other flights.'

'Impossible . . . that stretch of water has to be the busiest . . .'

'I know,' Carter agreed, bleakly. 'But there's been nothing. When the flight was ten minutes late being picked up by Crete Control they instituted the standard alerts. In the last twenty minutes they've sent up search planes to follow the flight path but so far . . . nothing from them, either.'

'And they can't raise them on the radio?'

'No, sir. They haven't stopped trying, of course, but no response. There was an Alitalia commercial flight about ten minutes ahead flying parallel five thousand above, but they reported no contact of any kind, sight or radio.'

'There must be a hundred ships . . . liners, fishing boats, Navy . . .'

'And it's still a lot of water, sir.'

'My god . . .' Ainslie whispered. 'She said there was no point wasting money on a . . . the plane was coming across anyway . . . she insisted . . .'

'I know.' Carter's shoulders slumped.

'What kind of a plane was it?' Ainslie demanded, standing up abruptly.

'A 707 converted mostly to freight with a limited passenger accommodation. Last maintenance just two weeks ago, reported perfect. The pilot was an experienced man . . . no problems there.'

'And now no plane.' Ainslie turned to look out of the window behind his desk. It had been snowing steadily since first light, and a thick drift lay on the windowsill, heaped against the glass, melting into lace at the edges from the heat within the room. 'Sabotage?'

'Possible.'

18

'Hi-jack?'

'Also possible. But there's been no contact.'

'Fuel status . . . ?'

Carter glanced at the notepad. 'If they're still in the air they'll have to make a landing in the next half-hour. Somewhere.'

'She *was* on it . . . ?'

Carter left the door and crossed the room slowly, heavily. 'Yes, sir. I have the passenger list here as well. Only nine of them, plus pilot, co-pilot and steward. It was carrying a lot of cargo, but nothing important. Just general stores, that kind of thing. It was a housekeeping flight, one of the regular shuttles we run . . .'

'I know. She was bringing back a lot of wedding presents. She didn't want to wait for them to go by ship . . . wanted you to see them right away.'

Carter sank down into one of the leather chairs and stared at the notepad while Ainslie went to the tray of bottles and glasses on the bookcase. The neck of the whiskey bottle clattered briefly against crystal. When he handed Carter a drink the General allowed his hand to rest momentarily on his aide's shoulder before returning to his desk to pick up the phone.

'Dave? Marsh Ainslie. Look, this flight that's overdue . . . yes, that's the one. My daughter is on it.' He paused, listening, marking his desk blotter with the condensation from the bottom of his glass. 'I'd be grateful . . . the minute you hear anything. I have to go to one of these damn meetings, but Larry will be here.' He took a swallow of whiskey and grimaced. 'Dave . . . do you have any indication that it might be a political hi-jack, anything like that? No, huh? Mmmmmm . . . Look, can we try to keep it out of the papers? I mean, it's our flight and our problem. Yes. Well. Do the best you can, I don't need reporters all over the place in addition to all the rest. Thanks.'

Carter glanced up as Ainslie replaced the phone and sat staring at his empty glass. 'Can't you skip the meeting, sir?'

'Not this one . . . anyway, it will keep me busy.'

His aide nodded and looked away, wishing he had a meeting important enough to occupy him instead of long hours of helpless waiting to endure.

Two hours later, Carter had Ainslie called out of the meeting and faced him across someone else's desk in an anteroom. 'They've found the plane, sir.' There was no sorrow in the green eyes, Ainslie was glad to see. Instead they were filled with a glitter of unmistakable rage. 'About sixty miles into the desert west of Adabad. The sand had been sprayed with a chemical that turned it into a landing strip as hard as rock. The plane was there. Empty.'

'*Empty?*'

Carter nodded. 'Completely undamaged, put down nice and neat, everything turned off and tucked up according to regulations. Maybe I shouldn't have said empty. The pilot and co-pilot were still in it, drugged. Cargo was all intact, nothing taken. But the passengers and their luggage . . . gone.'

'Any sign of another plane?'

'They have police and security teams in there now. They seem to think the passengers were evacuated by a helicopter. A big one.'

'And have there been any messages?'

'No. No messages, no demands, no explanations, nothing. Those passengers might never have been *on* the plane. Even the ashtrays were clean.'

'They kidnap nine people and stop to clean the *ashtrays?*'

'Yep. Removed the refuse modules, too.'

'That doesn't make sense, Larry.'

Carter leaned forward on his knuckles, flexed his shoulders. 'Oh, it probably makes sense, all right. But not sense that *we* can see. Yet.'

Ainslie rocked back and forth on his heels, his hands knotted behind him. 'A big helicopter, you said?'

His aide nodded. 'Long-range or heavy-cargo, yes.'

'But nine people and their luggage aren't heavy cargo.'

'No.'

Ainslie's eyes went to the map on the wall of the ante-room. 'Where would they take them?'

'Maybe *why* they took them will tell us that.'

'And what's going to tell us why?'

'I suppose the kidnappers will. Eventually.'

# Three

Timmy was the first to wake.

When he went to the window and saw the snow he realised why he felt so cold and nodded, satisfied. In the big
bed next to his smaller one both his parents still slept, his
father breathing heavily, his mother curled tidily alongside.
Timmy tried to rouse both of them in turn but their sleep
was beyond him.

When he tried the handle of the door it opened easily
onto a balcony that ran around three sides of an enormous
room, two storeys high. Below him he could see large comfortable chairs and sofas, a table with straight chairs, lots
of bookshelves and a big fireplace where a bank of massive
logs burned. It was warmer out here on the balcony.

He turned and looked down at the other doors. Tiptoe-
ing – he didn't quite know why – he went to the next one
and slowly opened it. Two men were asleep in there on twin
beds. One was Mr Skinner, who had lent him the binoculars, lying on his stomach. The other one was the big man
with the loud voice who had been sitting at the back of the
plane drinking out of a little silver flask. He slept on his
back snoring messily and unevenly, with little grunts in
between. Timmy tried to rouse Skinner but he wouldn't
wake up either.

In the next room he found Laura and another lady, also
sleeping. In the room beyond that two more men. A frown
creased Timmy's smooth forehead. He'd never seen grown
men holding hands before, especially across the gap between two beds while sleeping. He went further into the
room and discovered they weren't holding hands at all but
were handcuffed together: one old man with grey hair and

one young man with long, dark hair. How very strange.

Timmy shivered and went back out onto the balcony. It was so *quiet* in the house, except for the big man's snores. Slowly he descended the staircase against the far wall to the room below. There was a really big glass window in the front wall, and through it he could see the snow stretching away between thin spindly trees. The sky was white, or a very pale grey that was perfectly smooth and even all over. It didn't look very nice out there.

Under the balcony and the stairs he saw there were doors. The two under the stairs were locked, but behind the others he found a big modern kitchen, empty, a cold room with a big humming machine and smaller machines in it – washing machine and dryer he recognised, the others he didn't. Another room was lined with shelves from floor to ceiling, all filled with tins and packets of food. He couldn't read the writing on them, but they reminded him he was hungry. He was hungrier than he could ever remember being in his whole entire *life*, in fact. Running his finger along the nearest shelf he located a box with pictures of biscuits on it, hesitated, then grabbed. They weren't very nice biscuits, he decided, after he'd eaten five or six, but they filled his tummy up a bit. Carrying the open box he continued his explorations, wishing somebody would wake up. There was a big freezer in the room but the lid was too heavy for him. Everything was so big and he felt very small. His arm hurt, too.

Looking down at it he saw that there were several little holes poked into the inside of his elbow, with bruises around them. Now that was upsetting. Somebody had been sticking him with needles and it made him want to cry. He hated needles. *Hated* them.

Suddenly he ran back up the stairs and into the room where his parents slept. They lay exactly as they had when he first woke up. That was even more upsetting. He ran next door and shook Mr Skinner, hard, but only got a muttered groan and nothing more. Crying now, he went to the next room and started to shake Laura, nice Laura

23

with the wiggly nose and her face all pale under the tumbled brown hair.

'Laura . . . Laura . . . please wake up . . . please . . .'

Laura felt cold, too. All the blankets must have fallen off again. She stirred and reached down to pull them up, but there were no blankets. Just the sound of a child crying. She struggled to open her eyes which seemed to be stuck together. There *was* a child crying very near her, a small boy, crouched beside the bed on the floor, clutching a box of biscuits and sobbing helplessly. He was wearing a pair of binoculars. Her lips had been cemented, too.

'Timmy?'

He struggled up from the floor, still holding his box of biscuits, and peered down into her face imploringly. 'Everybody is sleeping . . . I can't wake anybody *up* . . . and there's nobody else here . . . and it's all snow outside . . . please . . . please . . . get up.' His face was streaked with tears, and he looked so desperate that Laura's arms automatically opened. He flung himself into them and sobbed into her shoulder while she tried to clear the muddle from her brain, looking around the room over his head and blinking rapidly. It was a luxurious room with bright curtains and rugs . . . snow? Had the child said snow?

Shifting Timmy gently she managed to sit up and saw the other woman on the bed next to hers. She remembered her getting on just before the loading ramp had been pulled away. Laughing and giggling she had literally fallen into the plane and had caught hold of the seats to steady herself. Even asleep she was incredibly beautiful – a shapely body well-defined by the pale green linen dress, long elegant legs, a flawless face surrounded by a rich mass of glowing chestnut hair. Timmy struggled in Laura's arms and she let go of him, still trying to make some sense of all this. He was tugging at her.

'Come and see . . . come and see . . .'

'All right, honey . . . all right.' She allowed herself to be pulled up and off the bed, her head spinning but clearing steadily as she moved step by uncertain step to the door.

Once there she stared out and down at the enormous room below with the vista of birch trees and endless snow that stretched from the big double-glazed window to infinity, or so it seemed. A movement to her left startled her and she turned to see a man standing in the doorway of the next room. Timmy ran over to him.

'Mr Skinner . . . Mr Skinner . . .'

Skinner had woken abruptly, moments before, jolted by a particularly obnoxious crescendo of snores from the bed next to his. It had taken him a while to orient himself, locate his glasses, clear his head. Now he stood holding onto the doorframe, one hand resting on Timmy's shoulder as he took in the room and the girl standing against the railing of the balcony a few feet away. Not a very big girl, with medium-brown hair curving under a pointed chin, wearing a rumpled jersey dress in a shade of blue that echoed the shadows under her eyes.

Laura, in turn, saw a stocky man in shirt and trousers, his tie slightly askew under an unbuttoned collar. He had a pleasant, slightly bemused face half-hidden behind wire-rimmed spectacles.

They stared at one another for a long, long time.

Professor Skinner decided the others would probably wake up soon, after they'd followed Timmy into the bedrooms and scanned the occupants. That was his name – Professor D. B. Skinner.

'David Benjamin,' he smiled after Timmy's inevitable question. 'I'm afraid you can't make much of DBS, can you?'

'No.' Timmy agreed regretfully. 'I'm still hungry.'

'So am I,' Skinner said. 'I imagine everyone will be. You're sure there's no one else in the house, Tim?'

'No, sir. Two of the doors were locked – I knocked at them and called but nobody came. There's food downstairs,' he added pointedly.

'We'd best take a look,' Skinner suggested over Timmy's head. The downstairs room was vast. The house was apparently the home of people with considerable wealth. Quality was evident in every item of furniture, and everything had been chosen by someone with a lively eye for colour and texture. Yet it did not have the perfect balance a professional decorator would have conferred. It was too idiosyncratic a collection. The books on the wall of shelves were higgledy-piggledy, paperbacks mixed with hardcovers, all obviously read and used. Laura took down one or two at random.

'I think we must be in Finland,' she said to Skinner when he came back from touring the house with Timmy. 'The books seem to be in Finnish, anyway.'

'Yes,' Skinner agreed in his soft, precise voice. 'The labels on the blankets and curtains in my room were also printed in Finnish. And the maker's name on the bottom of the bureau drawers.'

'Oh,' she murmured, feeling a little foolish. He'd been ahead of her.

'Or, alternatively, it could be the foreign home of an extremely chauvinistic Finn,' he added carefully, and came a few steps closer. 'I'm afraid the boy was correct – there seems to be nobody else in the house except those of us who were on the plane.'

'But . . . why are we here? Who brought us? There must be something . . .'

'Not as far as I've been able to ascertain. We'll keep looking, shall we?' He turned where he stood, letting his eyes run over the furniture and the walls, and then spoke with satisfaction. 'Ah . . . here we are.' She watched as he approached the fireplace and picked up an envelope that had been propped on the mantelpiece. She'd missed it entirely. On the front in rough printing was the single word: *Passengers*. 'You see?' he smiled, extracting a sheet of paper from the envelope. The smile faded as he read. 'Dear me.'

'What is it?' She came over to stand near him, worried by the sudden blankness of his expression. 'What does it say?'

'I beg your pardon?' He swivelled his body to face her. 'I'm terribly sorry . . . that was very rude of me.' Handing her the paper he went to look out of the large picture window, his hands clasped behind his back, while she read the note.

DO NOT TRY TO ESCAPE BECAUSE YOU WILL DIE IF YOU DO. THERE IS NO WAY OUT.

YOU ARE BEING HELD PRISONERS FOR REASONS WHICH DO NOT CONCERN YOU.

WHEN OUR ENDS HAVE BEEN ACHIEVED, YOU WILL BE RELEASED.

THERE IS FOOD ENOUGH.

THERE IS FUEL ENOUGH.

YOU WILL BE COMFORTABLE.

ACCEPT AND YOU WILL LIVE.

WE ARE SORRY FOR THE INCONVENIENCE.

'Very polite, aren't they?' Skinner said reflectively, his breath momentarily misting the window in front of him. 'Apologising and so on.'

'But how . . . ?'

'There you are.' He nodded at the vista outside and again she moved to his side. Beyond the window were the marks of many feet in the snow – or tracks made by a few people going back and forth many times. The marks led from the right-hand side of the house and continued down the cleared area to the edge of the lake – or what seemed to be a lake – stopping some yards out on the flat frozen surface. 'Deeper coming toward the house, lighter going away,' Skinner observed. 'We were carried here.' He turned slightly to face her. 'Rather like a left luggage department, you see. To be called for when required. By helicopter, I should imagine. A light plane would have left skid marks on the ice.'

'Carried – all the way from Adabad?'

'Apparently so.' He stepped away from the window and looked toward the child. 'Well, Tim, have you located it?'

'I think so, sir. The picture looks like coffee, anyway.' Tim was carrying a large jar. 'I can't read the words.'

'No, well, of course you can't, they're in a foreign language, aren't they?' Skinner smiled. 'Let's hope all the food has pictures on it, otherwise we shall be having a very strange meal indeed. I don't much fancy having tinned pineapple when I want carrots, do you?'

'I don't mind,' Timmy said cheerfully. 'I like pineapple.'

'Oh. Well, that's all right then. Come along, let's see if there's anything like a kettle in that rather splendid kitchen.'

Laura was still standing at the window, staring out at the tracks and the icy scene of naked trees and endless snow. She wanted to scream or cry or do something hysterical to suit the occasion, but Skinner's attitude seemed to preclude that. She didn't think he'd have much patience with irrationality.

'Miss Ainslie?' He was standing in the kitchen doorway.

'Yes?'

'I believe it would be helpful if we could prepare some kind of food for everyone. Blood sugar will be low after such protracted sedation . . . do you think you could lend a hand?'

'Oh, yes. I'm sorry . . . I was just . . .' She put the letter on a small table at the end of one of the sofas and crossed the room.

'It *is* very distressing,' he said with an unexpectedly sweet smile. 'If you wish to cry . . .'

'I don't wish to cry,' she interrupted defensively.

'Ah. Well then, there must be something very wrong with me, because I *definitely* feel like crying at the moment, from sheer frustration if nothing else. But the boy . . . would be very upset, I think. You see? So we must keep busy until the feeling passes away, mustn't we?' He nodded to himself. 'Yes, we must keep busy, Miss Ainslie. That would be the best thing.'

She was close to him, and saw that behind the lenses of his rather severe spectacles his eyes were a deep and vivid blue. Until she saw his eyes she would have called him a neutral man, a beige man, a monochrome. Now she was not so certain.

'I don't suppose . . .' she began, but her voice wavered despite her good intentions.

'Why don't you go into the store-room and collect some things from the shelves?' he suggested gently. 'Tim and I will have a look round for plates and things. Just select whatever you think would be simple to prepare and digest. Take as long as you like.' He smiled again and disappeared into the kitchen.

One by one the others appeared.

Timmy ran to the kitchen door with a yelp of joy when his mother entered somewhat unsteadily, her outraged husband behind her. She gathered Timmy up in her arms. When she released him her face was wet with tears. 'I thought . . . I was afraid that . . .'

'I've been helping Professor Skinner and Laura,' Timmy explained over-casually, going back to the kettle to switch it on again. 'We've been making food for everybody, see? You'll feel better when you've had some soup, Mom,' he added. 'Your blood sugars are low.'

'Are they, darling?' she asked with an uncertain smile.

'Why don't you go and sit at the table with Mr Goade and Miss Lasky and we'll bring the things through,' Laura suggested. 'We've been awake longer. That sick feeling goes away after a while.'

'No . . . I'll help. I'd rather.'

They had no sooner taken the things through than the last two passengers appeared on the balcony, the younger one half-supporting, half-dragging the older man who was apparently still very groggy.

'Hey!' the young man called down. 'Can somebody give me a hand with Pop, here? He still wants to stay sleepies for a while.'

Skinner had his hands full with a soup tureen they'd unearthed, so Tom Morgan ran up to help.

' 'Course it would be a hell of a lot easier if you'd unlatch me, you old so and so,' the young man grunted as they finally reached ground level.

'No,' the old man muttered. 'No way, Hallick.'

Goade, the big man in Army uniform who'd been in the room with Skinner, looked up sullenly from his place at the table and reached for the ladle of the tureen to serve himself more soup. 'What d'ya do, rob a bank or something?'

The young man glared across the table from where he was getting his guardian into one chair and pulling out another. 'What's it to you what I did?'

'Not a damn thing, sonny, not a damn thing.'

'All right then, shut up about it.' Hallick sat down with an angry thump.

'Would you like some coffee, Mr . . . Mr . . .' Laura was holding out a steaming cup to the older man.

'Denning, Miss. Frank Denning, Federal Marshal. Thanks.' He took the cup with his free hand and began to sip the black liquid awkwardly.

'What's going on, anyway?' Hallick wanted to know, watching Laura put down another coffee in front of him. 'What the hell is all this place and how come we're . . .?'

Skinner handed the letter to Tom Morgan who glanced through it swiftly and then slowly read it aloud. Even Goade paused with his spoon in the air to listen, although he'd read it when he'd come down earlier. Skinner had gone back to the kitchen for more soup bowls, and when he'd put them down with the spoons and the bread they'd thawed in the microwave oven, he seated himself quietly between Laura and Timmy.

'Goddamdest thing I ever heard,' Goade muttered through a mouthful of soup. 'If it was a hi-jack, why ain't we with the plane? If it wasn't, what the hell is it? Hey?' Nobody answered because nobody knew what to say. He straightened up in his chair and looked belligerently around the table as if he suspected they knew the truth and were intentionally keeping it from him. 'Come on, come on . . . what's the answer, folks?'

'We don't know, Sergeant Goade,' Skinner admitted, still looking at his plate. 'Do you have any suggestions?'

Goade eyed the smaller man suspiciously. 'What d'ya mean, do *I* have any suggestions? *I* don't know nothing about it. Last thing I remember is that bastard with the gas-mask – and now this. Why should *I* know anything?'

Skinner didn't reply. Laura had noticed he had become more and more diffident as the others appeared, apparently preferring to busy himself with the immediate problem of sustenance rather than take part in any discussion or conjecture. Now the overhead light reflected off the lenses of his spectacles and she couldn't read his expression at all.

For some reason his lack of response seemed to irritate Goade. 'You're so damn smart, I suppose, huh? Make a little soup and slice a little bread and suddenly you're God Almighty, asking me like that.'

Skinner raised his head. 'I only thought that perhaps, as a military man, you might be more accustomed to dealing with unusual situations than the rest of us. That's all I meant,' he said mildly.

'Oh.' Goade was only slightly mollified by this offering. 'Well, I'm not. Nothing like this anyhow. What about you, Denning? You're a cop.'

The Federal Marshal looked over the top of his cup as he finished his coffee. 'I've had no experience with hijackers. Or kidnappers.'

'He's just a messenger boy,' Hallick said gleefully. 'He collects things and delivers them, that's all he does. All he's good for these days.'

'Things, hey?' Goade grunted. 'Things like dumb kids hardly old enough to wear long pants? I can see you're a *real* dangerous assignment all right.'

'He's old enough to kill,' Denning announced. 'Old enough to commit murder . . . that's the charge I'm taking him back on.'

Goade looked at Hallick in surprise, and Hallick stared back with a grin.

'Oh, you *scared* him, Pop. Look at that, he's impressed *now*.' Hallick's face clouded. 'Except I *didn't* kill nobody, they only say I did, dumb fucking cops . . .'

'Please . . .' Anne Morgan interrupted with a glance at Timmy.

'What?' Hallick turned his head sharply to look at her,

then flushed. 'Oh . . . sorry . . . forgot the kid was here. Sorry, ma'am.' There was something appealing in his embarrassment, as if the shadow of a long-forgotten habit of better manners had suddenly fallen on him. Anne Morgan smiled, nodded, then went back to eating her soup. Hallick's eyes remained on her for a while, then returned to Goade as the big man spoke.

'My god, this gets better all the time,' Goade growled. 'Not only do I get hi-jacked and kidnapped, but I get stuck in the back of beyond with a killer, a cop, a kid, and some fancy-ass Professor. And me with only three weeks leave, too.'

'I'm sure we *all* had better things planned,' Morgan said pointedly. 'That doesn't make the situation different or better for any of us.'

'They've gone to a great deal of trouble to get us here,' Skinner began, then stopped abruptly, as if he'd started to think aloud and now was uncomfortable under everyone's focussed attention. 'Sorry.'

'No . . . go on, Professor Skinner,' Morgan urged, his eyes bright with curiosity. 'Say what you think . . .'

Skinner moved slightly in his chair then settled to stillness again. 'I don't *know*, mind you . . .'

'None of us does, Skinner,' Denning said.

'Ah. No. Well – simply assessing the time factor, you see. We were – captured – near the equator and now find ourselves near the Arctic. That alone would have involved considerable organisation, suitable transport, so on. And the . . .'

'What makes you think it's the Arctic, for crying out loud?' Goade argued. 'You *say* it is . . . you *say* Finland, but . . .'

'Finland, yes. I believe so. Norway or Sweden, perhaps, but Finland is far more likely. The landscape is typical, the books and other things . . . and the thermometer presently reads minus 29° Celsius which would have to . . .'

'I didn't see no thermometer,' Goade interrupted again.

'Just outside the kitchen window.' Skinner glanced briefly at the others. 'Of course it's on the north side of the house, but even so we can expect the ambient temperature to be about that. Considerably lower when night falls, of course.' He looked down at the bread on his plate, picked it up abruptly and took a bite. After swallowing, he added, 'Which again argues a latitude above 65 degrees north at this time of year. I'll be able to tell you precisely what latitude when the sun sets, naturally.'

'Oh, *naturally*,' Goade muttered sarcastically.

'And then, of course, there are the injection points,' Skinner continued imperturbably. 'I counted five on my arm. Allowing perhaps . . .'

'At least two days,' Denning said. 'At least two, maybe three.'

'Yes,' Skinner agreed, taking another bite of his bread.

'But they *can't* expect to keep us here for very long.' Sherri Lasky's husky voice broke in for the first time. She swept her heavy chestnut hair back from her face and smiled. 'I mean . . . they took most of my clothes away . . . even my shoes are gone. But they left my cosmetics alone, I can't complain about that. I'd feel naked without mascara and lipstick, at least.' She winked at Goade who stared back stonily.

'I noticed the same thing.' Anne Morgan put her spoon down. 'They've left the three of us just two full sets of clothing each, nothing else. Not even slippers.'

Skinner nodded.

'Well, Professor?' Goade demanded. 'What about that? What's the answer to *that* little problem?'

'It's quite simple. To prevent us going outside the house.'

'Uh-huh. Like maybe because if we *did* go outside we'd find something like a nice four-lane highway fifty yards behind those trees out back? God Almighty, why should we *believe* what they tell us? Are you just gonna *accept* it all?'

'There are no four-lane highways this far north,' Skinner said.

'Oh, yeah? What are you, a professor of highways and thermometers or something? What makes you so damn smart?'

'I'm an astronomer.'

'He teaches 'stronomy – he's going to teach it to *me* after dinner,' Timmy said confidently. The corners of Skinner's mouth curved up slightly, then firmed again as he looked down at his hands.

'Astronomy, for god's sake!' Goade exploded in derision. 'Then why the hell should I believe anything you say either? I'm not going to sit around on my fanny like a good little boy and drink *soup*. I bet I could go out and get help in an hour.'

'If it takes much longer than an hour you won't make it,' Skinner stated. 'Even if you had boots – which you don't – all the clothing we've got between us wouldn't be enough. With insufficient clothing the temperature outside is lethal. Within thirty minutes at the outside you'll begin to lose your sense of direction and your concentration. You'll become acutely distressed physically and emotionally. At the end of an hour you'll lose consciousness, if you're lucky, and in another hour you'll be dead.'

'You seem very sure of your facts, Professor,' Morgan said.

'I'm not afraid of a little cold,' Goade snorted.

'I spent six months with the British Polar Expedition,' Skinner explained. 'Technically it was summer, of course, but we always wore a great deal of protective clothing and never went outside alone. Certainly never for more than half an hour if there was a wind blowing. There's a wind blowing now.'

The house was very solidly built, but even so they could hear the wind whining at the corners, and beyond the big window the leafless birches swayed soundlessly, the only moving things in the vast wilderness.

'That's only a breeze,' Goade objected.

'The wind chill factor is very precise,' Skinner started to say. 'For every ten miles an hour the . . .'

'Oh, for crying out loud,' Goade snapped impatiently and pushed back his chair to stand up.

'Are you saying that we're being held prisoners in this house by the *cold*?' Tom Morgan demanded. 'We're trapped here by the cold, nothing else?'

'Nothing else is necessary,' Skinner pointed out with a shy smile. 'Ingenious, really, when you think about it. They've no need to watch us at all. We've little clothing and no footwear. There's not a coat, anorak or kagoule in the house. Each bed has one electric blanket and one thin overblanket, nothing more. As it's now only early December the weather will get progressively colder. There's no telephone, no radio, obviously. I'm sure what they said in the note is perfectly correct. There's no way out.'

Goade walked away from the table and gestured widely at the room around them. 'What about the way *in*? This is a house, people must live here sometime. Rich people, from the look of it. How do they get here? How did they get it built in the first place? Huh? There *has* to be a road.'

'*Not* necessarily,' Tom Morgan shot back. 'There's that lake . . . it looks like a big one, it might connect to a navigable river. I can see what looks like a boathouse down near the edge of it. Or they might have used helicopters to bring materials in, the way they brought us in. There's been money spent on the place – plenty of it. It's a mansion by anyone's standards, in terms of electrical equipment and furnishings, anyway. What would a few helicopters mean to someone who could afford this kind of summer place? Which is what it probably is – not a year-round home.'

'Indeed,' Skinner murmured. 'Indeed.'

'So they grab nine people off a goddamned flight from Adabad and plonk them down in a rich man's retreat in Finland, is that it?' Goade demanded from in front of the fire. 'They give us plenty of food and all the rest of it and then just leave us here to rot?'

'Hostages,' Denning said. 'The note said something about achieving their ends . . . they obviously expect someone to pay for our release. Simple.'

'But why?' Laura looked around in puzzlement. 'Why? Why *us*? Is anybody here important?'

'Only me, sweetheart,' Hallick grinned. 'Don't I look important to you?'

35

# Four

'Well, none of this tells me a damn thing,' Ainslie complained, dropping the folder onto his lap and staring at the seat in front of him.

'I guess it was the best they could do on short notice.' Larry sipped his coffee. When he put the plastic cup on the armrest the vibrations of the plane made circular waves that shimmered in the faint overhead light. He could see his own profile reflected with Ainslie's on the dark window, and beyond that the glow of the jets against the night sky. 'What about that professor? Is he into some kind of secret stuff, anything like that?'

Ainslie lifted a corner of the folder, then let it fall back. 'Hardly. He teaches astronomy at a small university in the Midlands. He's an expert on sunspots . . . or solar prominences, I guess they're not quite the same. He's some kind of international authority – sent out to Adabad to set up a solar observatory at the new university there. Otherwise he's what the British call a "don" – thirty-nine, widower, lives alone and has few close friends, hobby music. Ivory tower all the way. Pipe and slippers type.'

'Okay, what about the others, then?'

Ainslie shrugged. 'Morgan is a top free-lance civil engineer, spent two years out there building an irrigation system for the government, wife and kid along for the ride. Project now complete, taking up a new contract with a big oil company. Sgt. Goade is a supply sergeant for the military staff at the Embassy – they love him because he can get anything for a price, including booze which is a no-no in that part of the world. Denning is a Federal Marshal sent out to collect Hallick who jumped bail back in the

36

States and has been cooling his heels in Adabad for months awaiting extradition.'

'What did he do?'

A shadow went over Ainslie's face. 'The charge was rape and murder.'

'That's seven,' Carter reckoned. 'Who's left?'

'Miss Sherri Lasky, known professionally as just "Sherri". A nightclub singer. From her picture she looks like quite a girl.'

Carter studied it briefly and handed it back. 'I see what you mean. Any kind of record on her?'

'Nope. For all her exotic looks, Miss Lasky appears to be just a nice girl from Wyoming trying to earn an honest living. By singing, nothing else.'

'And Laura makes nine.'

'Yes. Nine perfectly ordinary people, if you discount Hallick. Murderers aren't ordinary. And he also happens to be the son of Joseph Hallick who is known as Joe the Snow, one of the major cocaine importers in the States, very big in the Organisation or Family or whatever they're calling it these days.'

'*That's it* . . . they don't want him taken back for trial! Maybe he knows too much.'

But Ainslie shook his head. 'They had plenty of time to break him out of jail . . . or kill him, if that's what they wanted to do. No.'

Carter thought for a while. 'Experts . . . there's three experts on that plane. Skinner, Morgan, Goade. Maybe that's it . . . what do you think?'

'I can't see any connection unless somebody wants to build a telescope on a mountain powered by black-market booze. But you're thinking along the same lines I am – they didn't want to just hi-jack *a* plane, they wanted *that* plane. Or somebody on it.'

'Like Laura?' Larry asked slowly.

'It's occurred to me.'

'Yes, me too. To get to you?'

'I'd think that if I were on some key assignment, but I

don't think the ACRE talks matter to anybody but the Scandinavians.'

'And the Russians.'

Ainslie gave a snort of laughter. 'Oh, come on. The kidnap was well-organised, sure, but not *that* well. We know the Russians hate the idea of ACRE being set up so close to their border but pressuring *me* indirectly isn't going to change a damn thing, I'm just not that important.' He closed his eyes to forestall any further questions, and had a sudden image of Laura – a series of images. The sad eyes at twelve when he tried to explain why her mother had gone away, the wide eyes at eighteen when she'd won the scholarship to Smith, the agonised eyes at twenty-two when her first fiancé was killed in Vietnam, the watchful eyes ever since. Such a quiet girl, so shy, so locked up within herself, preferring a book or a concert to parties and socialising. That's why he had been as startled as she when handsome Larry Carter, the demon womaniser, had suddenly started taking an interest. She wasn't Larry's usual sort at all – neither a beauty, a wit, nor a sexpot. Just . . . Laura. His Laura, his baby. The only person in the world he gave a damn about. Gone.

The plane landed in Adabad just before dawn, and as they disembarked the bright headlights of a staff car swept out from the shadows and came to a halt at the foot of the ramp. A young lieutenant emerged and saluted. Ainslie sketched a response and waited.

'General, my name is Grey. They . . . we've heard from the kidnappers, sir. Or terrorists, or whatever they . . .'

'Well, spit it out, Grey, come on,' Ainslie ordered, the cold night wind from the desert whipping his trousers around his shins and turning the sudden sweat on his face to ice.

'It's a package, sir, arrived at the Embassy about an hour ago, addressed to you personally, as if they knew you were coming. The security people have X-rayed it, there's no bomb or anything.'

'Let's go.'

The American Embassy in Adabad was, like many of the buildings in the tiny and rapidly expanding country, highly modern and blindingly white. In the rosy flush of dawn, however, with the fine filigree of concrete 'lace' on the façade, the surrounding pools of shallow dark water and the background of high gold-streaked cirrus clouds, it looked like a little girl's pink birthday cake set adrift. Silvery fingers of spray were thrown up from the pools and fell back tinkling. The lavish display of water in this desert land was more indicative of wealth and power than six armies and a heap of diamonds. Ainslie appreciated the subtle interplay of décor and politics, but wiped his face in irritation as a few droplets landed on his face. Laura had a dress in exactly that shade of pink, she'd been wearing it the day she left for Adabad.

'Sir?' Larry was waiting on the top step.

'Coming, coming.' Ainslie moved on. They rounded the pierced façade, came to glass doors, went through after Grey and followed him across the rich simplicity of the foyer to a more workaday corridor where the fine-veined marble was replaced by dark linoleum.

The tall tanned man stood up when they entered his office. Grey made introductions quickly because both the newcomers were more interested in the thick envelope on the desk than the man behind it.

'General Ainslie, Lieutenant Carter – Consul Bowden.'

Bowden's voice was liquid and warm but his eyes were not. 'General, I'm very sorry this has happened. The local police are being extremely helpful although there aren't too many of them...'

'I appreciate that, Mr Bowden, thank you. Is this the package?'

'Yes... the security people say it's quite safe to open it.'

'Thank you.' Ainslie grabbed the envelope with no pretence of control and slid a finger under the flap to rip it open. He spread the edges, looked in, then upended the envelope and dumped its contents onto the desk. Nine passports, eight of them the familiar grey-blue of his own, one dark blue and deeply embossed with a lion and unicorn in gold. A single sheet of thick white paper drifted away from them and nearly went off the edge. Bowden made a grab for it and handed it across. Ainslie took in the words with a sinking sense of despair.

WE HAVE YOUR DAUGHTER AND THE OTHERS. YOU WILL RECEIVE MORE INFORMATION AT THE EMBASSY AT FIVE O'CLOCK THIS AFTERNOON. PLEASE BE PREPARED TO FOLLOW INSTRUCTIONS.

# Five

By early evening they were bored.

Or gave every impression of being bored. After they'd eaten and cleared away the evening meal they made desultory attempts at conversation, finding out a little more about one another. No one wanted to think or talk about what might happen if the kidnappers did *not* achieve their ends, and so one by one they lapsed back into silence, staring at nothing. Laura was reasonably sure that they, like her, were very frightened, but the sensation was not immediate. Like moths drawn to the killing bottle, they were still lulled by the light. Left alone as they were, there was no one on whom to focus either their fear or their outrage. As a result, the house, for all its luxury, felt rather like a railway waiting room. Or perhaps air-raid shelter was closer to the truth. They smiled, they pretended, and they waited for the destruction to begin.

The exceptions to the general feeling of lethargy were Skinner and Timmy. The man because he seemed to be interested in everything, and the boy because he was a boy. Together they took a tour of the house, with notebook and pencil, and made lists of all kinds of things. How many tins and packets of food, how many sheets and blankets and towels, how many windows and doors, how many rugs scattered across the woodblock floors (there seemed to be some kind of underfloor heating because even without shoes they were comfortable), how many radiators, how many cakes of soap and rolls of toilet paper, all the furniture, all the appliances (and *that* was a long list), types and kinds of curtains, types and kinds of decoration (teak panelling downstairs, emulsioned plaster upstairs, insulating tiles on all ceilings except the main room which was open to the massive rafters), even down to the pots, pans, cutlery, china and glassware. Skinner did draw the line at counting the books, but at Timmy's insistence marked down the number of shelves – forty. The two locked rooms downstairs had proved – after Goade in a fit of frustration kicked in the doors – to be self-contained servants' quarters, each consisting of bedsitting room and bath. More items for the lists.

Laura suspected that much of this exercise was devised by Skinner to keep Timmy from being afraid. Of course, she might be attributing a kindness to him that was not really there. The nature of the device – making lists – seemed a rather unique one, and probably reflected much of his own personality as well. Perhaps he even had a reason for it, although he hadn't said so in so many words. He said very few words, actually, unless asked a question.

Anne and Tom Morgan seemed happy enough to let Skinner bear the brunt of their son's energetic curiosity. Anne Morgan was obviously a devoted mother, but wise enough not to let it show too much. Tom Morgan's lack of interest, however, seemed to stem from just that – lack of interest in the boy or what he was doing. He might have loved Timmy, but he seemed the type of man who suffered from a low theshold of irritation as far as children were concerned. The boy was warily respectful of his father, open and loving otherwise. The Morgans were a fairly attractive couple in their early thirties, but their social attitudes seemed to belong to people twice that age. Or, at least, Tom Morgan's did. Anne merely gave silent acquiescence to his opinions, her eyes usually on Timmy. From someone with a face as bland and unremarkable as Tom Morgan's, one might have expected equally bland conversation. Unfortunately what lay behind the face was less than pleasant and remarkable in its venom. Eventually, Morgan used up his supply of outrage at the iniquities of the modern world, namely the moral degeneracy, avarice and political extremism that had apparently brought them to their present situation. Once having delivered himself of this burden, his relief seemed great. So was everyone else's. Now he and his wife sat neatly together on one of the two long sofas that flanked the fireplace, holding hands and saying nothing.

Denning had finally and reluctantly agreed to remove Hallick's handcuffs as neither his prisoner nor anyone else was going anywhere. Laura was surprised to find she quite liked Joe Hallick. Denning had said he was a murderer but the boy (he might be over twenty but she could only think of him as a boy) had a chirpy defiance she almost admired. She found his reactions to Sherri Lasky a little less charming, however.

She put Sherri's age at around thirty. That was more a matter of her assurance than her appearance. There was no denying she was very, very beautiful. She seemed to take Hallick's almost compulsive flirting as her due, even subtly encouraged him, as if she needed to publicly demonstrate her power over men. Laura wondered whether, if she watched long enough, she might learn the knack. Despite being well educated and well travelled, she had never quite discovered how to develop that kind of totally confident femininity that Sherri (and her own mother for that matter) seemed to secrete and exude quite naturally. She *needed* to learn it, for Larry's sake. He had a brilliant future ahead of him and being her father's daughter was just not enough.

She gazed down at the book she'd taken from the shelves. It was in Finnish, of course, and she wasn't quite sure if it was a text on botany, a travel book, or a treatise on nature photography, but looking at the pictures helped to pass the time.

Sherri and Hallick had discovered a stereo unit built into the wall beside the fireplace, but a search through the tapes and discs stored below it had revealed only classical music, much to their mutual disgust. They'd put on some Debussy, which Laura loved, but Goade had complained so they'd taken it off.

Goade, of course, was the problem. Alternating between sullen glares and open aggression, he made the atmosphere far less pleasant than it might have been. He reminded them of their dilemma because he kept attacking everyone for their 'pathetic' attitude. Well, Laura conceded, maybe they were pathetic but there didn't seem to be many alternatives. She glanced over at Professor Skinner who was working at the dining table. What *was* he doing with that calculator?

Initially Skinner had been perturbed to find no clock in the house because his watch was still set at Adabad time, and it wasn't until it occurred to him to check with the central heating controls that he was able to correct to local time. He made sunset at 4:28. While the others were talking he huddled over tables and charts from his briefcase and eventually announced that as far as he could reasonably calculate, they were at 67° North, which put them just over the edge of the Arctic Circle.

'Oh, terrific,' jeered Goade. 'What a relief. I thought for a while we were stuck at sixty-six degrees, or, God forbid, sixty-eight.' Hallick laughed at that – but then Hallick laughed at just about everything.

Skinner began to put his papers back into the briefcase. He did it neatly and with a minimum of movement, as he seemed to do most things. Laura could see Goade had already come to some conclusions about the shy academic, and he wasn't far away from making them public. Every time he looked at the smaller man there was derision on his face. To her, Skinner's physical actions showed economy and control, but to Goade they obviously conveyed something else. When Skinner got up and turned to carry the briefcase up to his room, Goade spoke laconically from his chair by the fire.

'I like your handbag.'

Skinner froze, then slowly turned to face Goade and the others. 'Do you?' he asked quietly, looking down at the battered leather rectangle. 'It's pigskin, I believe.' He turned again and started up the stairs. 'Still,' he added,

'I'm sure your father didn't have much difficulty finding another wife.'

They all stared at Skinner's square back as he mounted the last steps and walked along the balcony to disappear into the bedroom. Hallick began to laugh but choked into silence as he glanced at Goade's reddening cheekbones.

'I don't think I'd push the Professor if I were you, Goade,' Denning said from the opposite end of the dining table where he was laying out yet another game of solitaire with a deck of cards he'd found. 'Something tells me he's not quite as gentle as he seems.'

'He's a cocked-up little old lady,' Goade grunted, getting up and scowling as he stepped over Timmy, who was playing with some pieces of wood on the hearthrug. '*Professor* don't mean anything, he's a goddamned old-maid schoolteacher, that's all.'

'I like him,' came Timmy's stubborn tones from somewhere around Goade's knee, and Goade looked down.

'Oh, yeah? Well, don't like him too much, sonny, he might give you a nasty surprise.'

Timmy looked puzzled, and Tom Morgan spoke sharply from the sofa. 'That was uncalled for. I'm sure we'd all appreciate it if you kept ignorant comments like that to yourself.'

Goade just snorted and walked into the kitchen. After a minute they heard a clatter of cutlery. It was the second time during the evening Goade had gone into the kitchen to make himself something to eat; there seemed no end to his appetite.

'What're you makin' them out to be, kid?' Hallick suddenly asked Timmy with every indication of sincere interest. 'Soldiers?' Timmy seemed surprised as Hallick joined him on the hearthrug.

'They're only pieces of wood, really,' he sighed heavily.

'Oh, sure. But that one . . . he kind a looks like he could be a soldier, don't he?' Hallick reached into his trouser pocket and pulled out a small paring knife. The firelight glinted along the short blade, and Denning half rose from

45

his chair, unseen by the others. With a quick movement Hallick picked up one of the pieces of wood and began to work on it with the knife. Denning sank back down onto his chair again, but held the balance of the cards unplayed in his clenched fingers.

'See? If I just . . . smooth down this side here . . . and cut off this little twig . . . there.' Hallick held up the bit of wood. Somehow, with a few cuts of the knife he had managed to convert it into a man-figure carrying a sword or rifle in one stiff arm. 'How about that? Any more pieces like that one?'

Timmy took the little figure from him in some awe, peered at it and then at Hallick. 'I think so,' he said eagerly, and crawled on his hands and knees over to the wood box next to the grate. After rummaging for a moment he crawled back with several small chunks of wood and handed them trustingly to Hallick who sorted them out and went to work with the knife again.

Skinner came out of the bedroom and looked down at the scene below. Timmy's eyes were shining as Hallick worked deftly to produce one crude figure after another from the small pieces of firewood, lining them up in a row.

Grief didn't often rise in Skinner now, except when he saw parents watching their children as the Morgans watched Timmy. They'd said the child in Margaret's womb had been a boy but he knew what four-month foetuses looked like and never felt he had lost a son. Only Margaret and the future they'd planned together. He folded his arms and leaned against one of the balcony supports, trying to assess his fellow captives. Sherri seemed happily absorbed in improving her manicure; the Morgans, Hallick and Timmy in the wooden army; Denning once again in his solitaire. Laura was reading a book, the curtain of her hair obscuring her face and catching a glow from the fire beyond. He watched for a while, but she didn't turn the page. Surely a picture of crags and bracken wasn't all that absorbing? He knew, suddenly, that she was watching the others from under her lashes, listening to them, hiding behind her hair like some small animal. He approved of her stillness and wariness. It was the best way for any frightened thing to gauge its danger.

Suddenly, from beneath his feet, Goade appeared with a half-eaten sandwich. He could see pink scalp between the thinning strands of blonde hair, the broad spread of the shoulders jutting out on either side. The big man's body was foreshortened by the angle, and Skinner had a sudden irrational impulse to find something large and heavy he could drop onto Goade and obliterate him once and for all, smashing him into the floor.

Anne Morgan stirred. 'It's getting late, Timmy,' she said. He looked up at her reproachfully.

'Aw, mom . . . I'm not sleepy.' But Skinner could see he was struggling to stay awake and obviously Mrs Morgan saw it, too. After a few more of Timmy's protests, however, Tom Morgan's patience snapped.

'Timothy!' he snapped. 'Do as your mother says, *no* arguments, march!'

For a brief moment Timmy looked almost afraid of Morgan. After giving the irate father a sour look, Hallick leaned over and nudged Timmy.

'Hey, kid,' he said, with an air of benign conspiracy, 'don't fight City Hall, it gets you *nowhere*, you know?' He grinned at Timmy's expression. 'Tell you what. I'll keep on workin' here until *my* bedtime, and when you come down in the morning you just see what you've got, okay? How's that?'

Skinner smiled. The idea of finding a surprise was evidently something Timmy hadn't considered. 'Something nice?' the boy asked hopefully.

'Well, I ain't no Phidias, but I'll do my best, that's all I can say,' Hallick promised solemnly. 'Better than just pieces of wood, anyway.'

Skinner straightened slowly and stared at Hallick. Where would a badly-spoken young murderer have come across a name like Phidias and known it well enough to use in its proper connection? Odd. He turned and went

47

along the balcony, passing Anne Morgan and Timmy on the stairs.

'Goodnight, Tim.'

'It's not really night,' Timmy objected.

Skinner stood back against the railing as they went up.

'Not here, no. But your body is still working on Adabad time . . . and it's about midnight back there. Anybody would feel sleepy at midnight.'

Timmy paused and looked back at him. 'Do *you* feel sleepy?'

'Yes,' Skinner answered frankly. 'I'm just going to make myself a hot drink and then I'm going to bed, too.'

'Oh,' Timmy said, digesting this. 'Joey's making me some soldiers.'

'So I see. You should have quite a collection by tomorrow.'

'Yep. An army.' He followed his mother and then turned at the top of the stairs. 'Laura's father is a *general*, with three stars. Would you tell Joey to make me a general?'

'All right,' Skinner assured him over his shoulders. 'I'll tell him. Goodnight.'

'And you'll take those binoculars off before you get into bed, young man,' Anne Morgan declared as she shepherded the boy into the bedroom. 'I don't mind you wearing them all day, but not all night as well.'

Skinner placed Tim's order with Hallick, and then went into the kitchen to mix up some dried milk and put it onto the cooker to heat. As he stood watching it he heard a step behind him and turned to see Laura.

'Would you like some cocoa?' he asked her.

'Oh,' she said in surprise. 'That would be very nice.' He mixed up more milk and added it to the saucepan. 'I haven't had cocoa at night since I was a little girl,' she told him. 'My father used to make it for me and I'd drink it while he read me my story.'

'I'm afraid I'm not much good at reading stories,' he apologised to the saucepan and heard her chuckle.

'Neither was he . . . he usually fell asleep before I did.'

48

He measured out the cocoa and added it to the milk, watching it spread across the surface and suddenly sink out of sight. 'Timmy tells me your father is a three-star general. Is that correct?'

'Yes. I'm an Army brat.'

He turned. 'I beg your pardon?'

She coloured faintly under his regard. 'Oh, it's just an expression.'

'Ah.' He turned off the heat under the saucepan and then glanced at her again. 'Tell me . . . is it conceivable all this is in some way connected with your father? Three-star generals are rather important, it seems to me.'

'Daddy wouldn't agree with you. But if it did have to do with him, why not just take me and leave the rest of you?'

'I've no idea. Does he do anything in particular, your father?' he asked casually, reaching for the sugar. 'The name Ainslie is familiar to me but I can't think why.'

She looked up at him suddenly and he was startled by the brightness of her eyes, a light tawny brown against clear whites, fringed by the long lashes she usually kept lowered. 'He's attached to the UN at the moment. He's in Oslo for the ACRE talks, and they elected him chairman. You might have read it in the papers. He's very good at organising people because he's got a terrible temper. It never actually explodes, mind you, but everyone always *thinks* it's going to, so they do what he says.'

'A valuable attribute in a chairman,' Skinner said dryly, lifting the pan from the burner and pouring the cocoa into the two mugs he'd set out as they talked. The cocoa filled the mugs exactly with none left over. He carried the pan to the sink and began to wash it out. 'That might be it,' he mused, jerking his hand back as he rinsed the pan. Whoever had built this house had certainly set the thermostat high, the water was scalding. 'ACRE is something to do with a city on ice, isn't it?'

Laura had a teatowel ready and took the dripping pan from him to dry it. 'Well, sort of. The letters stand for Arctic City Research Establishment. The Scandinavian countries are interested in developing their northernmost territories and have asked the UN for a massive grant to build a model city inside the Arctic Cir . . .' She stared at him, the towel suddenly motionless.

'Yes,' he concluded, softly. 'And here *we* are at the Arctic Circle.'

She finished drying the pan. 'But ACRE isn't political or anything. The Russians hate the idea, but nobody else does. It's just wasted land unless they can make it liveable.'

'Ah, well, perhaps it's merely a coincidence.' He handed her one of the mugs, took a sip from his own and grimaced.

'But . . . do you believe in that big a coincidence?' she asked.

He looked at her thoughtfully and she realised he was far younger than he initially appeared. Behind the old-man's spectacles were a young man's eyes, alive with conjecture. 'No,' he said, cautiously. 'I think one would find the statistics were against it, actually.'

When Skinner went upstairs he discovered Goade poking hurriedly through his briefcase. Pausing in the doorway he watched for a moment, then spoke.

'Want to borrow my lipstick, Sergeant?'

Goade pushed the briefcase aside and whirled around angrily. 'No – just wanted to see what kind of dirty photographs you like.'

'Ah.' He went into the room and began to remove his clothes from the bureau. He'd already decided to move down to one of the servant's rooms rather than share with Goade. 'Unfortunately my wife broke me of the habit some years ago. Sorry to disappoint you.'

The big man scowled at him in the mirror. 'Wife? You're married?'

'I was,' Skinner said. 'She died in a motor accident.' He stacked the few items the kidnappers had left him on top of his briefcase, closed the bureau drawer, and started out. 'We made a very attractive couple. People used to comment on how well we looked together – probably because we always wore matching dresses. Goodnight.'

When he was half-way along the balcony he heard the door slam shut behind him and smiled without much humour. Goade's insinuations were beginning to bore him. He knew his habits of precision grew out of solitude and the kind of work he did, but that didn't blind him to reactions of men like Goade. There had been women since Margaret died, although not many. Goade would never be able to comprehend that some men actually prefer celibacy to compromise. It didn't matter, of course, but he found it irritated him. He hesitated momentarily half-way down the stairs, then continued his descent. If it had never mattered before, why should it bother him now? It must be the situation. He was permitting it to unbalance him, and he could not afford to do that. Control. He had to keep in control. No emotions, no distractions. He could allow himself nothing.

Laura was at the foot of the stairs, waiting to go up, and he smiled at her. 'Good night,' he murmured. 'Sleep well.'

'What's the matter?' Sherri asked as Laura hurried into the bedroom.

'Nothing ... why?' Laura said, defensively.

Sherri turned but continued to brush her hair with long, even strokes. 'I don't know ... you look kind of ... excited about something.'

'I ran upstairs too fast, that's all.'

'Oh.' She continued to watch as Laura undressed somewhat jerkily and pulled a bathrobe on over her slip. 'I heard you laughing out in the kitchen with our little professor ...'

'He's not little,' Laura protested, pulling out drawers as if searching for something. 'He's a very nice man. I like him.'

'So I gather,' Sherri said dryly. 'You want to watch out for the nice ones ... they can tie you up into more knots than a kitten with a ball of yarn.'

It seemed a homely phrase for someone of Sherri's type, and Laura wondered if she had always been such a glorious Technicolor beauty. Someday, somewhere, she must have

51

been a little girl with no front teeth and a band-aid on her knee. Freckles, too, with that colouring. She stopped opening drawers and looked at the other woman.

'What do you mean . . . tie you in knots?'

Sherri shrugged, flicking her hair over her shoulders and starting to pull a few strands out of the brush. 'They make you care. Caring leaves you wide open . . . and that's when they say "Goodbye, baby, you didn't think I was serious, did you?" Stick to bastards . . . that way everybody knows what they're in for and you can enjoy the ride without worrying about what's at the end of it, you know?'

'Do you always stick to bastards?'

The beautiful shoulders slumped almost imperceptibly, then straightened. 'No . . . not always. That's how I know.' She faced Laura squarely, and Laura thought she saw pain in the enormous green eyes. Pain, sympathy, and a little anger. 'You've got to get tough if you intend going after anything special in this world. You're soft as butter, honey, and someday you're going to melt all over somebody and make a real mess of your life if you aren't careful.' She turned away suddenly. 'Oh . . . forget it. You don't want any free advice from me, for crying out loud. Why should you? I never even take it myself until it's too late.'

'Oh, please . . .' Laura said, awkwardly, reaching out to touch the silky skin of Sherri's arm. 'If I looked like you then I could do . . . get . . . whatever I wanted. But I don't . . .'

'You're a real pretty kid,' Sherri said briskly, dropping the strands of gleaming hair she'd pulled from the brush into the wastebasket. 'You could do a lot with yourself if you put your mind to it – but don't.'

'Don't? Why not?' Laura was surprised.

'Because looking like you do, you might get away with it. Men reckon girls who look like me can handle anything with a laugh, what the hell? But you . . . they want to look after you, protect you. Don't knock it.'

'But I hate that,' Laura said in despair. 'I'm *not* a fragile little figurine . . . I'm tougher than I look.'

Sherrie regarded her thoughtfully. 'Maybe you are at that, now I take a look at you.'

'Then . . .'

Sherri dropped down onto the edge of her bed. 'Look . . . there comes a time when you've got to add up your assets and work out how to use them. My assets are my ass and my boobs and my face. Men don't want to know I can cook and sew and all that crap, they want to know how quick they can get me on my back.' She laughed harshly. 'Pretty quick, unfortunately, but that's my problem.' She paused a moment, smoothing the peach satin of her petticoat, then went on. 'Forget what I said, honey. Don't get tough. Just get . . . careful, you know? That way you'll probably end up slaving over a hot stove and hanging up wet diapers and be happy as a lark doing it. So would I, funnily enough, if the guy was the right guy. But they never are . . . or, if they are . . . oh, hell . . .'

'But if you . . .' Laura began, then stopped, embarassed.

'If I what?' Sherri's eyes narrowed. 'If I didn't throw it in their faces? Hah . . . I *told* you . . . you got to use what you've got. Anyway, I've got a living to earn. I won't always look like this, and don't I know it.' She got up. 'This is beginning to sound like midnight in the girl's dorm. Next we'll be making fudge. You going to have a bath?'

'In a minute . . .'

'Then I'll go first . . . won't be long.' She grabbed her robe and went out, leaving Laura to continue her search.

She finally located her cosmetic case in the bottom drawer of the bureau and opened it, puzzled, certain she'd put it somewhere else. There wasn't that much in it, but what was there had been tumbled about and gone through. Sherri? That seemed unlikely; she had enough cosmetics of her own to stock a shop. Besides, Sherri wouldn't have poked holes in her night-cream and broken off the lipstick like that.

Who on earth had? And why?

# Six

The second envelope arrived at ten minutes to five. The taxi driver who delivered it was being questioned by the security people, but it was obvious he would be no help whatsoever. 'A man' had handed him the envelope and a respectable amount of money to deliver it to the Embassy. No, not a local, a European in sunglasses and a white suit. He'd spoken French with a slight accent but the taxi driver didn't know what kind of accent. And so on and so on.

In the envelope were four photographs. One was of Laura and another woman lying on twin beds, the others showed the Morgan family, Goade and Skinner, Denning and Hallick. The caption was succinct.

ONLY SLEEPING BUT IT COULD BE PERMANENT

There followed a brief series of instructions. Ainslie was to be taken four miles out into the desert on a certain road and left there at seven o'clock that evening. He would be contacted. He was to be entirely alone and no harm would come to him. Full details of the demands would be given to him and he would be returned to the same place on the road by eleven o'clock that evening.

They had a light meal in the Embassy dining room, arguing over the question of whether Ainslie should wear some kind of device by which they could keep track of him, if he was in personal danger, why the personal contact was necessary and other less obvious considerations. Ainslie poked a fork into his chicken and rice but ate little. Bowden watch him sympathetically.

'I don't think they'll try anything violent, General,' he finally said, taking a sip of ice water. 'The entire operation has been neat, businesslike and calm. We haven't had any public announcements, none of the usual terrorist organisations has claimed responsibility. I think you'll find money is all they're after, nothing else.'

'It *took* money to do what they did,' Ainslie objected. 'There are cheaper and easier methods of obtaining ransom than building a temporary airfield with expensive chemicals, for instance.' He dropped his fork onto the plate with a clatter. 'I tell you, it keeps coming back to the hostages themselves.'

'Or one of them,' Grey put in.

Ainslie's head jerked up. 'What do you mean . . . what do you know?'

Grey glanced uneasily at the Consul who avoided his eye. 'Sorry . . . just thinking aloud, sir.'

'Well, go on. Think some more.'

Bowden sighed. 'I believe Grey was referring to a somewhat confusing series of messages we've been receiving from a certain organisation with headquarters in Virginia.'

Ainslie's eyes narrowed. 'The spooks?'

Bowden's mouth tightened. 'As you say, "the spooks". First they demanded a full flight list. Then confirmation that all those on the list were actually *on* the plane when it disappeared. When the plane was found our security people here were instructed (in code, I might add) to go over it themselves, but I don't think they found what they were looking for. They came back angry.' He regarded Ainslie with some caution. 'I'm not saying it's relevant . . .'

'The hell you aren't,' Ainslie said. 'You're saying one of the people on that plane is a goddamn CIA agent.'

'I don't *know* that, General, and neither do you. The odd thing is . . .' Bowden hesitated, then apparently made up his mind. 'We have had similar enquiries from British Security.'

'Skinner?' Ainslie demanded.

'I knew it!,' Larry Carter exclaimed, throwing down his napkin. 'I knew it – he's just *too* innocent. I knew it.'

The Consul looked at him for a moment, then returned

his attention to Ainslie. 'I found it very strange he was on an American military flight.'

'Nothing strange about it, as a matter of fact. Just a courtesy. Apparently the flight he was booked on had a mechanical problem and they couldn't find him an alternative before the next day. The Dan-Air people knew we were going direct to London, picked up the phone and asked. I gather the whole thing was very casual . . . if the person has to get somewhere urgently . . .' he trailed off. 'I wonder where he had to be?'

'Yes,' Bowden nodded. 'He must have kicked up some kind of fuss because nobody else was transferred to your plane. Just him.'

Ainslie watched the Embassy car turn on the narrow stretch of two-lane concrete. As its red tail-lights winked away he jammed his hands into his pockets and looked around.

In the distance there was a half-shell of illumination over the town, and far off to the right the twinkling spires of the nearest oilfield. Above him the clarity of the desert night was pierced by a million stars, but the moon had not yet risen. It seemed as if the darkness around him could be held in the hand, felt, weighed. It was cold, too, in sharp contrast to the heat of the day that had suffocated him. Scuffing the sand at the edge of the road he began to pace back and forth, listening for the sound of a car, glancing back down the road occasionally for the first sign of headlights. This was an incomplete highway, dead-ended – if a car came, it would be coming for him.

But it wasn't a car. Faint at first, the chuffing beat of a helicopter eventually drew his attention. He scanned the sky then saw it, a distant star that moved across the face of the rest, low against the horizon. He kept his eyes on it, not sure that it wasn't just one of the commuter choppers run by the oil company. When its noise grew to a roar and it began to dip closer to the surface of the sand, he realised it was coming for him. It settled not twenty feet from him, the two figures within lit by the green glow of the instrument panel. One of them jumped out and came toward him, ducking slightly beneath the still-turning rotors.

'Ainslie?' the figure shouted over the wind and noise of the engine.

'Yes,' he shouted back.

'Come, please.'

He stepped off the concrete onto the sand. Closer-to he could just about make out the features on the dark face – whites of eyes, teeth, not much more. He could feel the blown sand in the air and squinted against it.

'You want me to get in?'

'Get in, yes.'

After the man had locked the door he reached down between his feet and passed something over to Ainslie who had taken one of the seats in the back. 'You put these on, please.'

Ainslie thought at first they were ordinary goggles but when he put them on he found they were totally impervious to light. He was blind. The man then grabbed his hand and shoved something into it.

'For the noise,' bellowed the now invisible escort, and he realised he'd been given ear-plugs. He nodded to show he understood and inserted one in each ear. The roar of the helicopter was still loud, but bearable. He felt the lurch as they left the ground. There was a moment of disorienting slippage, and then their attitude steadied. He had no option but to sit and wait.

'I hope the drink is to your liking,' his host said courteously.

'Very refreshing.' Ainslie put the glass down on to the brass table top between them and glanced at the man opposite. Very pale, not tanned. An extremely handsome man, dressed immaculately in a dark suit, white shirt, dark tie, gold cufflinks and a narrow flat gold digital watch, no other jewellery. His dark hair was thick but cut close to his head, and white at the temples. He looked more like an ageing film star than what his passport designated him to be. He'd handed Ainslie the Swiss passport when they had seated themselves on the wide patio that ran the length of the low white house. Ainslie had not been permitted to go inside, but through the sliding glass doors he could see a luxurious sitting room lit by the glow of hidden lamps. What else was hidden within? Laura and the others?

According to the passport, his host was one Felix Doppler, Swiss national, legal consultant, age sixty-two, identifying marks none, and he had entered Adabad yesterday.

'Do you want my identification?' he asked, handing the passport back.

'No, thank you, there is no need.' Doppler's voice was light and Ainslie had to lean forward slightly to catch the words even in the silence of the night around them. 'I would like to make my position clear immediately, General Ainslie,' Doppler said earnestly. His left eyelid had a slightly pronounced droop and Ainslie thought he detected a general stiffness in the facial muscles on that side. 'I am acting purely as a neutral intermediary in this affair. I have a certain reputation for negotiation.'

'I don't know you, Mr Doppler. I have no way of verifying anything you say.'

'No,' Doppler agreed. 'But when you return to your Embassy you will be able to do so, and no doubt will. I would, in your place. Let us proceed on that assumption.' He leaned back and took a gold cigarette case from an inner pocket, offering it to Ainslie and taking a moment to light both cigarettes. Ainslie noticed there was a decided tremor in the rather bony fingers and that Doppler held the case and lighter very tightly to disguise it. 'So. I am authorised to tell you, first of all, that your daughter and the other hostages are well, that they are comfortable and are being treated with respect.'

'Thank you – with the same reservation,' Ainslie replied.

A brief smile passed over Doppler's features, emphasising the stiffness on the left side of his face. 'Further proof of what I say will be forthcoming, General. Now, as to the conditions which must be fulfilled before the hostages are released . . .' He paused, and Ainslie felt his stomach tighten. Doppler sighed, flicked the ash from his cigarette, looked up at the sky. 'Some are simple, some are not.'

'There's more than one?'

'Oh, yes, I'm afraid so. Just as there is more than one hostage, perhaps.' He put his cigarette down on the edge of the ashtray, balancing it carefully. 'Frankly, General, I am operating on what you in the military call, I believe, a need-to-know basis?'

Ainslie nodded.

'Yes. My entire involvement in this rather unpleasant affair has been through a series of telephone calls, plus verification by my banker that a certain sum had been paid into my account. Only one man has contacted me. He has suggested that for convenience I refer to him as "Mr Brahms". I don't know why. And before you ask, no, I do not know who he really is.'

'Mr Brahms,' Ainslie echoed, puzzled.

'Whimsical, I agree. Now, first of all, there is a deadline for these conditions being met, as there always is, but it is *not* the usual matter of hours. Far from it. You have six weeks, General, to do what Mr Brahms requires. If at the end of that time the demands have been fully met, your daughter and the others will be returned alive and well. If not, they will never be seen alive again.'

'Six *weeks*?'

'Yes. I don't think you will call it generous when you hear what has to be done.'

'I see. And what exactly has to be done, Mr Doppler?'

Doppler stared at the cigarette burning in the ashtray but seemed disinclined to pick it up again. 'Money, first of all. The equivalent of three million dollars in gold to be deposited in a Swiss bank.'

'My god . . . three *million*?'

'That is the sum, yes. In gold. Next – the text of a speech, which I will convey to you at a later date, is to be read out at the General Assembly of the United Nations.'

'What?' Ainslie exclaimed. 'I can't arrange that . . . they won't allow any political rantings to . . .'

'I am told it is not "political" in the sense you mean. It is a speech on humanitarian attitudes that will offend no one . . . Mr Brahms apparently wants it on record, and he seems to be certain you can arrange it. You have many friends at the UN, General.'

'I may have, but . . .'

'Next . . .' Doppler continued. 'The release of three prisoners currently jailed in Amsterdam. I will give you a list of their names when you go. In fact, I will give you a list of all the demands in full, just so there will be no confusion.'

Ainslie was catching up. 'Terrorists?'

'I beg your pardon?'

'These prisoners . . . they're terrorists of some kind?'

'No. I believe the charge was burglary. Why should you think they're terrorists?'

'They usually are . . .' Ainslie stopped. 'Thieves? Criminals?'

'It is a legal nicety. The charge was breaking and entering, the sum involved was in the region of . . . three or four thousand dollars at most. Industrial diamonds, I believe.'

Ainslie put his hands over his face and rubbed his eyes, then leaned back. 'Your Mr Brahms certainly goes in for variety. Is that all?'

'No, I'm afraid not. Certain members of Embassies here in Adabad are to be recalled permanently. I will give you that list as well. Three from the American Embassy, two from the West German Embassy and two from the British Embassy.'

'This gets better all the time, Doppler.'

'No, it gets worse, I'm afraid. ACRE.'

Dropping his chair back onto four legs, Ainslie gave a grunt of understanding. 'Ah . . . *now* it makes a little sense. ACRE – that's why I'm involved, why Laura is involved?'

'Perhaps, I don't know. ACRE is to be cancelled, General. Or, alternatively, moved from the North Cape area to somewhere more acceptable.'

'Acceptable to whom?'

'To Mr Brahms, presumably. I cannot tell you what I don't know.'

'But ACRE doesn't even exist, we're only beginning to plan the thing, it won't be built for years yet.'

'All the easier to change its venue, I should have thought.'

'To what?'

Doppler shrugged. 'Greenland? Iceland?'

'Tell that to the Norwegians and the Swedes, they'll love it. ACRE is their project, not mine.'

'ACRE is a project of the UNDP. Surely *they* are the final arbiters of where it will be sited?'

'It's not as simple as that.'

'Well . . . I'm afraid that's your problem, not mine. Next . . .'

Ainslie's mouth tightened. 'How much longer is this thing . . . this ridiculous list?'

'You find it ridiculous?'

'I find it absolutely terrifying.' Ainslie stubbed his cigarette out angrily. 'This Brahms is obviously totally insane.'

Doppler watched his own cigarette teeter, then fall into the ashtray, smoke curling up from the still-glowing coal.

'I think not, you know. Not insane in the usual sense.' He put his fingertips together and stared at them. 'Mr Brahms speaks with the voice of the dead, General Ainslie. As a lawyer I've heard that tone of voice many times. Always from the lips of men with absolutely nothing to lose. Men who have, or think they have, no alternatives. It *is* possible he is insane, of course. It is equally possible that his values are simply not ours, his reasons not as easy to fathom as others might be.'

'You know who he is, don't you?' Ainslie asked suddenly.

'I told you . . .'

'No . . . I don't care what you told me. You know the voice, don't you?'

'I'm not sure. Perhaps after a few more conversations . . .'

'And you'll tell us . . . as soon as you know?'

Doppler stared at him across the tips of his fingers. 'He is paying me.'

'We can pay you, too. If you want to be neutral, here's your chance . . . you said you didn't like what you're doing.'

'If the negotiations are successful I intend to give that fee to the Red Cross, General. If you wish to match it, fine.' Doppler closed his eyes for a moment, his face paled and he caught his breath. But when he spoke his voice was calm. 'If Mr Brahms is who I think he may be, it will do you no good to know his identity. Indeed, I rather hope I am mistaken, for your daughter's sake. Were you to choose an enemy, I promise you it would not be this one.'

'You don't have to try and frighten me. I'm already frightened.'

'It would probably be wise to stay that way, General.' Doppler opened his eyes and smiled briefly. 'And now – the final demand. Quite simple by comparison . . . it will give you no trouble.'


'You know those names?' Ainslie asked Bowden, two hours later.

'Certainly. Ozawa, Groves, Previn, Mehta . . . superb conductors, all of them. Particularly in the modern repertoire.'

'I don't know anything about music,' Ainslie muttered. 'Goddamnit, the whole thing is absolutely crazy. She's been taken by some total and complete nut and we're supposed to deal with that? Impossible.'

Bowden dropped the typewritten sheet onto his desk. 'I agree, it makes no sense to us. But it must make sense to someone. Perhaps the man coming from London will be of some help.'

'Who's that? Who's coming from London?' Ainslie whirled away from the map on the wall and stared at Bowden.

'They tell me his name is Skinner.'

# Seven

Breakfast was not particularly successful. It progressed in silence, except for Timmy and Skinner who were conducting a quiet conversation at the end of the table just beyond Laura.

'And they chained her to a rock so the sea-monster could eat her up?' Timmy breathed. 'And she had to *wait* there ... she could see it coming closer all the time?'

'I'm afraid so,' Skinner told him. 'Andromeda was very brave because she was doing it to save her father's kingdom, remember. But then something wonderful happened.'

Timmy's eyes grew wider still. 'What?'

Skinner spread some butter with great precision on the corner of his toast and then put it down uneaten. 'She heard a wind ... a great beating of wings in the sky ... and down out of the clouds came Pegasus, the flying horse. On his back was Perseus who was the son of Zeus and much loved by all the gods. They had given him many gifts to make him a great warrior – the winged horse, winged sandals, a mighty sword, a shield as bright as a mirror, and a special helmet that could make him invisible. Oh, Perseus was a very splendid fellow altogether. He was just on his way home then, you see – from slaying Medusa.'

'Oh, I know about her ... she had snakes all over her head.'

Skinner smiled. 'She did indeed – not a very pretty sight. At any rate, as Perseus was flying through the sky he chanced to look down and saw what *was* a very beautiful lady chained to this great rock. He saw the sea-monster, too. So he swooped down on Pegasus and killed the monster before it could gobble Andromeda up. Then he struck away her chains with his sword and carried her off with him into the sky.'

'That's great. And then did he go off and kill more monsters?'

Rubbing his nose with his knuckle Skinner glanced over at Laura and saw she seemed as entranced as the child with the old legend. 'No . . . I'm afraid he took Andromeda home and married her.'

'Oh, pooh – that's *dumb*,' Timmy objected.

'Well . . . she was very beautiful, they say. Mind you, Perseus did go off and kill other monsters eventually. I expect he left her at home then. But they had a son, and that son had a son, and *that* son had a son, and who do you suppose *he* was?'

'Who?' Timmy demanded.

'Hercules.'

'I saw him in a movie, once!' Timmy said with great excitement.

'There you are, then,' Skinner said, and picked up his toast.

When Timmy had scampered off to play with his soldiers, Laura put down her coffee cup. 'That's a lovely story.'

'Yes,' Skinner agreed. 'They're all lovely stories, which is why they've survived. The odd thing is what *we* call constellations are really just arbitrary patterns of stars that in reality have absolutely nothing to do with one another. Some are thousands of light-years apart. It's only because from here on Earth we always see them in conjunction with one another that we attribute any connection to them. Purely for convenience, now, nothing more.'

'I'd rather think of them the old way.'

He smiled at his plate. 'So would I . . . even though I know better.'

'All the stars got dumb stories like that to go with them, do they?' Goade asked from the far end of the table. Skinner glanced at him.

'Most of the constellations do, yes.'

'Jesus.' Goade shook his head in disgust. 'That's some

kind of *science* you got there, Skinner. You teach that junk to your students, too?'

'By the time they get to me most of my students have learned and forgotten the myths, Sergeant. They're a very technical generation now. They don't intend to look and wonder, they intend to solve the whole thing by computer or climb into a rocket and find out first-hand.'

'You don't sound as if you approve of that,' Morgan commented.

'Of course I approve of it,' Skinner said crisply. 'The numbers are far more fascinating than the legends, but they would hardly interest an eight-year-old boy, would they?'

'Thank you for . . . giving so much attention to Timmy, Professor Skinner,' Anne Morgan said. 'I'm sure he'd be far more frightened if it weren't for your stars . . . and Mr Hallick's soldiers.'

Hallick actually blushed. 'Hey,' he said diffidently. 'I *liked* carving them things for the kid. I'll do him some more, later on . . . he's a nice little kid, you know?'

'What's that?' Goade said suddenly.

'What?' Denning asked.

'That noise . . . that noise outside. Don't you hear it?' Goade pushed back his chair and started across the room to the window. 'Maybe it's Skinner's winged horse, hey?' The rest of them heard it too, now, and began to get up. Goade was staring out of the window with a mixture of fear and excitement. 'It's a chopper . . . there's a *chopper* landing on the goddamned *ice!*'

The two men from the helicopter wore heavy arctic clothing, one in orange, the other in yellow. Their faces were entirely covered by knitted masks with slits for eyes and mouth, and their bodies were bulked out by the padded parkas and trousers. Both carried automatic machine pistols.

'Good morning,' said Orange. 'You will do as you are told and there will be no harm.'

Skinner was standing just ahead of Laura, his fists

clenched by his sides. There were incongruously cheerful designs knitted into the gunmen's masks, red and green stylised bird-like creatures with four legs and long claws. When the man spoke the birds seemed to stretch their wings, as if they were crawling across the blank face toward the glinting eyes.

'What do you want us to do?' Skinner asked quietly.

'Nothing terrible,' Orange said. 'Just to sit and have picture taken, that is all.' Their arrival had changed the atmosphere in the house totally. The unexpectedness of it and, above all, the ugly weapons they carried, made the situation suddenly very terrifying and very real. There was no sense of suspended time any more . . . the men were serious, and they brought a threat of death with them.

Orange turned to face Goade. 'You first.' Goade went pale, and then bright patches of red appeared on his cheeks. The warning was clear to Yellow, who lifted his gun menacingly, and Orange followed suit. 'We have no worry to kill you. Any of you, is that understood?'

'I understand,' Goade croaked, and the red patches faded.

'Good. You all understand this?' Orange looked at each of them in turn and they nodded obediently, like dolls. 'Ex-cellent. All today we want is pictures. Another day, perhaps more. Co-operate for yourself, please.' He nodded toward Yellow who stepped forward and took Goade by the arm, drawing him toward the dining table and pushing him into Skinner's empty chair. With a sweep of his arm the masked man pushed the plates and dishes out of the way. A cup and saucer tilted off the end and smashed onto the floor, spilling coffee across the polished wood. He reached into the front pocket of his parka and drew out a small camera to which was attached an electronic flash-pack. Then he reached in again and drew out a folded newspaper which he thrust at Goade, indicating he was to open it. Goade did so, and they saw the newsprint was in Arabic.

Yellow gestured that Goade was to hold the unfolded paper up to his chest with the headline facing outward.

When it was positioned to the gunman's satisfaction, Goade's picture was taken with a brief blue-white flare. Yellow nodded and wedged his camera against his gun to wind the film forward.

'Woman and child together, now,' Orange directed. One by one they were all photographed holding the paper. Skinner was last. He took the paper from Denning who had preceded him, and held it up as if scanning the news.

'See anything interesting, Professor?' Goade snarled from the chair he'd taken near the fireplace.

'What?' Skinner jerked his head around, nervously.

'When you are ready, please,' Orange said with some impatience.

'Sorry . . . sorry,' Skinner whispered and sat down holding the paper awkwardly in front of him. Unfortunately, just as the flashgun went off he flinched, and Yellow made a grunt of annoyance. 'Sorry,' Skinner apologised again, dropping the paper onto his lap and smoothing it out with quick, agitated gestures. 'I didn't expect . . . sorry.'

'Take again,' Orange commanded.

Once again Skinner lifted up the paper and held it gingerly in front of him, this time managing to confine his reaction to a slight start as the flashgun went off. He looked questioningly at Yellow.

'Will have to do,' Orange decided, and Yellow wound the film fully forward before tucking the camera back into his parka and zipping it up. 'Is anything needed here?' Orange asked. 'Medicines? Anything?'

'A lift home would be nice,' Goade said.

Orange ignored him and gestured to Yellow, who started up the stairs. They all watched in some perplexity as he went from room to room, collecting something he kept wrapped up in a towel he'd taken from the first bathroom. When he came back downstairs Orange indicated the open door of the room Skinner had taken over and Yellow went in there, too. When he returned, having checked the other servants' room as well, the towel was bulging with things that clinked and clattered.

'We take razors so you will not shave. We leave box in

67

hall, you open when we are gone only. Come back maybe tomorrow, maybe next day. Thank you.' They went out closing the inner door behind them. The hostages heard the outer door slam and after a moment saw them cross in front of the window and start back to the helicopter.

'When they come back we'll be ready for them,' Goade snarled.

'Why, can you fly a helicopter?' Skinner enquired curiously.

'Nah . . . but there's got to be a radio in it, doesn't there?'

'I'm sure they've considered that possibility, Sergeant. There would be no radio . . . so there would be no point in causing trouble, would there?'

'Goddamn pansy-ass,' Goade muttered, but apparently took the point.

Silently beyond the double-glazed window, and then with a faint clacking roar, the helicopter's rotors began to turn. The vanes flopped into life, rising with centrifugal force until they were a grey blur. The orange craft abruptly lifted from the ice and began to move away. Within two minutes it had entirely disappeared behind the intertwined birches.

Hallick was the one who remembered the box and went out to drag it in. Just a large cardboard carton without markings. Inside were cigarettes, three bottles of brandy, apples and oranges, several toys for Timmy, including a tiny helicopter exactly like the one they had just watched fly away, a large bottle of aspirin, a thick stack of paperback novels in English, copies of the previous day's *Telegraph*, *Guardian*, and the Paris edition of the *Herald Tribune*, and even several packets of sanitary towels. At the very bottom there was a large box of very expensive Swiss chocolates.

'And who said there ain't no Santa Claus?' Hallick grinned. 'Hey?'

# Eight

Captain Edward Skinner was a more vivid version of his academic brother. Where the Professor shown in the passport photograph was pale and blurred, the British Naval officer standing in front of Ainslie was dark and sharp-eyed. Passport photos are notoriously unfair, but Ainslie felt sure all the more energetic genes in the Skinner line had passed to this younger brother. Even the way he had entered Ainslie's temporary office was indicative – straight through the door and across the room, a brief salute followed by a firm handshake, a quick comprehensive perusal of the surroundings, and Captain Skinner was on station.

He had asked to see Ainslie alone.

Taking time to let his impression of the Captain sink in, Ainslie poured out coffee before starting. 'Good flight, Captain?'

'Delayed five hours by fog in London, otherwise fine. Have there been any further developments?'

'We made contact with the kidnappers last night,' Ainslie answered, handing him his cup and outlining his meeting with Doppler. He showed Captain Skinner a copy of the demands and waited for his reaction. The Captain laughed.

'Incredible,' he said, handing back the sheet. 'Can you meet any of them?'

'The money has been guaranteed by the oil company who have Morgan under contract. We've been in touch with the Head of the BBC World Service on the concert thing, he's getting back to us today. As for the rest, what would you think?'

'I can hardly speak for the UN, but I expect we can help you with the Hague on those prisoners if they're what Doppler claims and nothing else.'

'We?' Ainslie poured cream into his coffee and stirred.

Captain Skinner reached for and handed over a small flat leather folder. Ainslie put down his cup to take it and flipped the cover back. After a moment he returned it and took another look at the man it had identified. 'Why the uniform, then?'

'Oh, I'm a naval officer, I have every right to wear it. It makes an excellent cover; even David thinks I'm just a desk-bound sailor.' The Captain grinned. 'And I usually am. In this case, no.'

'I see.' No matter what the identification said, Ainslie's instinct still told him he could trust this man. 'In this case, you're what, then?'

Captain Skinner took a sip of his coffee. 'A brother, and an agent of Her Majesty's Combined Security Services. That's the order *I* prefer but my superiors reverse it, of course. Whatever they've sent me to do, General, my main concern is for David. I'm ... very fond of him.'

Ainslie nodded. The Captain's voice had warmed considerably when he spoke of his brother. 'You said agent. In what sense an agent?'

Captain Skinner finished his coffee abruptly, put the cup and saucer back on the tray, and seemed to change the subject. 'You've done very well to keep this out of the papers for as long as you have.'

'It was simple enough to issue a cover story about instrument failure and a forced landing in the desert. We telegraphed in the passengers' names giving various excuses. It being a military flight gave us some control. I don't know how much longer we can keep it secret, though.'

'You'll have to, General. You'll get all the help you need, because it's vital that no one begins to wonder about what's happened to those nine innocent people aboard Flight 816.'

'But they aren't nine innocent people, are they? They're

eight innocent people and one goddamned secret agent, aren't they?' Ainslie retorted. '*That's* what you want kept quiet.'

The Captain's eyes flickered and he reached into his jacket pocket to draw out a rather battered packet of cigarettes and a box of Swan Vestas. 'Do you mind if I smoke?' he asked, offering Ainslie one. Ainslie shook his head and waited while the man lit up and tossed the spent match into the ashtray on the desk. 'You've been told about that, then?'

'Not directly. I put seven and six together and came up with ninety-one. Look, Captain, I appreciate you've got to get this said. Why not get it over with so we can concentrate on getting your brother and my daughter back from this madman who's holding them, all right?' He frowned. 'Is your brother the agent?'

'I don't think so.'

'You don't *think* so? Don't you *know*?'

'Unfortunately not. The only man who knew dropped dead in Beirut the evening before the flight.'

'Jesus wept . . . what next?' Ainslie banged the desk and swivelled his chair around to stare at the map on the wall.

Captain Skinner drew on his cigarette and began to walk slowly around the office. 'Background first. About eighteen months ago we discovered that someone was milking both your government and ours of considerable sums of money under the guise of securing intelligence on Middle East political activity. I believe you call it a rip-off? I'm not a hunting and shooting member of my Service, General. Much as I'd like to think of myself as James Bond, the fact is I'm an accountant.'

'An accountant?'

Captain Skinner grinned over his shoulder. 'Yes, just an accountant. Even spies have to be paid and paid for, you know. Someone has to keep track of the pennies, and one of the chaps who adds up the numbers is me. Anyway, as I said, we discovered that this operation was going on under our highly trained noses, and had been going on for some time. When we began to get correlations with your people we contacted Washington and put together a co-operative investigation. It's been most illuminating. Needless to say, most of the money being drained off has been yours since you have so much more to spend than we do. But our losses have been considerable as well. Not only that, we found a lot of this money was getting kicked back into pockets we thought could be trusted. *And* some of it was going into pockets where it had no right to go. We don't mind paying for our *own* spies, General, but we hate to subsidise the Russians. It grates.'

'I can imagine.' Ainslie turned his chair back to watch the Captain pacing.

'All right. We mounted this investigation between us and we found out a lot of things about one another that perhaps didn't want knowing, but we had no option. It hasn't been an easy alliance, these things seldom are. One of the things it was necessary to do was to put together tallies of payments, so we could sort out the real from the fake. That involved putting together all the names of agents and double agents run by both sides, as well as agents of other intelligence agencies – the Israelis, the Arabs, the Germans, the French, and so on. You see? All this was done, collected, correlated, and so on by the man who died with such bad timing. He was an excellent man, but he had a fetish about stopgaps. This is to say, he felt the fewer people who know something the fewer there are who can betray it. *Somebody* had to put it all together. And remember, this is an internal problem, really . . . auditing, that's all. He was the filter, the narrow place in the pipeline . . . it all had to come together with him. It wasn't plans for some doomsday weapon, it was just accounts receivable.' Captain Skinner paused to stub his cigarette out in the ashtray and immediately lit another. 'So, they left it in his hands and he got it all down to manageable proportions. Then, maybe because he didn't trust his usual contact, he found someone on that plane he knew and trusted to bring the stuff back to Head Office. Just a messenger, a postman if you like. Or postwoman. And all that he or she is carrying is a set of lists. Just lists. But, when a computer gets on to it, patterns will come out. Patterns and names. He'd already sent through some early stuff – and that told us that some of the names coming up will *not* be ones we'd like to find. The thing could go very high. Very high indeed.'

'My God, no wonder you're worried.'

'Exactly. Now the lists are useful to us in *that* way, but they could be useful to, say, the Russians or the Chinese in quite another, obviously. Not only would they reveal agents who have successfully stayed undercover for years, but they would also be the means for blackmailing all kinds of people.'

'Why haven't our own people told me this?'

'You're being told now. Somebody had to be in charge of the thing and Britain won the toss. I do believe they actually tossed for it, in the end.' Again, the briefest of smiles. 'One can almost visualize the scene – heads we win, tails you lose. Incredible.'

Ainslie was shaking his head in despair. 'So *that's* the real reason they've been kidnapped? To get this information?'

'Ah, well . . . that's another difficulty, you see. *You've* been given quite a lot of proof that in fact they've been taken for other reasons altogether. This Doppler fellow, the demands, the passports and photos and so on. It may well be our carrier has been caught up in something else quite unrelated to his mission. Indeed, may be as trapped and desperate as the rest of the hostages, although for quite different reasons.'

'So it could be your brother after all.'

Captain Skinner nodded. 'Yes, it could be David. His astronomical papers would be ideal for encoding information, they're mostly numbers. It could be anyone considered trustworthy enough to handle what was really just a routine transmission of secret information from A to B. Even your daughter, for that matter, although I should think it highly unlikely.'

'Highly,' said Ainslie with an edge of sarcasm.

'Yes. We do have one thing on our side, of course. Despite our late lamented chap's fetish for secrecy, he was bright enough to realise the possible dangers, so he put a guard on the mail run, as it were. Unfortunately the plane had taken off before we could catch up with his appointee, but it sounds as if the job was put into capable hands. One of your people, as it happens, in keeping with the spirit of point-counterpoint.'

'And who's that?'

Captain Skinner sank down into the chair on the far side of the desk and stretched. 'His name is Goade. Sergeant John Goade. I understand he's one of your best.'

# Nine

Between them Hallick and Goade had finished one bottle of brandy by nightfall and had started on the next. Goade became more abusive and sullen, increasing his barrage of insults toward Skinner, who ignored him. Laura, sitting across from Skinner, saw that the remarks were heard, if not responded to. There was a glint in his eye that reminded her of the pilot light under a boiler in which the pressure was steadily rising. But he continued to sit quite still, reading every item in every newspaper, seemingly not with them at all.

'What I want to know is who's going to back me up when they come again?' Goade persisted. 'As far's I can see, Timmy would be more help than old pussy-sit-by-the-fire over there. Morgan's muscles are all in his neck, Denning's past it. Looks like just you and me, Joey boy, hey?'

'You'n me, babe,' slurred Hallick, concentrating on pouring another brandy.

'They'll be ready for you, Goade,' Denning said from the window where he was staring out at the last glow of sunset.

'So what? If they want to take more pictures – and they gotta do that to show we're still alive – then they gotta come through that door 'cause there ain't no other way in.'

Hallick swivelled to look across the room at the door. 'That very door?' he asked gleefully. 'That very door over there, right there?' He had progressed through the various stages of inebriation with textbook ease, and had now reached a state of childish merriment in which every word held a secret hug-himself meaning. He stood up and went unsteadily across to inspect the door from a distance of inches. 'You're right, Goade...'

'Of course I'm right,' said Goade smugly.

Hallick turned and started back through the room. 'It is definitely a door ... couldn't be anything else.'

'Oh, go to hell,' Goade poured himself another drink. Hallick stopped, rocking back on his heels.

'Oooooooooh, bad talk, you shouldn't talk bad talk, Goade, it shows a lack of covabulary resources, see?'

'No kidding,' Goade muttered.

'No kidding, old Goade, old boy. There are children and ladies present, you mussent forget that. Hello, ladies. Pretty ladies, too, every one of them.' With great deliberation he approached each of the women in turn. After inspecting Anne Morgan, who avoided looking at him, he pronounced. '*This* is a little-mother type lady.' Moving on, he gave equal consideration to Sherri. 'And this is an honest-to-god raving beauty, here, this one. Doesn't need lipstick and stuff at all. Look at that.'

'I wouldn't say it was her who's raving,' Goade observed.

Hallick stopped in front of Laura. 'And this one is ... what *is* this one, I wonder?' He put out his hand and lifted Laura's chin. 'What kind of lady are you? No glasses – can't be Marion the Liberian. No boobs – or hardly any – can't be Marilyn Runmoe. No kids – can't be a little mother. I think she must be one of a vanishing species. A Nice Girl. Are you a Nice Girl, Laura? I *like* Nice Girls.'

'Do you?' Laura asked. She wasn't upset by Hallick's perusal, despite Denning's warning. For some reason he reminded her of Timmy with his seriousness and his attempts at classification. She sensed no menace in him whatsoever.

'Oh, yes indeed I do.' Hallick released her chin and turned to find Skinner regarding him over the top of the newspaper. 'Well, hell*o* there, Prof-baby. Thought you'd gone to sleep. Do you like Nice Girls?' Skinner stared levelly at him without answering until Hallick's attention broke and he wandered back toward Anne Morgan. When

76

he was some distance away, Skinner lifted the paper once again.

'*He* don't like girls at all,' Goade sneered.

Hallick turned to regard his drinking partner. 'Wrong, Goade. You are *wrong*, Goade. He likes them all right, but he doesn't know what to do about it, that's his problem. Doesn't know where it's at, does he, honey?' Anne Morgan stared down at the carpet as Hallick swayed in front of her, and pressed back against the cushions when he leaned down to peer into her face. 'He sees it and he zips his fly over it but he can't remember what it's for. *I* know what it's for, though. You'd better believe I do.'

'Please . . .' Anne Morgan protested in a whisper.

'Please? Please what, honey?' He started to reach for her just as Morgan came out onto the balcony and stared down.

'Hey . . . get your filthy hands off my wife!' he shouted angrily, starting for the stairs.

'Uh-oh, Joey . . . you're making waves,' Sherri said suddenly, getting up and grabbing Hallick's arm, winding it around her own waist and pressing herself up against him. Blearily he stared at her, then grinned.

'Why if it isn't the Raving Beauty. Hello, Rave.'

'Hello, Joe. Is there any of that brandy left for me? You never ever offered me even a little drop . . . you're a mean, mean man.'

'Ohhhh, I'm sorry, honey. C'mon . . . you can have *all* you want,' Hallick said expansively. Sherri half-led him across to the brandy bottle. As he poured a glass for her he leaned over to whisper into her ear and she gave a wriggle and ran her hand up his spine to entangle her fingers in his hair.

'Is that a promise?' she asked, huskily.

Morgan, who had arrived to find his target gone, stared at the pair of them as they whispered and touched one another with increasing familiarity. 'Are you all right, Anne?' he asked his wife irritably, his eyes still on Sherri and Hallick.

77

'I'm fine, Tom. He's just drunk, that's all. Forget it.'

'Well, *she* isn't . . . they're cut from the same cloth if you ask me. I'm glad you put Tim to bed early.' He threw himself down on the sofa next to his wife. 'Little slut,' he muttered. 'Crawling all over him.'

'She only did it to distract him, Mr Morgan,' Laura found herself saying. 'She . . . she probably knows how to handle men like that without getting hurt.'

'Yes . . . I'm sure she's had plenty of experience,' Morgan said, a little too loudly. Sherri turned, gave him a lazy, insolent wink, and then leaned over to whisper something in Hallick's ear. He turned and stared at Morgan, then started to laugh. 'I bet your ass,' he choked.

Skinner folded his newspaper and put it carefully on top of the others by his chair, glancing at Sherri and Hallick, then away.

Goade peered between the two beside him and called across, 'I see you managed to hold onto *that* newspaper all right. Too bad you couldn't hold onto the one this morning – never saw such a pathetic sight in my life – you were so scared I thought you were gonna bust into tears.'

'Oh?' Skinner said, getting up to toss some wood onto the fire. 'I'm glad you thought I was nervous, Sergeant. Let's hope they thought so, too.'

Morgan tore his righteous indignation away from Sherri and Hallick and looked at Skinner with curiosity. 'You mean you did all that on purpose?'

'Hmmm?' Skinner returned the poker to its stand. 'As a matter of fact, yes. Did it look all right?'

Laura felt something in her chest let go, although she hadn't been aware of a tightness there before. She watched Skinner as he suddenly grinned at Morgan. It was like seeing a boy momentarily look out of a man's face, a boy no one had seen before but who had been in there all along.

'What did you do, David?' Denning asked, coming away from the window to stand behind Laura's chair.

Briefly, Skinner explained, and Morgan began to laugh. 'I'll be goddamned . . . you were quick.'

Skinner shrugged. 'I had ample opportunity to look at it each time one of you held it up. No one may notice it at all, but I had to try. Unfortunately, they won't be using that method again.'

'Why not?' Laura could feel Denning's hands pulling the fabric of the chair tight against the frame as he clenched it.

'Basically it isn't worth the bother. They had to import that paper so that the people who see the pictures will assume, quite naturally, that we're being held in the Middle East. He was very careful to get anything out of the background that would indicate otherwise. A plain table and a plain wall, nothing else.'

'But what will they do to show we're still alive, then?' Morgan wanted to know. 'That's the whole point of the photographs, isn't it?'

'Oh, certainly,' allowed Skinner, bending down to pick up Timmy's helicopter from the hearthrug. Straightening up he began to twirl the blades around with a forefinger.

'Well?'

Skinner put the helicopter onto the end table. 'Oh . . . the beards, of course. They took our shaving things so that we'd have to let our beards grow. Each time they take a picture the beards will be more pronounced. They'll show we're alive – dead men don't grow beards – and they'll show a progression in time.'

'But *we* don't have beards,' Laura pointed out.

'They'll pair the women with the men,' Denning said.

'Yes,' Skinner agreed pensively. 'That's why we'll have to work out what we're going to do pretty carefully . . . we can't know who will go with whom, but if we . . .'

'Do?' Goade demanded. 'What'ya mean, *do*?' He was obviously chagrined to find Skinner had not really been afraid.

'Well, I've been considering our position here . . .' Skinner began tentatively.

'Oh, God, here we go,' Goade confided to the rafters. 'He's been *thinking* again.'

Denning turned toward the big man angrily. 'Look,

Goade, I've just about had enough of you. All you can think about is using your stupid fists which will probably end up getting us all shot. David has at least done something constructive . . . *not* getting drunk, *not* pawing women, and *not* shooting off his mouth.'

'Ohhh,' taunted Goade with childish exaggeration. 'Now the little man is a *big* man because he knows a little Arabic, hey? My, my . . . let's all get down on our knees to Skinner the Wonderman. My ass.'

Skinner sighed and gave a short, embarrassed gasp of laughter.

Denning moved over to the fireplace and leaned down to throw a match into the fire after lighting a cigarette. He grinned at Skinner. 'How about it, "Wonderman" . . . like to hear a little hymn of praise?'

Skinner flushed. He swivelled to look at the old man, found his intent was friendly, and relaxed. 'What do you suggest?'

'Well, let's see . . . we could start off with "Lead, Kindly Prof" then swing into "I Dreamt I Dwelt in Finnish Halls", vamp a few bars of . . .'

Goade gave a sudden curse and threw the empty brandy bottle against the base of the wall behind him. The crash and slither of flying glass made them all jump.

'That was very silly,' Anne Morgan rebuked him.

Goade made a face and drank some brandy straight from the second bottle, muttering, 'Oh, that was silly, Goade, what a silly billy you are, Goade, *what* a naughty man.'

'You were saying, David?' Denning asked.

'What?' Skinner was staring at Goade strangely and it seemed to take him a moment to hear Denning's query. When he turned his head the light reflected off his spectacles, giving him a blind, empty expression. 'Oh. Yes, sorry.' He smiled at Laura vaguely without focussing, then gave a slight shiver and became recognisably himself again. Laura felt like shivering, too. Instead of the boy coming out of hiding this time, something else entirely had taken over Skinner's face. She wasn't sure what it was, but it made her stomach hurt.

'Sorry,' Skinner said again and looked at Denning's cigarette. 'I wonder if I might have one of those?'

Denning looked surprised, but held out the pack for Skinner who took one and lit it with a brand from the fire. He coughed slightly and took the cigarette out of his mouth to look at it wryly. 'Been years . . . I'm not sure if I can still . . .' He sighed and took a deep drag that seemed to stay down all right. 'You see, the pictures will be our only way of communicating with the outside world, so I think we should plan a way to use them, if we can, to do just that. The first thing that occurs to me is hand signals of some kind, but they can't be too obvious. Do you suppose they'll continue to use that table and chair?' He twisted around to look. Anne Morgan had gone out to the kitchen and come back with a dustpan and brush. She walked over and began to sweep up the fragments of glass. Goade watched her efforts with satisfaction, as if he fully planned to explode another missile as soon as she'd finished cleaning up the first. When she'd completed her task, however, he simply poured out another portion of brandy, staring into the amber liquid as if within it were suspended a first-run western. Anne Morgan paused next to him as if she wanted to speak, thought better of it, and went back into the kitchen. They heard her emptying the broken bits of glass into the bin. Skinner nodded to himself.

'Sergeant Goade?'

'That's me,' Goade said to the brandy.

'I wonder . . .'

'So do I.'

Skinner blinked and after a moment asked, 'I wonder if you know any Morse Code, Sergeant?'

Goade scowled at the brandy and then at Skinner. 'Nope, no Morse Code.'

'Oh.' Skinner's shoulders sagged slightly in disappointment. 'What a pity.'

'I know Morse Code,' Anne Morgan said from the kitchen doorway.

'Good heavens!' Skinner exclaimed in amazement. 'Do you really?'

She came slowly into the room, her face carefully averted from Sherri and Hallick who were now intertwined on a dining chair, Sherri on Hallick's lap. 'Yes, I . . . I believe I can remember it.'

'You *believe* you can remember it? Come on, honey, you *know* you can,' Tom Morgan said with what almost sounded like exasperation. He took his own eyes off the amorous couple at the opposite end of the table from Goade and glanced at Skinner. 'Anne has an eidetic memory.'

'What's an eidetic memory?' Denning asked curiously.

'Total recall,' Skinner said, staring with gratification at Anne. 'How absolutely splendid . . . what a great gift.'

'Not really,' she said placidly. 'It's more of a burden, I'd say.'

'You mean you can remember everything? Everything you've ever read or heard or . . . everything?' Laura whispered, fascinated.

'She only has to read it once and it's in there for good,' Tom said with a kind of embarrassed pride. 'Until she wants to get it out again . . . and then out it comes, just the way it went in. Morse Code is no problem, is it, honey?'

'Incredible,' Denning said from the fireplace.

'Increbidal!' shouted Hallick suddenly, pushing Sherri aside and getting up from the chair with a glazed expression in his eyes. He took a few steps toward Anne Morgan who had nearly reached the group in front of the fireplace and grabbed her arm, startling her. 'Lemme look at this increbidal lady with the magic head . . .' He put his face close to hers and she pulled away. He looked reproachful. 'Hey . . . don't do that . . . I ain't going to do nothing to you . . . I think you're very . . . don't *do* that!' he said angrily as she continued to back away. 'Hold still . . . hold *still* when I tell you . . .'

Tom Morgan started to get up and Denning took a step forward, but it was Skinner who got there first. The next moment Hallick was sliding off the wall next to the kitchen door with an astonished expression on his face.

'I'm frightfully sorry,' Skinner was saying to Anne. 'Are you all right?'

'I . . . I'm fine . . .'

Goade looked from the two of them to Hallick and back. 'That was the luckiest goddamn punch I've ever seen.'

'It wasn't a punch . . . he never hit me,' Hallick contradicted in a thin voice.

'I think it would be an excellent idea if you went to bed, Joe, don't you?' Skinner suggested quietly. 'I think the party's over now.'

Denning went over to jerk Hallick onto his feet. 'Come on, dumbo . . . the Professor's right. Bedtime.' He looked over at Skinner with a pensive expression, shook his head, smiled, and took an unprotesting Hallick up the stairs and into the bedroom, kicking the door shut behind them.

'My, my . . .' Sherri cooed archly from where she was leaning against the table. 'That was *very* impressive, David.'

'I didn't mean it to be,' Skinner said flatly.

'Well . . . it was,' she smiled, and Morgan made a noise that broke half-way between anger and derision.

'Shopping for a replacement so quickly, Miss Lasky?' he asked with a sneer. She took her eyes from Skinner's face, measured Morgan and found him wanting.

'Why . . . are you volunteering?' she challenged. Morgan seemed to bring out the very worst in her, and she constantly threw his moralising back in his face.

Laura stood up abruptly and announced, 'I'm going to make some sandwiches. Is anybody hungry?'

Skinner beamed at her. 'What an excellent idea. I'll help, shall I?' But when they came out with the snack only Goade and Denning were there and it wasn't a particularly cheerful meal.

Skinner sat alone in the darkened main room. He hadn't been ready for sleep and as the others went upstairs he'd switched off the lights and pretended to go back to the kitchen to make his cocoa. Now he had settled himself with the headphones that were connected to the stereo, hoping

Mozart and then Delius would bring him the peace he couldn't find in himself. Sunk in the big chair he watched the others going back and forth along the balcony. It was like a stage constructed and illuminated for his private amusement. There were two bathrooms on the upper floor, one at either end of the balcony. The stately dance of emerge from bedroom, walk, pause, knock, wait or enter which his unwitting cast performed in turn was fascinating. Tom Morgan was the last. He peered down into the dark pit of the main room, hesitated a moment, then turned off the balcony light and disappeared into his room.

After a few minutes Skinner's eyes adjusted to the gloom and the furniture slowly took shape again in the dim combination of dying firelight and rising moon. The recording of North Country Sketches came to an end and the arm of the turntable lifted itself from the disc to drop slowly into its rest. He made no move to take off the headphones but sat quite still in the chair staring into the dull red glow of the fire.

The visit of the gunmen that morning had seemed to bring out everyone's worst traits. Goade had become more abusive, Hallick's alcohol-stimulated libido had in turn triggered off Sherri's, Morgan's pompous sense of righteous indignation had been given a focus, Anne had become even more withdrawn, and he himself had lost his temper. They were disintegrating, subtly but surely, after just a few days. Laura and the child were so far unchanged. Outwardly unchanged, at any rate, God knew what was happening inside them. He felt his temper slipping again and fought it back into its kennel. More Delius, perhaps. He began to get up, then froze as he heard one of the doors open onto the balcony. No light showed and he couldn't tell positively which door it was. Slow footsteps followed. Careful furtive steps. Another door opened and closed. He sat on the edge of his chair, frowning, the headphones dangling from his hands. Who had gone where? Not to the bathroom . . . the steps hadn't gone to either end of the balcony, just started and stopped somewhere in the middle. He'd nearly given up trying to figure it out when again a door opened and closed. More footsteps, but not furtive this time. These were hurried and uneven. Whoever it was ran along the balcony and half stumbled down the stairs. A darker shadow crossed the faint oblong of light that came through the big picture window and then hurled itself into one of the chairs. Even in the darkness he had recognised her. After a moment she began to sob. He tried to speak quietly, so as not to startle her, but the sound of his voice brought an abrupt halt to the misery, and he could visualise her strangling herself in an attempt to regain her control.

'I think you'd better move down to the other servants' room,' he told her softly. She didn't answer, and he sighed. 'Was it Hallick? Did he try to . . . ?'

Laura realised who it was and answered reluctantly. 'I suppose it must have been but he didn't touch me – he went straight to Sherri's bed. They thought . . . they . . .'

'They had arranged it previously and thought you were asleep. I'm sorry.'

Laura slowly struggled upright in her chair and stared at the square figure in the chair opposite. 'Why should *you* be sorry?'

'I really can't imagine, but I am. For that, for all of it.' The silence stretched, and he got up and went over to the stereo, winding the lead around the headphones and stooping to tuck them underneath. 'One could see it was going to happen sooner or later, of course . . . one would have hoped they'd have more restraint, but people don't always function according to other people's rules, do they?'

'It's not that I'm a prude . . .' she murmured.

'It's not a matter of morality, rather one of simple good manners, I'd have thought.'

'I'm *sure* they thought I was asleep.'

'Indeed? They hardly allowed you much time for it, I must say.' He was startled to hear her giggle, suddenly.

'They hardly allowed much time for anything. He just came in the door and . . . bingo.'

He straightened and peered at her outline in the chair. 'Bingo?'

The giggling became more pronounced. 'Yes . . . five

steps over to the bed, one creak of the springs, two gasps, and . . . bingo . . . they were off and . . .'

'A veritable triumph of marksmanship, considering his condition,' he heard himself say.

Laura erupted into stifled laughter. He stood by the faint green light of the stereo, trying to remain serious and sympathetic, but the more she laughed the more he wanted to laugh, too. His mouth began to fight him. In the end her attempts to stop laughing were even funnier to him than his own not to start, and just as ineffectual. It was hysteria, of course, hysteria arising from tension and exhaustion, nothing else.

Laura could see him, now, or at least make out the glint of his spectacles, the shape of his head, the white of his teeth and the pale outline of his shirt. When she had realised what was actually happening in the bed next to hers she had been dumbfounded. Then, when the gasps and movements increased in intensity she could no longer stand it and had fled – quite unnoticed, she was sure. She *wasn't* a prude, but she couldn't pretend to be asleep. Not with it so close, so . . . right *there*. She'd run out seeking solitude. Now she was very glad Skinner was here, laughing as helplessly as she. Somehow that made it all right, made her see how insane it all was. Skinner tried to bring himself under control, only to set them both off again by blurting: 'Between Goade leaping back every time I come near him, and now Sherri and Hallick reverting to the primitive . . . oh, pulsating sexuality, your magic spell is everywhere.'

He dropped into his chair, reached up and pulled his glasses off, wiped his eyes, and eventually they coasted to a stop. 'Oh, Lord . . . this is all so *bloody* ridiculous. Sorry.' He clapped his glasses on again and scowled. 'You must think me a complete idiot,' he muttered after a while.

It was so easy in the dark. 'No, I don't,' she told him truthfully. 'I think you're probably the least idiotic person I've ever met.'

He sighed again. 'Thank you.' The laughter had drained them, left them exhausted with a kind of temporary peace.

He leaned his head against the rough texture of the upholstery and listened to the rustle of her dressing gown as she settled herself more comfortably in her chair. After a while he spoke in a reflective tone. 'Do you know . . . I realise our situation is absolutely extraordinary, and yet . . . I don't actually feel any less comfortable *here* than I do on any given day *anywhere*. I teach nine months of the year and usually travel during the summer. I live in a little house in a little town, the same place I've lived for years. I've never furnished it beyond the basic necessities because it isn't really a home, it's simply where I live. That being the case, my work aside – I might as well be here as there. Does that strike you as peculiar?'

'No.' She tried to make him out in the shadows. He was a complete stranger, she knew little about him, yet the only name she could put to the feeling she had at that moment was recognition.

'Are you afraid?' she asked abruptly. She had been. She wasn't, now.

'Not yet,' he answered. 'Not yet, I don't think.' Suddenly he stood up and walked past her to stand at the window, looking out. The sky was clear. In the blackness above he saw and automatically catalogued old friends in their familiar glittering patterns. The moon was growing brighter behind the house, giving a ghostly illumination to the snow and the intersecting lines of birches and firs.

'I don't understand . . .' she paused, staring into the fire as a log broke in a rush of sparks and then fell, its glow darkening.

'What?' he asked, softly.

'Why you're so calm about it all, I guess. Everyone else has gotten angry, or upset in some way. But not you.'

'And not you.'

She plucked at the edge of her robe, twitched it over her knees. 'I've had my . . . less noble moments. I just had one, in fact.'

'The crying, or the laughing?'

'Both. You just . . . watch.'

87

'Yes, well . . . that's my profession, isn't it? Watching. When you're dealing with objects that existed millions of years before one and will continue to exist millions of years after one . . . day to day doesn't seem to have as much impact, somehow.' He bent his knees slightly to locate Aldebaran. 'And also . . . I've taught myself not to waste time on inessentials. Oh, not beautiful things or interesting things, they're always essential. But struggling for position, trying to be first in every race, that sort of nonsense. After my wife died I did a lot of that, but one day I began to hear the sound of all those feet pattering after all those rather meaningless triumphs, and mine were louder and faster than any of them. It seemed rather a silly noise to be making. So I . . . stopped making it. I will not change the world, I will not be rich or famous or wonderful in any way. I'm all I have and so now I spend myself a little at a time.' He chuckled. 'Except for my occasional forays into talking utter and absolute balderdash . . . sorry about the Sunday supplement philosophy, so late at night.'

'It's the best time for philosophy.'

'The self-justification of an unambitious man, I'm afraid. Not very impressive.'

' "And there is no object so soft but it makes a hub for the wheeled universe," ' she whispered.

'I beg your pardon?'

She blushed in the darkness, and tried to summon back the laughter. 'Oh, you talk philosophy, I spout poetry . . .'

'Say it again.' She repeated the phrase for him and he considered it. 'Wordsworth?'

'Tsk . . . the chauvinism of the English knows no bounds. Whitman, actually.'

'Oh. *Song of Myself*?'

'Yes,' she acknowledged, and felt her own chauvinism pinching a little. 'Anyway . . . your philosophy may not be world-shaking – that would defeat its object . . . but it *is* impressive.'

He put a quaver into his voice. 'Ah . . . you've made an old man very happy, my dear.'

She smiled, then stopped. 'Is that how you think of yourself, as an old man?'

'It's how my students think of me . . . who am I to argue with all those shining eager little faces?' he mocked himself.

Laura sighed and relaxed into the chair. 'Everybody thinks of me as a little girl,' she confided. 'My father calls me his "baby", Larry thinks I can't get from one side of the street to the other unless he draws me a map, my mother says I have the dress sense of a six-year-old. But I'm not a child, any more than you're an old man. Why don't people really *see* one another, I wonder?'

'I teach astronomy, not the psychology of perception. All they have to go on is the clues we give them. Perhaps you want to be seen as a child, perhaps I want to be seen as an old man. Perhaps we're both very successful at hiding ourselves, so it ill behoves us to resent it when it works against us.'

Laura nodded. She liked talking to him, she decided. Or perhaps it was just the sound of his soft, careful voice in the darkness that comforted her. He was such a strange man. Every time she thought she knew what he was, he turned into something else, right in front of her eyes. Or ears. Timmy saw Skinner as patient and gentle, Goade saw him as prissy, Morgan seemed suspicious of his intelligence, Sherri didn't even seem to see him at all. Curious. Suddenly, she turned in her chair to look at him standing at the window with his back to her, outlined by the moonlight as he looked up at the sky, and was stunned by what she felt.

She saw him as a male animal.

It was as if he were stripped naked. She could imagine every inch of him with complete clarity, and yet it was an abstract vision, almost cubistic. A rectangle bisected halfway up its length, topped by a sphere on a heavy stalk, his backside two squares set low and slightly indented at the sides, the whole of his body a smooth tawny colour that paled slightly over the stretch of buttocks, shoulder blades, and the hard muscles of his calves. She knew, positively *knew* that's what he would be like. Stocky, square-built men had never attracted her, the few men she had been drawn to physically had invariably been tall and lean, like Larry Carter. And yet, in that moment, she saw in Skinner's body true power. Power at rest, but power nonetheless. It was the threat of the sudden turn, the confrontation, the eyes compelling and the hands opening that gave her stylised image of him vibrant sexual overtones. It *had* to be the result of what had happened in the dark bedroom upstairs. She must have been aroused without realising it by the sounds made by Sherri and Hallick, there was no other explanation. Because this coolly intellectual stranger, a compact domino masked in ill-fitting clothes, had suddenly and almost overwhelmingly filled her with a physical hunger she had never before experienced. *She* had never initiated lovemaking with a man, and yet she wanted to, now. She wanted to go to him, touch him, confirm her vision of masculinity and promise, arouse him, and be taken. Especially his mouth . . . she wanted his mouth to . . .

'I suppose you know all the stars by heart,' she ventured shakily.

'Hmmm? Oh, yes . . . since I was a boy. They never change.' He dropped his eyes to the trees again. 'Of course, the stars *are* changing all the time . . . but never enough in one lifetime to comprehend except by hypothesis. Almost all my work is hypothesis, you see. We don't really *know* very much at all – and just when we think we do, somebody discovers something that turns it all upside down again. Guesswork, that's all it is. You can't touch a star, hold it in your hand, ask it what it's *doing* out there. Even if you could, I imagine there would be a language problem.'

'Yes . . . well . . .' She couldn't stay here. It was impossible to stay here feeling the way she did when he was just standing there thinking about his work. And she didn't really want what she thought she wanted, of course she didn't, it was just – what had he said? – bloody ridiculous. 'I think I'll take your suggestion about moving to the other servant's room. It would be better anyway . . . I'm not used to sharing.'

90

'It has its tribulations,' he commented wryly, still looking out the window.

She got up and made herself walk toward the door. 'Good night.'

He glanced around at her and smiled. 'Good night.' As she passed behind him he caught the faint scent of warm flowers, incongruous in the face of all the snow outside. He returned abruptly to his contemplation of the scene and frowned. Backing along the window he stood at the corner and looked across the front of the house as far as he could see. The moonlight was quite bright, now, and the shadows cast before it were almost sharp-edged, strewn out in a pattern that suddenly made no sense whatsoever. He cleared his throat and raised his voice slightly. 'Laura?'

She was at the door of the bedroom and turned quickly at the sound of his voice. 'Yes?'

'Can you sew at all?'

# Ten

'What time does that paper hit the streets in Beirut?'

Carter consulted his notebook. 'It leaves the presses around five-thirty in the morning. A copy could be taken any time after that – if they've got a contact in the press-room there's no need to wait for street distribution.'

'And what times does Goade's watch show?'

Carter looked at his notebook and then at the pictures tacked on the board in front of them. On the top row were the eight originals of the hostages taken with the newspaper, and below it enlargements of various areas of the pictures. 'It says eight-fifty, but there's no way of knowing whether that's morning or evening . . . there's no natural light in the pictures, just flash.'

'If it's morning they could be within three hours of Beirut, or less.'

'Yes. But if it's evening . . . they could be anywhere.'

'The boy is wearing pyjamas . . . like he just got up.'

Captain Skinner shook his head. 'He could also be ready to go to bed . . . that doesn't mean anything, either.'

Ainslie contemplated the pictures for a moment, then spoke with conviction. 'It's morning.'

'You seem pretty sure, sir.'

'I am. *She* hasn't got any make-up on,' he said, pointing at Sherri Lasky. 'Women never take their make-up off before nine o'clock, but they sometimes don't put it on until after breakfast.'

'Maybe she hasn't got any make-up with her.'

'Yes, she does. Look here.' He picked up the first pictures they'd got from the kidnappers, the one of Laura and Sherri asleep on the beds. At the edge there was the top of a bureau or table, and on it were various bottles and jars. 'Laura doesn't use that brand so it must be Miss Lasky's,' Ainslie concluded.

'All right, I'll buy that,' Carter conceded, making a note. 'So they're within three hours or less of Beirut.'

'Three hours travelling by what method?' Captain Skinner asked quietly. 'By car that's perhaps a hundred miles . . . but by helicopter at least twice that. And by plane . . .' He shrugged.

Ainslie scowled and dropped the photograph back onto the desk. 'Anything else, Larry? Those so-called forensic experts must have some ideas.'

'Ideas, yes sir, lots. But facts . . . no. All conjecture, they said.'

'Spit 'em out.'

Carter took a deep breath and let it out. 'Okay. In this enlargement you can see the inside of the kid's elbow. We counted five or maybe six injection points, most of them nearly healed, but the bruises take longer. They say that if they were sedated right after they were taken, which seems likely considering the pilots were drugged, then they were kept under for some time. But they haven't been drugged for the last day or two. They all look clear-eyed enough, although we can't see Goade's face all that well because of the light streaks. This one looks a little looped, though.' His pencil tapped Skinner's picture.

Fortunately the flash hadn't reflected off his spectacles and his eyes were clearly visible, one drooping a little more than the other, both bleary. 'Can't see *his* elbows holding the paper up like he is . . . but it looks like they've kept him under for some reason.'

'What about it, Captain?' Ainslie turned to the man on the couch. 'Is your brother apt to have given them trouble so they'd have to keep him quiet?'

Captain Skinner grinned but it was a humourless effort. 'David? That's pretty unlikely. He's a very quiet man, probably wouldn't even have *spoken* out of turn, much less tried anything physical. He tends to watch and wait. I'm not saying he doesn't have a temper . . . he's got a god-awful temper, in fact, but it takes a great deal to set it off. I'd expect trouble from Hallick, Goade, even Morgan if they maltreated his wife or child – but not David. Not yet, anyway.'

'But eventually?'

'If they pushed him enough. I hope they don't, for their sakes.'

Carter turned to stare at him. 'What do you mean . . . you make him sound . . .'

'What?' Captain Skinner asked, with a raised eyebrow.

'I don't know . . . dangerous, I guess.'

'Any man with a white-hot temper is dangerous, to himself and the people around him, I'm afraid. David knows he can be destructive if he loses control, so he never allows it to happen.'

Carter looked at Ainslie. 'I thought you said he was the pipe and slippers type?'

Ainslie shrugged. 'What else do your photo experts say?'

'They think they're all being kept together. Goade's picture was probably taken first – those light streaks usually occur at the start of a roll that's been slightly exposed during loading. They also say that *probably* means it's a fairly expensive camera – most cheap ones take cassettes. Anyway, you can see his hands clearly enough – his knuckles are pale, scared or angry they said. But he crumpled up the paper and you can see those crumple marks in all the rest of the pictures because most of the others seem to have grabbed it further up the page. And maybe the Professor was taken last. Maybe. We blew up *his* watch – here – and it reads 9.03, an interval of some thirteen or fourteen minutes, if their watches were more or less synchronised. It would have been enough time to take all the pictures if they moved straight through the sequence. About right.'

Captain Skinner got up from the couch and came over to stand next to the board, leaning close to inspect the photographs as Carter continued his report.

'The wall behind them is natural teak. Now you don't find that out here too much because of the climate and the insects. So they make it someplace with air conditioning, an office maybe, or a rich man's house.'

'What about that house where you met Doppler?' Captain Skinner asked, still inspecting the photographs. 'Did you get inside?'

'No.' Ainslie shook his head. 'I only saw the one room through the glass doors and that had white walls.'

'Have they located the house yet?'

Again Ainslie shook his head, ran his fingers through his hair and pressed his palms against his temples. 'No. I told them I counted off twenty-three minutes in the air but it's impossible to tell a change of direction in a heli-copter. They don't bank, they pivot. Twenty-three minutes straight puts us out of Adabad in three directions and over the sea in the other.'

'What about a ship?' Carter suggested suddenly. 'A yacht . . . all that panelling . . . they could be on a yacht, couldn't they?'

'Yes, that's good,' Captain Skinner approved, still bent forward at the pictures. 'I know someone who can check that out for you . . .'

Ainslie was watching him now because he sensed a ten-sion in his body that hadn't been there before. 'What is it, Captain?'

Captain Skinner straightened. 'Would it be possible to get an exact translation of this front page?'

'Larry?'

'Well, sure . . . take an hour or two, but sure. Why?'

'It might be nothing . . . there's just . . .' He took a hand out of his pocket to tap his brother's photograph. 'His eyes, first of all. Not only is he winking, but his eyes are almost crossed.'

'We figured that was the sedation,' Carter said.

'No . . . I think it's deliberate. When we were children we had a signal just like that . . . nothing obvious, but it meant something like "I'm telling a lie, back me up". Very useful when trying to get out of scrapes . . . we got into a lot of scrapes, David and I.' He closed his eyes for a moment, then opened them wide. 'Anyway . . . that looks very like it to me. He might guess I'd have a chance to see the pictures . . . it would have been worth a try, anyway.'

'But how could he be telling a lie in a photograph?' Carter argued with some impatience. It all sounded a bit vague to him.

'Perhaps he means the picture is telling a lie,' Skinner suggested. 'You see his hands? Everyone else held the paper with their hands pretty well opposite one another, the way you do naturally. But not David . . . the left one is a good six inches higher than the right, and his fingers are spread out awkwardly, too. David is fussy about his hands because of playing the piano so much . . . and he's never awkward. I think he's pointing *to* something.'

The other two went closer and peered at the photograph. The observation was valid – the Professor's hands did look odd.

'Does your brother read Arabic?' Ainslie asked.

'Why do you think he was sent out to set up that solar observatory? He's damn good but still young in academic terms. He spoke the language – that is what made the difference. He speaks six languages, actually, all with an absolutely atrocious accent but comprehensible enough to get by. What he can't speak he smiles, I gather. It seems to work.'

'He must be brilliant,' Ainslie said.

'He's a member of Mensa. David has a mind like a nosey sponge – he simply has to find out because he likes knowing things. Doesn't matter what it is, he just feeds on fresh information in case he might need it *sometime*. He plays piano to nearly concert performance standard, he reads voraciously, walks miles and keeps fit, writes textbooks and does an amazing amount of research – all simply because he has nothing *else* to do. He's a lonely man . . . he has to fill his hours or go mad.' Captain Skinner looked back at his brother's photograph. 'He wasn't always like that, of course. Probably one of the most vicious rugby blues they ever had at Cambridge and not a bad amateur actor, either. But when Margaret died, he changed. Locked himself up and hid the key. When it gets too bad with him . . . he comes to us and I guess pretends for a while that my family is his, that he's a part of something. We wish he'd come more . . . but . . . he doesn't.'

'How long were they married?' Ainslie asked, not quite certain why he wanted to know.

'Six months. Childhood sweethearts, all that kind of thing. He took it very badly.' He turned away abruptly and walked over to the window, his hands thrust deep into his pockets.

'Get onto that translation thing, will you, Larry?' Ainslie asked quietly, watching the uniformed figure at the window. Carter nodded and went out. Ainslie turned to look at the photograph again, his eyes drawn irresistibly to Laura. She'd understand that kind of man, he thought. She had pain like his once and had reacted the same way. Went inside herself and closed the door. He'd never been able to find the key, any more than the Professor's brother had.

The words Professor Skinner had been pointing to proved to be *sun*, *cold*, and *midnight*.

'Mean anything to you, Captain?'

'No. I guess I was wrong. But it was worth a try.'

'Maybe it will make sense later on.'

The Englishman nodded, almost smiled. 'Maybe.'

At nine that evening Grey burst into the dining room, his face red with excitement. 'They've found them . . . they think they've found them!'

It was a small house on a twisting back lane in the old city. They walked the last five hundred yards because the car couldn't get any closer. The police had been watching the house since late that afternoon because of a chance piece of information they'd picked up from one of their regular informers. A man in an American Army uniform

97

had been seen briefly at one of the windows of the house, and the house was known to them as having been used before by 'suspicious' people.

'What do they mean by "suspicious" people?' Ainslie whispered to Grey as they went down the uneven pavement between the dark houses.

'They didn't say, exactly,' Grey whispered back. 'I guess you know they don't like us much . . . oh, they like our money and all that . . . but a lot of the locals resent the changes they think we've brought because of the oil. This Hammad . . . the cop in charge . . . he hates our guts.'

'Don't tell me some American GI got his sister pregnant?' Ainslie joked.

'Oh . . . you know about that?' Grey said in surprise. 'He was an oil company clerk though, not a soldier.'

'Jesus Christ, doesn't anything ever change?' Ainslie grumbled to Carter.

'What?'

'Nothing . . . never mind . . . this looks like it up ahead.' Ainslie turned up his jacket collar and stifled a sneeze. In Oslo he'd stayed as healthy as a horse, here in a hot desert country he'd come down with a headcold. Even his sinus passages were against him.

Grey introduced them to Captain Hammad, a hatchet-faced man with a mouth like a bad-tempered barracuda. They huddled in an archway looking at the house across the way and Hammad grudgingly told them that as far as they knew the uniformed man was still in the house.

'One man goes in, nobody comes out . . .'

'You know the man who went in?'

'We know. Not a good type.'

'Criminal . . . political . . . how do you mean, "not good"?' Captain Skinner asked with intense curiosity. Hammad turned to look at him and Ainslie saw that his eyes seemed to have no pupil . . . just dark brown centres that melted into the whites with no delineation.

Hammad stared at Captain Skinner for while, then turned away without answering his question. 'We will be going in now,' he announced softly. 'My men are in position.'

'Are they armed?' Captain Skinner seemed very anxious. 'There may be women and a child in there . . . if there's shooting . . .'

'Excuse me, please,' Hammad interrupted, and slipped out of the archway and into the next shadow soundlessly. They had two more glimpses of him before he seemed to disappear entirely, engulfed by the darkness.

'Insolent bastard,' Ainslie muttered.

'You must understand, General, we actually have no status here,' Grey tried to explain. 'They needn't have notified us at all . . .' Carter dug an elbow into his arm and he shut up.

The night seemed to stop around them, waiting, and then the silence was split by a shot, followed swiftly by two more. Captain Skinner moaned and hit the wall with a clenched fist. Then another shot was heard and Ainslie's control snapped. He ran out of the archway and up the cobbled street toward the house. After a moment, Captain Skinner dashed after him. Grey grabbed Carter's sleeve, his mouth opening and closing like a guppy's.

'Yeah . . . I know . . . we have no goddam status,' Carter snarled, and pulled away from him to follow the others. 'I'll write a report on what you can do with your status, Grey.'

As Ainslie reached the door of the house it burst open and a man cannoned into him, knocking him back against the wall. Hammad was close behind, but just as he was raising his gun to fire at the man's back, Captain Skinner tripped over a loose cobble and crashed headlong into Hammad's knees. It looked almost like a perfect rugby tackle. The shot went wild, and so did Hammad, cursing and kicking at the uniformed Englishman to free himself. He ran shouting down the street into shadows. Another policeman came out of the door and his foot ground the fallen Skinner's hand into the cobbles with a crunch of bones and tendons. Then he, too, ran down the street with

99

his gun raised. With a wordless howl of pain Captain Skinner fell back onto the stones, clutching his hand and raising it into the moonlight where it seemed to swell visibly as he watched. Ainslie pushed himself away from the wall and caught Skinner under the arms, first dragging him upright and then towing him white-faced into the house where there seemed to be a great many people, none of whom they wanted to see.

Carter entered behind them and they stared wildly about, Captain Skinner clutching his forearm to support and protect the crushed hand, Ainslie still half-choking to get some breath into his lungs.

'Through there . . . try through there!' Carter shouted over the noise of the arguing policemen, all of whom seemed to be trying to get the blame in first. He put a hand under Ainslie's elbow and conveyed them between the windmilling arms and bulging eyes to a half-open door on the far side of the room. A younger policeman stood by it as if trying to prevent someone leaving or entering. He stepped back automatically at the sight of the three uniforms, then gave a half-salute that ended in a faltering flop of his arm.

The second room was larger than the first but seemed more crowded because of all the furniture it contained. Desk, bureau, washstand, wardrobe, three chairs, bed. On the bed, stretched neatly and full-length, was a man wearing an American Army uniform.

Carter started to turn back out of the room to search the other corner of the house but stopped at the sight of Grey who stood behind him staring in.

'Is he dead?' Grey gasped.

'I don't know . . . get out of my way, will you?' Carter shoved past him and dived through the milling swarm of policemen. Grey slowly entered the room and joined Ainslie and Captain Skinner at the side of the bed.

'Where's Larry gone?' Ainslie asked in a thin voice.

'To look for the others I guess . . . but the cops are saying there's no one else in the place. He's not dead, is he?'

'No . . . but his breathing's not too good. Why? You know him?'

'Don't you?' Grey demanded. 'That's Johnny Goade.'

The local doctor who attended the Embassy staff was binding Captain Skinner's hand when Carter came into the office and very deliberately kicked a chair out of his way. It skidded over the linoleum but remained upright, coming to rest against the side table.

'Well?' Ainslie demanded.

'It's Goade, all right . . . but he's so far under he won't wake up until the middle of tomorrow.'

'Can't they give him something to bring him out of it?'

'They tried, but it didn't work and they won't give him any more because they say it might kill him.'

'Meanwhile the kidnappers are taking the rest of them further and further away,' Ainslie groaned. But Carter was shaking his head.

'Uh-uh. There's no way the rest of them could have been kept in that house, it's too small. They must have separated them right after those second pictures were taken, it's the only explanation.'

Captain Skinner gave a grunt of pain and the doctor murmured an abject apology as he continued to work. Carter glanced over.

'Is it broken?'

'No . . . only bent, he says. It's not his bloody hand, of course.' The Englishman spoke through his teeth.

Carter stared at him for a moment without seeing him, then drew closer to Ainslie and spoke in a whisper. 'Sir, your wife's on the phone.'

'My who?'

'Mrs Ainslie, sir. Sorry, Mrs Potts I guess it is, now. Apparently somebody told her you were here, and why. It may not be in the papers – but . . .'

'Oh, hell.' Ainslie's eyes showed fear, the first time Carter had seen it there since they'd heard about the plane going missing. 'Oh, shit,' Ainslie amplified. It was the first time

Carter had ever heard *that* from him, either.

'She's very upset, sir. I think you should talk to her . . . she's crying and . . .'

'Grace *always* sounds like she's crying. Damn, I hoped she wouldn't find out I was here.'

'It's a small place . . . people talk . . .'

'How come it's a small place when she wants to find *me*, and such a big place when we want to find Laura? It's not a country, it's a goddamned accordion. *You* talk to her, will you?'

'I did . . . I tried to . . .'

'Sure . . . thanks . . . never mind.' Ainslie walked slowly to the desk and picked up the phone. Even before he got the receiver to his ear he could hear the wailing and the weeping, and sighed. Freud was right, he decided, life *was* just one goddamned thing after another. It was going to be a long hot night. He hated long hot nights.

# Eleven

Skinner had forgotten the sheer pain of being cold.

Before he'd even got around the corner of the house his nose had begun to burn. The sub-zero air froze the inner membranes every time he took a breath, then thawed when he exhaled, only to freeze again, thaw again. They had not been able to wait for a still day. He had hoped the wind would die down by midday. It hadn't. As a result, even behind the crudely knitted mask and mittens he felt his flesh tightening and stiffening against the bitter restless air. Soon both face and hands would begin to ache. He crossed his arms and jammed his hands between elbows and body. Once around the corner he had some protection but not much. The crude seams of his suit were already etching a line of ice down his body as the wind pried at them and penetrated.

It had taken them two days to make the suit. Work had been interrupted once by the return of the gunmen for another set of pictures long before he was ready for them. They had done the best they could, but he wasn't very hopeful that their second message would be as clear as the first – if that had been noticed at all. During the picture session they had been terrified that the gunmen would make another tour of the bedrooms and perhaps notice some of the missing items, but they had stayed downstairs, taken their photographs and departed. Denning had asked for a prescription to be filled, Goade had asked for more brandy (and a ride home), and Anne Morgan had asked for more toys for Timmy. If the gunmen *had* gone upstairs they might well have been annoyed. Six towels, one thin over-blanket, one sheet, four pillows, one bedroom curtain, four insulating tiles from the ceiling, a rubber bathmat, and a pair of shower curtains were now missing from the inventory of the house. They would have wondered where they were. Skinner knew where they were – he was wearing them.

'Look,' he had explained to the others. 'If we *know* where we are we can *say* where we are in the pictures. I'll look around once during the day, see if that *is* a boathouse down by the lake, see if there *is* a road or a town in sight. Then I'll go out again at night and get precise bearings from the stars. But it will take time and I'll need something to wear.' He was sure Laura at least thought it was just another 'project', like the lists he'd made with Timmy, but she worked as hard as the others, perhaps even harder, and had the sore fingers to prove it.

His shuffling progress through the deep snow was as comical as his appearance, he supposed, and he avoided looking in at the window when he came level with it. They were all standing inside watching for him. Goade, too, no doubt, still filled with the hilarity he'd given vent to when Skinner had finally emerged from his room wearing the home-made arctic gear they'd put together.

Layers, that was the secret of insulation. Not a big thick overcoat but a series of thin 'overcoats' that trapped dead air between them. He'd known what was needed, but not how to manufacture it. It was Sherri, in the end, who had made the pattern and supervised the sewing.

'I was making my own clothes from the time I was ten,' she'd told him. 'We grew grain, not money. Store-bought clothes were for town folks, not us.' This practical side of her nature seemed at odds with her constant *femme fatale* act, but he was grateful to her.

They had the kitchen shears to cut it out, and the two curved needles from the poultry trussing kit to sew it together. Everything else was a compromise. First they'd painstakingly unravelled one of the rough-weave bedroom curtains to get thread. That was Timmy's job. What they didn't use for sewing was either braided into drawstrings for wrist, waistband, hood, and ankles, or knitted into the balaclava and mittens that now protected his face and hands. Anne Morgan had done the knitting. Sherri, Laura, and Skinner himself had made the suit. Denning's arthritis made his fingers too stiff for the work, and Goade refused to have anything to do with the entire operation, except to make comments from time to time about Dior turning over in his grave. The boots were Morgan's contribution, aided by Hallick. The result was somewhat spectacular in its own way, but not entirely satisfactory as Skinner was beginning to discover.

He'd had to stand in his underwear while Laura took the measurements, a procedure that seemed to embarrass her far more than it did him. She called them out to Sherri who translated them into newspaper patterns. Then they cut out an inner suit of towelling, soft and absorbent. After that the snowsuit itself – sheet, loose feathers, and blanket quilted together into jacket and trousers. And then a last layer of plastic shower curtaining which they rubbed with cooking oil to keep it flexible in the cold. It was the shower curtains that had caused the trouble. It was hardly *his* fault they'd been patterned with bunches of flowers and grapes caught up in green leaves. That had been far preferable to the alternatives from the other bathrooms – multi-coloured parrots, mermaids, or the gaping lines of impossible fish blowing equally impossible bubbles.

Goade had very nearly ruptured himself. 'I love it, I love it!' he shouted, pounding the arm of the sofa. 'Too bad we haven't got a bell to go on the tip of his little hood, hey?'

Skinner had nearly stifled in the heat of the house while Morgan and Hallick put on the 'boots'. Lacking any kind of glue (although they'd made several malodorous attempts to produce some) they had settled on a base of insulating tiles and rubber bathmat, bound on by strip after strip of blanket, until he looked like a double-gout patient. If he could have stayed on the surface of the snow it would have been fine, but the snow was deep and already the outer blanket strips were sodden. Dry cold was bad enough, wet cold was lethal. He had to move quickly, but he could not, and so was balanced on a knife edge between time allowed and area to be covered.

Wearing his glasses was probably a bad idea, but it was either putting up with the smears of cooking oil that kept them from frosting over or being unable to tell he was about to walk into a tree until it was too late. At least they'd keep his eyeballs from freezing. For a while.

He was past the window now, and could not resist glancing at the others through the glass, freeing one hand momentarily to give a brief wave and then returning it to its haven against his body. The bulk of the chimney was next, snow caught in the crevices between the irregular stones, very picturesque. And then he was next to it – the real reason he'd insisted on all of this, the truth that had only revealed itself by its 'moonlit shadow on the snow. He paused a moment and turned side-on to the wind. The exterior of the house was magnificent. Broad planks of dark wood overlapping horizontally, broken on this south side by the chimney and the picture window to his left, and to his right . . .

Three long narrow windows stretched two storeys high, breaking the lapstrake lines of the cladding. Their glass reflected the birches, the snow, the sky, and himself – ridiculous in his brightly patterned snowsuit. He'd been quite correct. The house was twice as big on the outside as it seemed on the inside.

Giving a small grunt of satisfaction he waded over to the nearest of the tall windows, but they were curtained and he couldn't see what lay within. Slowly he continued around to the back, stopped and looked around at his tracks, already being filled in by snow that was being blown off the surface and over the edges of each shapeless step.

There was no door into the other half of the house.

No door, no break of any kind in the long lines of the overlapping boards. Nothing at all.

He made a brief sortie into the woods to the rear but

106

there was no indication of a path or lane in any direction. Returning to the house he doggedly completed his circuit. He twisted his face in gargoyle grimaces, bringing a hand up to punch himself on the nose. It hurt, so it was still alive. He leaned against the corner of the house, trying to keep his breathing light so the cold wouldn't penetrate the depths of his lungs. His cramped muscles screamed for oxygen but he could only allow them a metered flow – the bill for gasping was too high out here. After a while standing still and losing what body heat he'd built up was even more expensive, so he left the shelter of the house and started down the treeless avenue that led to the lakeside. Once out of the lee of the house the arms of the wind met again, pushing him toward the shore some eight hundred metres ahead. The small wooden structure was *not* a boathouse – it stood some twenty metres short of the lake's edge. He shuffled toward it, turned the handle and stepped inside. A sauna, of course. It couldn't have been anything else in Finland. Quite an elaborate one, too. An outer changing room, and beyond, the sauna proper. It was windowless, but by the light from the door he could just make out the low wooden benches that lined the walls on all four sides of the stone-filled pit in the centre. At the far end was another door, leading to the lake where one's overheated body could find exhilaration by sudden immersion. While his body was quivering and shaking in self-defence against the bitter cold he found the pleasure of such a prospect eluded him. He went through the far door and continued down to the edge of the lake.

As far as he could see ahead there was only the flat ice. By squinting he could just make out the farther shore, a mere thickening in the line of the horizon. He tried to summon up from his memory some semblance of a map of Finland, but it was no use. He didn't know if he'd ever examined one, except during his schooldays. They, like everything else, were a long way off.

On this side the shore stretched away on either hand until it, too, became a thin featureless line. Three miles across? More? And length – no way of telling. The freezing air was deceptive and his eyesight untrustworthy now. One always doubled or even trebled distance when estimating under these conditions, nothing was ever as close you'd like it to be.

The stillness, apart from the wind creaking the trees behind him, was absolute. Stepping tentatively onto the ice, he went a little way out from the shore, feeling no give beneath him. Already the thickness must exceed half a metre, depending on the slope of the bottom. The surface was not slippery, the constant etching of the wind had seen to that, but he went carefully because he was already beginning to lose sensation in his feet. He'd have no warning if he came to a fault or weak spot, and a sudden soaking was the last thing he needed. Overhead the sky was an even, featureless grey without a discernible moving cloud shape. The diffused light gave a surrealistic dimension to the bleak scene. It wasn't until he turned into the wind and saw the house that he felt human again. The wood used in the lapstraking was apparently creosoted, and the dark rectangular bulk with the silvery reflections in the windows was a startling contrast. The roof, he saw, was steeply inclined to allow snow to slide off. Smoke was being whipped away from the chimney by the wind. The thin streamers reminded him, if he needed reminding, that beneath them lay warmth and a haven from the silent emptiness that was slowly freezing him to death.

Once back on the shore he turned around and began backing into the wind toward the house, down the long avenue, past the little wooden sauna, glancing over his shoulder every once in a while to orient himself and trying to follow his own tracks. His entire body was beginning to ache. Twisting his face and flexing his fingers and toes he listened to the dry crunch of the snow under his feet and the eerie creaking of the wind-rubbed branches on either side. Behind his spectacles his eyes were watering, the tears gathering below the lenses on the yarn of his mask and freezing, as his exhalations were freezing beneath his nose and chin. He banged himself on the nose again, loosening the crystals of ice, but didn't feel the impact. Too long. He'd stayed out too long.

By the time he finally reached the house the ice had caked his eyelids shut and he was afraid to touch them for fear of shattering his spectacles or tearing the flesh of his eyelids away with the ice. His hands could not grasp the wooden knob of the door, and he banged feebly a couple of times until they realised, and came. Just before he went in he leaned down and took two handfuls of snow, pressing it over his glasses to protect them against the sudden warmth of the interior. He had no sensation of cold from the snow, except under his nose where his breathing had regularly warmed the skin of his upper lip.

Someone grabbed him and helped him through the entry into the big room beyond, and he heard someone else slam the outer and inner doors behind him. Slowly the snow in his mittened hands began to melt, running between his fingers and down his wrists.

'We've run a hot bath for you,' he heard Tom Morgan say.

'No . . . no . . .' he managed to articulate as they led him along. 'Run a cool bath . . . a cold bath . . .'

'But . . .' someone else protested.

'You heard him,' Morgan's voice snapped. 'Do what he says . . .'

'Hang in there, Prof,' came Hallick's voice on his other side; it was Morgan and Hallick who were guiding him along. The last of the snow slid away from his face and his glasses instantly steamed over leaving him as blind as ever. He could hear bathwater running, now. Eventually they held him still and he felt the suit being taken off. Lacking any method of fastening they'd sewn him into it and now had to cut him out of it. He could feel hands fumbling along the seams, felt the jerk and snap as the threads were parted, and then heard a woman's voice gasp, 'My god . . .'

The stiff suit was pulled away from him and the knitted mask eased over his head. Finally he was able to take his glasses off and felt the ice on his eyelids melting and running down his face. The sudden warmth of the room was as agonising as the cold outside had been. Staggering slightly he pulled away from them and went into the bathroom. He slid into the water still in his underwear, leaving his bound feet hanging over the edge of the bath. Morgan followed him in to the bathroom and began unwinding the strips of cloth until Skinner could pull his feet free and submerge them in the water. He knew it was cool water but it felt warm to him. Leaning forward he took a breath and submerged his face. In a little while he would turn the tap with the red circle. In a little while, but not yet.

He slept for a while cocooned by the electric blanket, although he'd had no intention of doing so when he climbed under it, and was about to get up when Laura came in carrying a tray. Her eyes widened at the sight of his exposed body and he grabbed at the bedclothes, pulling them up to his chest. He realised it wasn't his nakedness that worried her, but the sight of his ice-burned skin. He thought he detected the glitter of sympathetic tears and spoke gruffly. 'It looks bad but it isn't. It's just like getting red-cheeked on a winter day . . . only a little more extensive. It will go soon.'

She smiled tentatively and he smiled back. 'I've brought you some hot soup and a cup of tea,' she said, setting the tray onto his knees and then perching herself at the end of the bed.

'The universal panacea,' he commented, picking up the spoon. When he'd finished both he set the tray to one side and leaned back against the pillows with a sigh. 'Are you drying out the suit?'

'We hung it in the generator room. Why?'

'You'd better bring it into the warmth . . . it has to be completely dry before I go out again tonight.'

'You can't . . .'

'I said I'd go out *twice*, once to explore the surrounding area and once to calculate our position by the stars.'

110

'You're a very stubborn man,' she chided.

He settled into the pillows and folded his arms over his chest. 'Not really. I simply prefer to finish one thing completely before I start another. Call it a fetish if you like, but I'm going to finish what I set out to do because I won't be comfortable until I have,' he said in a reasonable tone.

'Stubborn.'

'Obsessive?' he suggested.

She smiled despite herself. 'Stubborn.'

'Determined? Noble? Dedicated?'

'Stubborn.'

'You mean you would prefer me to be *merely* stubborn, is that it? Very well, I am a stubborn man. And you are an obstinate woman.'

She stared at him, amazed. 'Me? How can you possibly think that?'

'Very easily. It's written all over your chin.'

Involuntarily she reached up and touched her face, then looked at him in chagrin as he began to chuckle. The trip outside had burnished his skin and his eyes were very blue against the higher colour, the corners crinkling up as he laughed gently at her. She couldn't understand it.

Who was this other man who was smiling at her out of Skinner's face?

Whoever he was, he seemed to be as confused as she was, suddenly, and looked away. She stood up. 'Shall I tell the others you'll be out soon?'

He was pushing the spoon around the tray, making it spin slowly with his index finger. 'Yes, all right. It won't take me a moment to dress.'

When Skinner emerged Laura saw there was no sign of the other man in him who had startled her so much. Wearing his usual wrinkled shirt and trousers, with his glasses back on his nose and his shoulders in their habitual droop, he looked as he always looked. Like a shy, scholarly professor of astronomy bemused at finding himself on the ground instead of high among galaxies and constellations.

111

'Well?' Goade demanded. 'Any sign of Santa Claus out there?'

'I'm afraid not, no,' Skinner said in a soft, regretful voice. 'The wooden structure is a sauna, not a boathouse, there are no roads in sight nor anything else except trees, snow, sky and distance.'

'All that for nothing,' Morgan carped bitterly. 'You looked half-dead when you came back – for nothing.'

'Well,' Skinner said mildly, continuing past them toward the bookshelves that covered the far wall, 'I wouldn't say it was for nothing. All information is useful.' He felt a touch on his arm and looked down.

'You were brave, Skinnie,' Timmy said.

'Tim . . . don't be disrespectful,' Anne Morgan remonstrated.

Skinner smiled. 'I told him he could call me Skinnie – it's what my students call me, although I'm not supposed to know. They could have made it something worse, I suppose,' he added reflectively, then looked down at the boy again. 'And I wasn't brave at all, Tim. Just . . . stubborn.' He glanced at Laura who was standing by the fireplace. 'I just wanted to know . . . you see?'

'Oh.' Timmy thought about this. 'But nobody else wanted to do it.'

'No, well . . . there was only time to make one suit, wasn't there?' He turned to Anne Morgan. 'Could you draw me a map of Finland from memory?'

She shook her head. 'My memory isn't photographic, I'm afraid.'

'Ah . . . pity.' Almost idly he went down to the ladder that stood in the corner and began to slide it along its track across the face of the shelves. He rested his hand on one step, looking down at the floor as he went the whole way to the opposite corner, then turned and ran the ladder back again, slowly. When he'd returned to his starting place he looked at them over his spectacles. 'I wonder if we might take a look among the books for an atlas?' He started back along the shelves, coming to a stop about two-thirds of the way along. 'Yes,' he said, running the ladder back and forth gently beside him. 'Yes, that would be a constructive beginning.'

'But the books are all in Finnish,' Hallick objected from where he was sitting on the arm of Sherri's chair, twining a strand of her hair around a finger and letting it go.

'Oh, indeed, yes they are,' Skinner agreed, mounting the ladder right to the top and leaning forward to examine the shelves more closely. 'But maps are pictures, latitude and longtitude are numbers, so it won't make any difference. That lake out there is very big, certainly big enough to be on a map. It might save me going out again tonight.'

'Well, that seems worth doing,' Laura said, coming across to start pulling likely volumes from the shelves.

'Indeed,' came Skinner's distant tones from over her head. 'Indeed.'

There was no atlas on the shelves.

They had paused for dinner, said goodnight to Timmy, worked on and on, looking even for histories or biographies, anything that might have had a map. One by one the others had lost interest, and in the end only Skinner and Laura persisted. He climbed carefully down the ladder and glanced around at the others. Goade, Denning and Morgan were playing cards, Hallick was carving more soldiers, Sherri and Anne Morgan were seated on opposite sofas not looking at one another.

'I'd hoped to avoid this,' he remarked quietly. 'But I have to know.'

Laura was on the floor in front of the shelves with a stack of books beside her and looked up, startled. 'Avoid what?'

Skinner didn't reply immediately, but put a hand on the ladder and gave it a strong shove that sent it sliding with a hiss of metal on metal to the far end of the wall where it banged and bounced back a few inches. He began poking and prying at the books that had been hidden behind the ladder. After a moment he stopped, leaned forward slightly, and then straightened. 'Of course,' he said to himself. 'Fool.' He took hold of one of the shelf dividers, his fingers catching in a groove that lay just beyond the edge on either side, and gave a sharp yank. There was a click, and the entire bank of shelves in front of Skinner and Laura began to move toward them in a unit.

He grabbed Laura and dragged her bodily up and away, holding her against his chest with one arm and reaching up to adjust his glasses with his free hand. Silently the shelves continued forward for a distance of about a foot, then began to slide to the right, finally coming to rest and leaving a gap of some four feet in width and eight feet in height directly in front of the two of them. A black gap from which a breath of moist cool air flowed momentarily, causing Laura to shiver against him. His arm tightened.

'Perfectly logical, of course,' he breathed, his lips only inches from her cheek. 'Solitude within privacy within isolation.'

The shock of a large dark space suddenly yawning where none should be filled Laura with terror, but the strength of his arm across her and the solidity of his body behind her somehow kept the fear in her head without allowing it to escape. As the others crowded around them he released her abruptly and went forward into the gap.

'What the *hell* . . .?' Goade choked as Skinner's white shirt glimmered briefly and then disappeared.

'Found the switch . . .' came Skinner's voice, and the space beyond the bookshelves was suddenly flooded with light. He reappeared in the gap. 'Right where it should be for a left-handed man, of course.' Then, with his hands clasped behind his back he turned away from them, walking into the room he had just seemingly produced from thin air. They followed him like stunned sheep.

'Son-of-a-bitch,' Goade muttered.

It was one vast room, as high as the main room behind them but longer. The furnishings were both luxurious and simple. Skinner, to their left, was perusing some of the shelves that lined that entire wall, and also filled the spaces between the tall windows on their right. Against the far wall was a long gleaming mahogany table, empty save for a pile of papers and a jar of assorted pens and pencils. In front of the table stood a perfectly ordinary office swivel chair, turned slightly as if its occupant had only just stood up and moved away, although there was no one in the room except themselves. The floor was deeply carpeted wall to wall in dark crimson. The long windows were covered with heavy velvet curtains in the same shade of red and hung in thick vertical folds to the floor. In the centre of the room were two rows of buttoned leather chairs with small tables between each pair. The chairs were set in a slight curve around the object that dominated the room – a massive grand piano in the same gleaming mahogany as the table. As they stared around, too dumbfounded to ask even the obvious questions, Skinner left the shelves and moved with some reverence to the piano. He hesitated a moment, then gently lifted the curved wood and exposed the keyboard. Leaning forward he struck a few keys at random, then some chords in a soft progression. The rich vibrant tones filled the room with only the faint hiss of a humidifier as background. Nobody seemed able to do anything but stare at the room and at Skinner, who continued to play chords at random, lost in the sound he was producing.

'What the hell is it?' Hallick finally asked for all of them.

'Oh . . . it's a Boesendorfer. He wouldn't have anything less.'

Laura went forward and stood next to Skinner as his strong, square hands struck chord after chord on the ivory keys.

'*Who* wouldn't?' she asked. He smiled at her over his glasses and then sat down on the bench. 'Axel Berndt, our host,' he said and gestured with one hand while the other continued to play, runs now, and half-melodies. 'This is his work-room. Those are all manuscripts on those shelves there and there . . . in between the windows are probably

115

references on theory and composition, that sort of thing. He may not know we're here, of course.'

'You know exactly where we are, don't you?' she accused.

'I do *now*,' he said amiably. 'I only suspected before. We can smash up the bottles tonight . . . and I'll need that Morse Code, Anne, if you'd be kind enough to write it out for me?'

Laura sat curled in one of the leather chairs, listening to Skinner play Chopin. Before that it had been Bach, a little Mozart, some Ravel, and now back to Chopin again. He was totally absorbed in the music, his head tilted slightly to one side, the muscles of his shoulders occasionally tightening the shirt across his back as he reached for low and high notes.

Having answered their demands and questions until he had no more to give, the others had finally gone to bed, leaving them alone at last. The sliding door was back in place, isolating them with the music, leaving the others to darkness and sleep.

They were captive, Skinner had told them, in the summer home of Axel Berndt, possibly one of the twenty richest men in the world. A sad, tragic man, he said. His wealth had started with an inheritance and had grown through his own efforts and ingenuity into a great fortune. Munitions, heavy armament, steel, industrial machinery, electronics, cosmetics: Berndt companies made them all. And, in the classic tradition of such things, the money had brought him luxury but not happiness. In the early sixties Axel Berndt had been in a train crash in which he lost the great love of his life. In trying to rescue her he was terribly burned, and had never shown his face in public since. He lived behind his money, moving from house to house around the world. And in the summer he always came to *this* house to do the one thing that gave him pleasure – compose music. The Finnish retreat was well-known but had never been photographed – remaining a secret like most of the things Berndt cared about. For three months every year, no matter what the state of the world or his empire, Axel Berndt wrote music. Skinner had noticed the initials AB on the water taps, and on some of the tools in the generator room, but had said nothing. It had seemed *likely* – but he hadn't been certain until he'd found the piano. There *had* to be a piano, he said. And there was.

Laura thought that the eventual reactions of the others to this information had been the strangest part of it all. Goade had been furious, of course, because Skinner hadn't said anything before.

Denning had gone quiet, while Hallick had begun whirling an annoyed Anne Morgan around in ever-increasing circles. He seemed convinced that once Skinner had got their location out via the photographs it was only a matter of hours before they were rescued. When a very ruffled Anne had pointed out in some irritation that for him that would hardly mean freedom, he had switched instantly from glee to resentment and accused her of hating him like everyone else. Anne had turned to her husband for protection from Hallick's spleen, only to find him talking to Sherri at Berndt's worktable, and had shortly afterward stalked off to bed with a 'headache'. It was left to Denning to calm Hallick down. Sherri had finally grown tired of Morgan's sermonising and had proceeded to lure Hallick out of the room on a trail of whispers. Morgan then rounded on Denning furiously for not keeping his prisoner under control. In the end, Laura had been very happy to see the lot of them gone.

Skinner had finished the Chopin and was flexing his hands to ease the strain.

'David?'

'Hmmm?' he turned on the bench and smiled at her. 'Any requests from the lady in the front row?'

'Do you think they *will* see the message? In the photograph?'

He rubbed the back of his neck and then turned fully around. 'I don't know. We can only try. The other two messages don't seem to have got us anywhere, do they? One does not hear the thunder of rescuing feet, does one?'

'No, one does not,' she smiled, watching him take off his glasses and polish them absently on the front of his shirt. Without their camouflage he looked very tired. 'Are you through playing?'

'No. But you don't have to listen, you know. I have four more days' practice to make up, it will take me quite a while.'

'I *like* listening.' She looked down at her hands. 'I don't think Joe really *wants* to be rescued, you know.'

Skinner stood up and walked across to the shelves of manuscripts, taking one out at random and flipping through it. 'I don't suppose he does. As Anne pointed out with an unerring lack of tact, he doesn't have much to look forward to. The situation might be intolerable for the rest of us, but for him it's a holiday, isn't it? Well,' he amended, replacing the manuscript and extracting another, 'at least a change of jails. And he has a few extra gratifications here he might not expect to get again, once Denning takes him back.'

'Sherri, you mean?'

He smiled briefly. 'Among other things, Sherri, yes. Also the unprejudiced esteem of an eight-year-old child, luxurious surroundings, the company of some *splendid* people,' he twisted his mouth wryly, 'and your bread.'

She laughed. 'Now there's no call for you to turn nasty along with all the rest of them, is there?'

He brought the manuscript back and propped it on the piano.

'Not everyone can be expected to blossom in a situation like this.' He put his glasses back on and leaned forward to peer at the music.

'You have,' she said, and instantly regretted it. His expression, when he looked over his shoulder, was one of total amazement.

'What an extraordinary thing to say.'

She thought so, too, and wondered where it had come

from. 'Is that some of Axel Berndt's music?' she asked hurriedly.

'I think so . . . shall we see what it's like?' He sat down again and after a few false starts played the piece through. It was very lovely, a simple flowing melody set against some quite complex modulations and progressions. When he'd finished, he shook his head. 'I shall have to work on that, I think. Very deceptive piece.'

'Like the man himself?'

He closed the manuscript. 'Perhaps. One can't help wondering whether he's cognizant of all of this, or part of it. Do you suppose he could have taken us hostage in order to break a strike at one of his factories?'

'That's absurd.'

Chuckling, he began to play Chopsticks. 'Of course it is . . . as we ourselves are absurd, dear Miss Laura Ainslie, all of us . . . some bickering and arguing, some indulging in sex for purposes of anaesthesia, some giving vent to moralising attitudes toward one another, some running around in the snow and then playing Chopin like an arthritic kangaroo, some baking very *brown* bread,' he glanced owlishly over his shoulder at that, 'all of us washing our socks and looking out of the window to complain about the weather when at any moment, if things don't go the way they want, those two men could come back and shoot all of us bloody well dead, dead, *dead*!' His voice rose and he finished with a crash of discordants. He let his hands slide from the keys into his lap, sat for a moment with his head down, tried to laugh, couldn't. 'Forgive me.'

'David . . . why don't you make up your practice to-morrow? I know you like to finish things when you start them, but . . .'

'All right,' came his meek reply. He struck a few notes, let his hand linger, continued to play as if he simply could not stop himself.

'I'll make some cocoa . . .' she offered, getting up. He nodded and played on. It was the first time she had seen any sign of weakness in him. It had only been a momentary loss of control, and for some reason instead of making him appear less, it made him seem more. Stifling an impulse to go to him, she went instead to the sliding door and pressed the button to activate its mechanism, watching it move away from her and then aside, revealing the dark room beyond. She left it open because he wasn't playing loudly enough to wake anyone now. They all must have been asleep for hours. And she'd be carrying the mugs of cocoa when she came back. There was enough illumination for her to get to the kitchen without bumping into anything. She reached inside to flick the switch and froze. It was just as well she'd left the sliding door to the music room open. Soundproofed the way it was, he would never have heard her scream otherwise.

Anne Morgan lay on the kitchen floor beside the big pine table, her nightgown up around her waist, her legs wide. There were red marks around her neck and a pool of blood lay under her head like a crimson cushion. Her eyes did not blink as the light directly over her came on.

She was dead.

# Twelve

'Can you describe the men who kidnapped you?' Ainslie asked.

Sergeant John Goade shook his head slowly, his eyes still not clearly focussed on the two uniformed officers standing by his bed. He seemed confused by the fact that one wore an American Army uniform and the other a British Naval uniform. Both men wanted information and he wasn't sure which of them was the more senior, being unfamiliar with British insignia. The American General seemed to ask most of the questions, but the Britisher seemed more worried by the answers. He knew he should snap-to for the General, but somehow it all seemed to be too much trouble at the moment – both of them had an odd habit of occasionally drifting up toward the ceiling and their voices would get small and far-away. He tried very hard to please them.

'I never . . . saw them . . . too well. Food brought in the dark and drugged mostly, I guess, sir.'

'Did they talk to you, ask you anything, did you tell them anything about your assignment?' It seemed to Ainslie that Captain Skinner should be asking these questions but he was apparently disinclined to do so.

'No assignment, sir . . . on three weeks' leave . . . they treated me right enough . . . didn't seem to want anything, sir . . . except to keep me there.'

'What happened to the others?'

'What others, sir?' Goade's eyes slid toward one another, independently, and then drifted back to centre.

'The other passengers, dammit!'

Goade's forehead creased with concentration. 'Just me,

sir . . . ran out of gas . . . pulled over . . . they came up . . . don't remember anyone . . .'

'I see.' Ainslie looked over at Captain Skinner who was lighting yet another of his steady chain of cigarettes. 'I presume this is all part of his training?'

Captain Skinner looked up, startled, through the match flame. 'What?'

'Refusing to tell me anything. Whose side does he think I'm on, anyway? Show him your identification and let's get this thing going.'

Captain Skinner seemed disinclined to do this, either. He took a few drags of his cigarette and regarded the dreamy and confused man in the bed thoughtfully. 'Why not let me talk to him alone, General?'

'*I* want to know what happened . . . where the others are . . . why they were separated . . .' He frowned. 'What's all this about running out of gas, anyway?'

'I suggest you let me do the finding out. You trust me, don't you?'

'Oh, for God's sake, man . . . it's not a question of that!' Ainslie exploded in frustration. He turned away from the bed, walked to the window, came back. 'You think that's better, do you?'

Captain Skinner allowed one of his brief smiles and flicked his ash into the wastebasket by the bed. 'I think we should remember what the doctor said about his condition. He's been kept in a dark silent room for some days, apparently, drugged and so on. What was that phrase the psychiatrist used . . . "primal function patterns"? He's disoriented because of sensory deprivation. Like the prisoners of war in Vietnam, say. He's trying hard to hang on to the edges of things . . . but he may not remember much, and what he does remember might not be clear or even true. I've had some experience in this, I'm sorry to say . . . why don't you let me handle it alone? If we're one-to-one and I identify myself, it may work better.'

'Does he know you?'

Captain Skinner shook his head. 'No . . . but there are

122

standard rote identification procedures, other ways . . . I can make sure he knows he can trust me. After that . . .'

'All right, all right . . . it's plain as hell *I'm* not getting anywhere. Go ahead . . . I'll wait outside.' Ainslie scowled and stormed out of the room, venting his irritation on the door as he slammed it shut behind him. He leaned against the wall with his elbows on the windowsill, the hot sun frying the back of his neck from the outside, his temper from the inside. The long sunlit corridor was virtually empty. They had made sure Goade was placed in a little-used part of the new hospital, his custody under the juris-diction of the Embassy security corps. The Adabad police were furious, but since Goade was a member of the American Armed Forces and had committed no crime, it was taken out of their hands. About twenty yards away a security man lounged at the junction of this and the cross-corridor, otherwise Ainslie was alone. If there were patients in the other rooms, they weren't getting much looking-after. For fifteen minutes not a single nurse passed by.

Finally Captain Skinner opened the door and came out. Beyond his shoulder, for just a moment, Ainslie saw Goade's face against the pillow. He looked as if he'd passed out.

'Well?'

Captain Skinner sighed. 'He never even got *on* the plane, General. He was taken out on the way to the airport and has been held here in Adabad ever since. Whoever is in those pictures isn't Goade, never was. If the picture hadn't been streaked like it was we might have known that sooner. He's obviously the same size and more or less like him, but it isn't him.'

'It's somebody after the man Goade was supposed to guard, is that it?'

'So it would seem.'

'So all this *is* to do with your deal after all?'

'So it would seem,' Captain Skinner repeated, looking very unhappy. 'I'd really begun to hope it wasn't, you know. Easier the other way.'

'Who was he suppoed to guard?'

'The courier was to identify himself on the plane as soon as possible ;Goade's assignment was strictly riding shotgun on the journey. He was to watch the courier, make sure no one interfered with him – or her – during the flight, and hand over to Heathrow Control after landing. Just a last little job before he went on leave, nothing more.'

'So whoever took his place doesn't actually know who the agent is?'

'No. Unless, of course, they got the identification procedure out of Goade when he was drugged.'

'Oh, Christ.' Ainslie looked at the other man sympathetically, and they began to walk slowly down the hall.

'It still could be ...' Captain Skinner began.

'What ... could be what?' Ainslie said quickly.

'An unfortunate coincidence,' Captain Skinner said slowly, patting his uniform jacket pockets for his matches. Ainslie got out his lighter and obliged. They paused for a moment, still some distance from the security man. Captain Skinner blew smoke in a long steady stream, then spoke. 'That thing your aide said ...'

'That Larry said?'

'Yes. He said that list of demands you got from Doppler read like something put together by a nut who was sick of writing to the *Times* and decided to settle all his gripes in one fell swoop.'

'Oh, yeah ... I think he was just trying to be funny. He's a bright enough guy, I don't mean he isn't, but not all that long on understanding what makes people tick, if you see what I mean.'

'Even so ... what I said myself about my man being caught up in this kidnapping thing accidentally could still hold true. Maybe whoever took Goade's place wasn't after any courier at all, just part of the kidnapping plan. Maybe he's with the passengers as a kind of eavesdropper or something – in case they try to break out or whatever, he can tell the guards and prevent it.'

'That's pretty complicated ... if they have enough

124

guards the hostages couldn't break out anyway, could they? Why put a stool pigeon in?'

'I don't know . . . God, *I* don't know, do I?' Captain Skinner was getting peevish. 'Maybe they don't *have* a lot of guards. Maybe this Brahms guy *likes* things to be complicated. How the hell do *I* know?'

'Okay, all right, take it easy,' Ainslie muttered, startled by the sudden eruption from the Captain. The hands holding the cigarette he'd lit had been shaking. 'I'm sorry,' he added, with some difficulty.

Captain Skinner glanced at him. 'Oh . . . so am I. Nothing makes any bloody *sense* . . . or if it does, I can't see it and it's getting to me. I shouldn't let it.'

'It would be easier if it wasn't your brother.'

'And your daughter,' the Captain allowed. They stared at one another for a moment, accepted their vulnerability, turned and continued down the corridor in silence. The smoke from the Captain's cigarette hung in the sunlight for some time before it hazed away.

The second set of pictures arrived the next afternoon, and this time Goade's face – or the face of the man claiming to be Goade – was not obscured by light streaks. Captain Skinner immediately sent a copy of the photograph by wire to his London staff, hoping they could clarify whether the substitution should worry them or not. If the man wasn't a known agent, it might be possible to identify him through Interpol.

The answer came back in less than three hours, and from the Captain's point of view it was less than satisfactory. He put down the telephone and stared bleakly at Ainslie and Carter.

'The man in the picture is Alan Webb. He used to be one of ours. We thought he was dead.'

'Dead?' Carter exclaimed.

'Yes. About three years ago there was a . . . cock-up. Webb was shot in . . . well, he got shot in the course of duty, let's say. And disappeared. We thought he'd been

125

taken, but about a week later a body was washed up on a beach wearing his clothes, carrying his ID, and so on. The hands were too pulped to take prints, but we accepted that it was Webb. No reason to think otherwise, he'd always been trustworthy, a good man. Very good, in fact. Obviously we were wrong. About the body, about him.'

'You mean he arranged his own disappearance, wanted you to think he was dead?'

'Apparently. Or somebody did it for him. Either way, there he is.'

'Did you know him?'

'I'd seen him a couple of times, no more. They made the ID on bone structure, ear shape, so on. He's had some plastic surgery they said. Not a lot, but enough to fool people who didn't know him well. We don't make identification on the parts of the face you can change that way for just that reason. Having your whole face altered isn't really necessary, it's a long and complicated procedure, very painful, very expensive, not worth it. Lips, ears, boney prominences of the forehead, jaw length . . . that's the kind of thing we can use. It's Webb, all right. Or so the computers say.'

'Why didn't you identify the body that way?'

'I told you, we had no reason to doubt it was Webb, then. And the head had been smashed about some on the rocks . . . *now* we know why, of course. Then – no.'

They stared at the picture in silence. At all of the pictures. In some ways they were reassuring. The hostages looked more relaxed than they had in the pictures taken with the newspaper. On the other hand, they looked less well-groomed.

'I guess they took their shaving things away so they couldn't use them for weapons,' Ainslie mused, staring at the photograph of his daughter and the Professor. There were only four shots this time: the Morgan family together, Sherri Lasky and the prisoner Hallick, Goade and Marshal Denning, Skinner and Laura.

'She's almost smiling,' Larry said, leaning over Ainslie's shoulder.

'Yeah . . . *almost*,' Ainslie agreed. 'But I wouldn't say she looks like she's at a cocktail party or anything.'

Larry laughed. 'If you ask me she looks *exactly* like she does when she's at a party. As if she wishes she were somewhere else listening to records and reading a book.' His laughter was wry and turned on itself by anger.

Captain Skinner looked up from the photograph of Sherri and Hallick. 'Your daughter not the sociable type either, General?'

Ainslie shook his head. 'Maybe she's had to go to too many. When you get to my rank there's a lot of entertaining to do, dinners, parties, receptions, so on. For the past year or so Laura's been my official hostess, whatever you want to call it. She's damn good at organising parties, making sure everything is ready at the right time, the food perfect, the guests compatible. But once she's got the thing underway, she'd just as soon melt into the woodwork as stand around and make the right noises.'

'She'll get to like it,' Carter said emphatically. 'She'll change.'

Ainslie looked at his aide in some irritation. 'If she gets back at all,' he said heavily.

Carter looked chagrined, then slightly defiant. 'She'll get back, all right. We'll get her back. Look . . . they don't look scared anymore, do they? Or hungry? Or hurt? If you ask me what Doppler said must be true, they're being looked after all right. Just because the men haven't shaved doesn't mean anything . . . they're all sitting easy there, hands folded, relaxed, ca . . .'

'*Dammit*!' Captain Skinner's unbandaged fist hit the desk so hard that Carter jumped along with the overflowing ashtray. He and Ainslie stared at the suddenly altered man across the desk. 'Dammit, David . . . I'm sorry!' Captain Skinner shouted, grabbing all the pictures up and staring at them hard, one after another. 'I never looked . . . I never bloody looked!'

'Looked at *what*?' Ainslie demanded.

Captain Skinner thrust the four photographs at Carter. 'Get the hands blown up . . . come on, come on . . .' he commanded. 'Get those bloody photo experts off their backsides and tell them to enlarge the hands, all of them ... come *on!*'

After a nod from Ainslie, Carter took the photographs and went out, peering at them with a puzzled expression.

'Take it easy,' Ainslie cautioned as Captain Skinner jumped up and began to pace around the office, banging his unbandaged hand against his leg, faster and faster, calling himself a bloody fool every time it connected. 'What did you see?' Not only was he curious, it also seemed to him that the Captain would probably detonate himself if he didn't get it off his chest.

Captain Skinner whirled around to face him. 'David *was* pointing deliberately at those words in the newspaper,' he said, the words tumbling out half-formed. 'And he used hands again on that second set of photographs ... I should have stuck to it, I should have realised he'd go on trying ... that's the way he is. He always goes on, until he finishes what he starts. Always.'

'And?'

'I could just about have made it out without the enlargements but it's best to be sure . . . all the people in those pictures *weren't* sitting with their hands folded, General, they were making letters with their hands, spelling out some kind of message. Trust David . . . my god . . . I'm such a bloody bloody fool.'

'You mean ...'

'I mean David is trying to tell us where they *are*, don't you see? It's the only way he can tell us, the only method open to him, those damn pictures.'

Ainslie leaned back in his chair, astonished. 'Is he always so . . . clear-headed? I'd never have thought of that in a hundred years, I'd be too damn scared.'

Captain Skinner gave a short gasp of laughter. 'I'm sure he's scared, too. I told you, his mind never stops. And I guess they don't have much *else* to do but think, anyway – I don't expect they've laid on occupational therapy for them, or anything, do you? Basket-weaving, sewing mail bags, making ...'

128

'Hey . . .' Ainslie said sharply.

Captain Skinner closed his mouth with a snap, forced his hands down, took a couple of deep breaths, let go. After a minute he came back to the desk and dropped into his chair.

'Seems to me your mind doesn't stop too long in one place either, does it?' Ainslie said with deliberate slowness. 'Just . . . settle, will you? It's going to take a while for those pictures to get processed. Running around in circles and calling yourself names won't make them come back any faster.'

'I know that,' the Captain growled.

'All right, then.' The impulse to jump up and follow Skinner around in his circles had nearly got the better of Ainslie, but he was older and his joints were a little stiffer. He swivelled his chair from side to side for a bit, then opened a drawer and got out a cigar, clipped it, lit it, watching the other man until he saw the tension begin to slide from the shoulders. 'Tell me about the criminals,' he said, removing a fragment of tobacco from his lower lip.

'What?' The Captain's head jerked up and he stared across the desk.

'I said . . . tell me what your people have found out about the prisoners Brahms wants released from prison,' Ainslie said carefully.

'The prisoners? Oh . . . yes, the prisoners.' Skinner began slapping his pockets, finally drawing a folded sheet of paper out from the inside of his jacket. He produced a pair of horn-rimmed glasses and clapped them on. Ainslie suddenly saw a stronger resemblance between the brothers than he had previously, and smiled to himself, wearily. If there was some professor in this one, was there some secret agent in the other? He liked this one, would he like the other one, too? He thought probably he would, at that. Captain Skinner began to read without enthusiasm.

'Rudolf Winefeldt, 23, Jan Velden, 25, Karl Boyar, 20. First two are second offenders, Boyar is a first-timer. No previous criminal record on him. He was in university but dropped out last year after some kind of trouble over a girl, joined one of these religious sects, went underground.'

'You mean . . .'

'No. Underground with a small "u" . . . drifted out of sight, however you like to put it. Orphan brought up by his grandparents, brilliant boy but unstable, emotional, and so on. The first his family heard from him in over ten months was when he was arrested for this burglary and went on trial. They tried to help but he refused to have anything to do with them. Apparently wanted to plead guilty but the lawyer for the other two convinced him to go for trial. According to the police he almost begged to be put away.'

'Why didn't they give him a suspended sentence?'

'A watchman was injured during the burglary and that escalated the offence. But his sentence was lighter than the other two got. He's a Swede, the other two are Dutch. Some pressure was put on the Swedish government to extradite him but . . .'

'By whom?'

'I'm still trying to find out. It was unofficial . . .'

'You think they'll let them go?'

'I think so – under heavy surveillance, of course.'

'Hoping they'll lead us to Brahms?'

'Hoping they'll lead us to any bloody thing,' Captain Skinner said, tossing the paper onto the desk and twisting his hands back together in front of him.

'Has anyone talked to the prisoners?'

'Yes . . . of course, what do you think? They know nothing, they are astonished, confused, hopeful . . . either the best actors off the stage the world has ever known or actually not involved in the thing.'

'What about this Boyar, the one who wanted to go to jail?'

'He still wants to stay in jail. I guess they'll have to shove him out at the end of a stick . . .'

'Is he *scared* to come out?'

Skinner shook his head. 'No, nothing like that. Wants to pay "his debt to society" . . . or words to that effect. Over-developed sense of guilt, very religious, very penitent,

130

that's all there is to him. Handsome kid, nice manners, not like the other two. Doesn't have anything to do with them, now, either. Doesn't have anything to do with anybody, in fact. Sits in his cell and reads the Bible. *And* the Koran. *And* the Talmud. Whatever he can get hold of in that line. Where the *hell* are those pictures?'

Ainslie glanced at his watch. 'In the developing fluid, I imagine.'

Captain Skinner grinned down at his hands. 'Have you noticed that whenever I get excited you get calm, and whenever you get excited, I get calm?'

Ainslie smiled around his cigar. 'I noticed. Seems efficient enough. As long as *somebody's* keeping his head, I guess we'll be all right.'

The grin faded slowly. 'Yes . . . *we'll* be all right,' Skinner said softly.

When the enlargements came back, they confirmed the Captain's theory. They were still wet and Carter had to peel them apart to lay them out on the desk. 'This what you wanted?' he asked, still puzzled.

There was really no question.

Professor Skinner was holding his fingers in what looked like the numbers six and seven. Laura had formed the letter N. From the others they got the letters T, A, F, L, I, and another N. When Carter heard what the Captain was getting at, he tried to work it out.

'TAFLIN? What the hell's *that* supposed to mean?'

'They couldn't know what order we'd read them,' the Captain shot back impatiently. 'In fact, they might not even have known who'd be photographed with whom, come to think of it. So we have two numbers and seven letters. I don't think the child is making anything.'

'Just a funny face,' Ainslie said drily. 'So it's anagrams, is it? I used to be good at anagrams . . .' he reached for a pencil and paper, 'FLAT, TIN, FIN . . .' Ainslie was writing so quickly he nearly broke the pencil point.

'I think it would probably be faster by computer,'

Captain Skinner warned. 'I wonder if David meant those to be numbers, or if he wanted us to take the words for the numbers . . . that would add SIX and SEVEN to our possibilities.'

'It shouldn't take long,' Carter predicted. 'How many possible combinations could there be?'

As it happened, there were 5,040 possible combinations of seven letters. Having seen that, they decided the Professor had meant the numbers to be numbers. They hoped so, anyway.

'Captain,' Carter declared, looking at the long strip of computer read-out paper, 'I don't think your brother realised what he was handing us.'

Captain Skinner sighed. 'Oh, I imagine he did. But at least he's trying.'

'Yeah,' Carter agreed, heavily. 'Very.'

# Thirteen

'I didn't . . . I didn't!' Hallick whined, his hands over his face.

Denning stood beside his bed, still rumpled from the sleep from which Skinner had roused him, clutching Hallick's arm with one hand, the other back to strike again. Only Skinner's intervention had prevented him from beating Hallick senseless.

'You little pervert, you crawling little . . .'

'I didn't touch her . . . I never . . .'

'Why . . . *why*? Aren't you getting enough from Sherri you got to go after another one and kill her?'

'Perhaps you'd better take a look first, Frank,' Skinner urged, tugging at Denning's sleeve until he finally released Hallick. Still shaking with fury, Denning went over to the bureau and picked up the handcuffs.

'I knew I should've left these on . . . *knew* it!' Quickly he shackled Hallick's hands to the bedpost, pinching the metal circles until they dug into the flesh of the wrists. Hallick lay with his hands above him, his eyes dazed and a bruise already darkening along his cheekbone. He seemed totally unable to comprehend what was happening, and Skinner frowned, wondering. He and Denning went down the stairs. Laura was huddled in a chair in front of the fire, her hands over her face but making no sound.

They'd thrown a tablecloth over Anne's body, but Denning whipped it completely away, exposing her to the bright light once again. Skinner closed his eyes then forced them open as Denning knelt down and peered at the marks around her throat. After a moment he reached out and took hold of her jaw, rocking the head slightly from side to side.

'Looks like he tried to strangle her first,' Denning observed, his face pale but determined.

'Then where is the blood coming from?' Skinner whispered, leaning against the cabinet behind him and gazing at his own reflection in the black window over the sink.

Denning turned the head so that Anne's dead eyes were staring at the base of the sink, and grunted. 'Head's bashed in . . . right in . . .' He looked up vaguely and then squinted, leaning forward to peer at the corner of the big pine table. 'Blood on this corner of the table, David. Looks like he tried his usual tricks and in the struggle she hit her head. Maybe she didn't start to bleed right away . . . maybe he . . . got on with it and then . . .' But he was shaking his head even as he spoke. Getting down further he took a closer look at the blood-matted hair and tentatively probed with his fingertips. 'Funny . . .'

'What is it?' Skinner asked, wishing he could gather enough of himself together to go over to the sink and get a glass of water.

'Wrong shape . . .' Denning looked up at him. 'Wound's the wrong shape, she was stove in with something long and narrow, not a corner of the table. It feels . . . oh, Jesus.' He snatched his hand away and the head thumped slightly as it hit the floor. Staring at his bloodied fingers he rocked back onto his heels, then sat down on the floor. 'I went right through . . . edge of the . . . her skull's like paper . . .' He looked sick suddenly and for a minute Skinner thought he was going to pass out.

'Are you all right?' he asked anxiously.

Denning shook his head as if to clear it, took a few deep breaths. 'Been a long time since I . . . haven't been a working cop for years . . . years.'

'So it wouldn't have taken much of a blow to kill her?' Skinner asked, coming back to the point more to distract Denning than to gain information.

'I guess not . . .'

'But that doesn't make sense, Frank,' Skinner objected. Denning was trying to get up and Skinner went forward to give him a hand.

'I should have kept him cuffed . . . every minute I should have . . .'

'There was no point . . .' Skinner said as they stood there supporting one another. Denning turned sharply, nearly making Skinner lose his balance.

'No point? There's your point . . . right there. One dead lady. What the hell did you think I was taking him back for . . . writing dirty words on the goddamn wall? I *told* you he was a killer.' He shrugged Skinner's hand off and walked over to the sink, reaching for the tap and stopping with his hand outstretched. Skirting the body, Skinner came across and looked down. A broken glass lay in the stainless steel sink, and next to it a white smear that looked like melting aspirin tablets.

'She said she had a headache . . .' Skinner began, then turned to look at the door of the kitchen. 'She came down to get some water to take her aspirin . . . somebody came up behind her and . . .'

'Hallick came up behind her, you mean.' Denning growled.

'Do I?' Skinner asked. 'You said he was a rapist, too.'

'Well . . . look at her!' Denning gestured with his head.

Skinner did, reluctantly. Anne's position was still an overtly sexual sprawl, and he wished Denning had replaced the tablecloth. She looked so . . . so . . . wrong. Pushing his glasses back up onto the bridge of his nose with a shaking hand, he tried to formulate what was bothering him. 'Her nightdress is pulled up, her legs are apart, yes. But she doesn't look like she was raped . . . she looks like she was . . . arranged.'

'What the hell does that mean?' Denning demanded, half turning to look as well, then turning away again.

'I don't know,' Skinner admitted. 'I thought men who raped liked . . . the struggle.'

'Supposed to be a big part of it, I guess. So?'

'She wouldn't have struggled much if she was already unconscious, would she?' he asked, going over and picking up the tablecloth to cover the body. 'Is that how he killed the other one?'

'What other one?'

'The one you're taking him back to be tried for. Did he hit her on the head?'

'I . . . I dunno. I don't know the details, I was just sent out to get him, that's all.'

'Oh?' Skinner let the tablecloth drop, then stood staring at the edge of the pine table. There was blood there, but not much. And that was wrong, too, of course.

'Suppose Hallick wasn't a killer,' he postulated.

'What? Dammit . . . he's a killer all right,' Denning snapped.

'No . . . you don't *know* that,' Skinner said with precision. 'He hasn't been convicted yet, has he? He's a suspected killer, that's all.'

'You sound like some kind of . . . lawyer.'

'But suppose he wasn't even a *suspected* killer, suppose he was just another passenger like the rest of us, and this happened. Who would you suspect then?'

Denning moaned. '*I* don't know . . . look, David, we got a dead woman here and we got a killer . . . a "suspected" killer upstairs. They had to have good evidence to get extradition so that's that, it's good enough for me. Why make problems where there's none? It's *obvious*.'

'Yes,' Skinner conceded. 'Yes, it's very obvious, isn't it?' He looked through the gap in the door at Laura, still sitting in front of the fire, her hands in her lap now, but unmoving, expressionless. 'What isn't so obvious is what we're going to do when the gunmen come back tomorrow . . . they've missed today, they're bound to come tomorrow, aren't they? What do we do then?'

Denning was picking up the broken pieces of glass and placing them on the drainingboard gingerly. 'I don't understand . . .'

Skinner gave a hollow gasp that might have been laughter, probably wasn't. 'The whole bargaining point of hostages is that you *threaten* to kill them, but you *don't* kill them, you see? You just threaten. Once you start killing them it leaves the people you're bargaining with no hope.

136

Now, they've waved those guns about and said they would kill us if we didn't behave, yet they've gone to a great deal of effort to make sure that we're not only safe but comfortable, too. They're looking after us very well . . . very well indeed. *But . . .*'

Denning had turned on the water to wash the blood off his hands and was now getting another glass out of the cupboard for himself. 'But . . . what?'

'If one of us is dead . . . we all might as well be dead because we're useless to them. Not only that – we're witnesses to murder. Oh, not *their* murder, no. But that isn't how the law sees it . . . you know the law. What happens if a death occurs during the commission of a felony?'

'What?' Denning challenged.

'I believe . . . I believe it is automatically considered first-degree murder, no matter what the circumstances. That's right, isn't it?'

'You're telling it, not me,' Denning ground out, filling his glass and drinking the cold water steadily until it was gone. He put the glass down on the drainingboard next to the broken fragments with a thump. 'I wish to hell you'd get to the point.'

'The point is that when the gunmen arrive tomorrow, Anne *can't* be dead. She has to be alive, so that they can take her picture. We need that picture taken. Frank – we have a message to send, remember? Our only chance is to get that message out before the gunmen come back the next time. If they come back and find out she's dead tomorrow, they won't wave those guns. They'll have to use them, because they'll have no choice.'

'You can't be serious' Denning gaped at him.

Skinner turned away, clenching his hands together, and looked again at Laura through the door. They would kill her, they would kill all of them.

'You have got to be the coldest son-of-a-bitch I've ever met,' Denning said, stonily.

Closing his eyes, Skinner forced his hands apart. 'Possibly. We haven't really got time to discuss my shortcomings as a human being, Frank. I may be cold, but I have no wish to die. Do you?'

'That's a damn silly question.'

'Then I suggest you suspend your equally damn silly attitudes and accept the facts. We have no time to be nice or squeamish or anything else. My watch says it's after three in the morning. In my opinion that leaves us very little time. I'm not going to enjoy it any more than you are, I assure you, but it has to be done and I can't do it alone. Make up your mind right now, Frank. The longer you spend wringing your hands, the less time we have to live. Which is it to be?'

'What has happened here?' Orange demanded, looking around the room.

The main room looked like a hurricane had come through on a detour from the West Indies. A couple of the chairs were overturned by the dining table, there were glasses scattered around, half-eaten sandwiches on the furniture and floor.

'We had a little party,' Goade shot back belligerently. 'What's it to you what we do as long as we don't go anywhere?' He kicked aside a plate. 'Did you bring any more brandy with you . . . maybe some scotch this time?'

'We bring . . . I think better we take away again,' Orange said stiffly.

'And my tablets . . . you brought my tablets, didn't you?' Denning asked anxiously. Orange glanced at him – he certainly looked in need of some kind of medication. His face was grey and his voice was shaking.

Orange turned toward Hallick who was half-in, half-out of one of the chairs at the dining table. He face was a mass of bruises and swelling, and he was handcuffed to the leg of the table. 'You have fight, this one?'

'We have fight this one,' Goade smirked. 'We have *good* fight this one.'

That, too, was visually confirmable. Both Goade and Denning had reddened knuckles, and Skinner had a black eye. Morgan's eyes were swollen and he looked like he had the hangover to end all hangovers. Laura's eyes were reddened, too, as were Timmy's. Orange tilted his head.

'The boy . . .'

'Was frightened by all the shouting,' Skinner said. 'He was *not* drinking.'

'No matter what anyone says,' Goade added sarcastically.

'You clean place up,' Orange directed. 'We take pictures.'

'You want it clean, clean it yourself. We like it this way . . . it's homey, you know?' Goade said, turning away. Orange was looking around, counting.

'One missing . . . where is other woman?' he asked.

There was a silence, then Laura spoke. 'She's ill . . . she's in bed.'

'Show me.'

Laura hesitated, then went across to the door of Skinner's room and opened it. Orange followed and peered in. There was a strong smell of brandy in the room. Anne Morgan lay in the bed, eyes closed, the covers nearly hiding her. 'Wake up . . . need pictures.'

Taking a deep breath, Laura said, 'I'll try . . .' and went into the room, closing the door behind her. Crossing his bloodied fingers behind him, Skinner asked whether they wanted the pictures taken in the same place.

'Yes . . . at table. Move things away . . .'

They did as they were told and the pictures were taken of Hallick and Sherri, Denning and Goade. Orange went back to the door of the bedroom and opened it. Laura was bending over Anne Morgan, shaking her.

Looking up she stammered, 'I can't wake her . . .' She had stains down the front of her dress and a pool of what looked like vomit was on the bedclothes. 'She was sick and then passed out again.'

Orange made a grunt of disgust and gestured to Yellow. 'Carry her out.'

'I'll do it,' Morgan said, suddenly. 'You keep your

damned hands off her.' Timmy started to sob and clung to his father. Morgan patiently removed his hands and thrust the child at Skinner, who picked him up and held him against his shoulder.

'I don't see why you can't leave her alone,' Skinner intervened mildly. 'You can photograph the child with Miss Ainslie and me, and Morgan in there with his wife . . . why make her any sicker than she already is?'

Yellow turned his masked face toward his companion with a questioning tilt.

'Do it . . .' Orange directed. 'We cannot waste time here . . .'

When it was done, he waved his gun at them and spoke with disdain. 'This is bad, what happened. These . . . injuries . . . look bad in pictures . . . make difficulties, you understand?'

'We understand perfectly,' Skinner assured him, still holding Timmy on his lap. Morgan came out of the bedroom and closed the door behind him, looking ill and distraught. 'I suggest you simply tell the truth . . . they'll either believe you or they won't. At least we're all still alive, aren't we?'

Sherri started to laugh and Hallick looked over at her through slitted eyes. 'Shut up, you goddamn slut,' he articulated with difficulty through his broken mouth. Sherri shut up.

'It is on your own heads what this does . . .'

'All right, all right!' Denning suddenly snapped.

Orange stared at him for a moment, then asked his usual question. 'Is anything needed here?'

'More brandy,' Goade said. '*Lots* more.'

'Perhaps some tranquillisers?' Skinner suggested. 'You can hardly expect us to . . .'

'We bring.' Orange gestured to Yellow who picked up the camera and followed him out the door. They watched until they appeared outside the window, and then Denning went into the entry for the box.

'Do you think it . . .' Morgan began in a broken voice,

140

when there was a shout from Denning, and a blast of cold air came into the room. As they stared in horror Denning's shirtsleeved figure appeared outside the window, struggling through the snow after Orange and Yellow. They could see him waving his arms, half-hear his shouts and yells.

'My god,' Skinner exclaimed, putting Timmy down and standing up. 'What on earth is he doing?'

Orange and Yellow had turned from the helicopter and were coming back toward Denning, guns upraised. They seemed to be shouting at him to go back, making menacing gestures with their weapons, waving their arms. But Denning shouted back, and it looked as if he were arguing with them. They were close together now, and a particularly violent shove from Yellow sent Denning sprawling into the snow.

'Those bastards . . . he's an old man,' Goade flared and ran out of the door before anyone could stop him. Yellow and Orange were still shouting at the fallen Denning, but they only caught tatters of the sound through the open door as it was torn by the wind that shook the birches and sent flurries of snow up from the surface of the fresh fall like smoke rising. Goade was a part of the landscape, now, his big broad-shouldered body hunching forward steadily. Suddenly Yellow looked up and caught sight of him. He reached out and tugged Orange's sleeve and they began to back up, for all the world as if they were afraid. Considering what the expression on Goade's face must have been, Skinner thought it altogether likely. Then Yellow seemed to recollect the gun he was carrying, and raised it. The big man paid no attention. He kept moving toward Denning, and finally Yellow raised the gun and fired.

High on the big window a line of stars appeared, lines crazing out from central circles. Incongruously, even as the ugly chatter of the gunshots died away, there were several small metallic sounds. The spent bullets had hit the outer sheet of double glazing, but distance and that last impact had stopped them. They lay on the wooden frame like dead flies.

Goade had stopped where he was when the gun went off,

and he was still motionless. Orange and Yellow stared at him, then began to back off toward the helicopter, clambering in and slamming the door shut behind them. Through the open door they heard the engine of the helicopter start, and still neither Goade, the fallen Denning, nor anyone within the room moved a muscle. As the roar from the engine increased in volume and the whirling rotors blended into a blur, something did move, however.

The lines from the bullet holes began to extend and suddenly the outer glass of the big window gave a shiver and collapsed, falling down and out in a series of glittering shards onto the snow, leaving only jagged fingers of glass still clinging to the wooden frame. It seemed to happen silently because of the roar of the engine. And slowly, because they were so shocked that everything seemed to be happening slowly. Still nobody moved. And then, as the helicopter rose from the ice and began to swing away, Goade shook himself and began walking again through the snow toward Denning in that same determined way. By the time he had reached him the helicopter was a mere dot in the sky against the even white of the low clouds. Goade reached down and helped Denning to his feet, supporting him as they began the long walk back to the house.

Suddenly Timmy began to cry. He ran toward the door of the bedroom where his mother lay, but Morgan reached out and caught him, lifting him up and holding him tightly against his chest.

'Mommy . . . I want Mommy,' Timmy sobbed, struggling.

'Let Mommy sleep,' Morgan said in a choked voice as he buried his face in Timmy's shoulders.

As Skinner moved toward the open outer door to help Goade with Denning, he saw Laura start to shake. He stopped, unsure who needed him most. He met her eyes across the room, saw them fill with tears, and turned toward her. But she shook her head, made a gesture of despair, and ran into her room, slamming the door shut behind her. So he went out into the snow instead.

*

When he knocked on her door an hour or so later there was no response. Opening it quietly he looked in and saw her lying across the bed, face down. He started to close the door again, but she lifted her head. 'David?'

He went in and pushed the door shut behind him, stood for a moment and then went over and sat down on the edge of the bed. She had let her head drop again into the coverlet.

'Denning wanted his tablets,' he announced after a while. 'That's all he wanted, just his tablets. It's a wonder he didn't burst a blood vessel anyway, running through the snow like that.'

'Did he get them?'

'They were in the box all along ... underneath ...'

Suddenly his arms were full of her and he hardly knew what to do, she was shaking and trembling against him, sobbing into his shoulders. Awkwardly he tightened his arms and stroked her hair. Sherri's eyeshadow had smeared down and across his cheek, and his black eye was black no longer.

Laura could only cling to him, grateful for the solidity of his body and the quiet tones of his voice, sheltering in his arms. 'It's all right ... it's all right ... it's over now. All over now. It's all right.' But it wasn't, and they both knew it. He waited patiently until her sobs became chokes, gasps, and finally hiccups before he let go of her.

'You're all wet ...' she stammered finally, sitting upright beside him.

'Well – I may not be the most absorbent handkerchief in the place, but I'm certainly the biggest,' he tried. 'Anyway ... some of that is from the snow. I took her ... I put her outside.'

What else he had done, the terrible thing he'd had to do, still sickened him. Perhaps when Denning recovered he'd tell him about it. Perhaps he wouldn't. He was no detective and perhaps Denning wasn't, either. But the demon in him that had to *know* was appeased – at least for the time being.

'I'll clean your room up in a minute,' she said, sniffing

hugely and wiping her swollen face with her fingertips.

'No need . . . it's all done.'

'I'm sorry I ran away . . . I just couldn't . . .'

'You were wonderful,' he assured her. 'They were convinced she was alive, I'm sure they were. And the mess will wash out of the sheets easily enough, won't it?' That final touch, the fake vomit she'd made out of heaven knew what and hidden in a bowl under the bed, had clinched it. They would never have touched Anne after seeing that . . . Laura had been right, nobody, not even gunmen, fancied being spewed over by someone who was drunk. 'You were wonderful,' he repeated.

'Timmy . . . Timmy didn't see you . . .'

'Sherri took him upstairs right after. I wrapped Anne in a sheet and heaped snow over her . . . I don't know what we're going to tell him now, though.'

'You'll think of something,' she said with perfect confidence.

He smiled and shook his head, staring down at his hands. 'I'm running out of ideas,' he told her.

And time, he added silently.

# Fourteen

'Maybe that *isn't* another N at all, maybe it's an E.'

'If that *isn't* a second N then you've got to make another computer run.'

The air conditioner in the window was developing a whine between clatters. Outside the few drops that blew from the fountains onto the cement paving disappeared in seconds, dried by the midday blast of the sun. The streets were empty of people and cars, the sensible slept or sat quietly in darkened rooms, waiting for the worst of the day's heat to pass.

All three of them had long since abandoned any pretence at formality. Carter and Ainslie had sweat patches darkening their khaki shirts on chest and spine as well as armpits, and even Captain Skinner's white cotton broadcloth was translucent in the same areas. Their jackets were thrown across the sofa, and Ainslie's tie was draped rather nonchalantly from a map pin, partially obscuring Greenland and the east coast of Brazil.

Carter undid another button and exposed the sheen of perspiration that glistened on the evenly developed pectorals of his smooth chest. The blonde hair on the back of his neck was glued to the flesh in curly tendrils. Even so, while Ainslie and the Englishman looked unkempt and uncomfortable, Carter only glowed more healthily in the heat. It was the lifeguard look, the Captain decided. Put a bottle of suntan oil next to Carter's elbow and he could be an advertisement in any woman's magazine. They'd sell a million. He wasn't quite sure why he resented Carter's physical perfection, but he did. It was a slap in the face to ordinary men everywhere.

Out of sheer desperation they had ignored all of the seemingly meaningless combinations of letters the computer had given them and concentrated first on the whole words the letters they'd discerned in the photograph made up. There were still an awful lot of them.

'NAIL, FAIL, TAN, NIL, FAT . . .'

'67FAT?'

'67FAT what?'

The phone was next to Ainslie's elbow but it was Carter who answered it, reaching across and dragging the instrument toward him as he lifted the receiver.

'General Ainslie's off . . .' he stopped abruptly, then covered the mouthpiece. 'Sir . . . it's Doppler.'

Ainslie dropped his ballpoint and reached for the receiver.

'Ainslie here.' He listened a moment, then nodded at the other two. 'Yes, Mr Doppler, I'm listening. Yes . . . yes, I understand. The same time as before? All right. Would you consider letting me bring someone else . . . yes, I appreciate that, but . . .' There was a long staccato from the telephone audible to the others even across the desk. Ainslie sighed and shrugged his shoulders at them. 'Very well . . . whatever you say. Yes, I'll have a report on the demands ready. Yes . . . tonight then.' He put down the phone, stared at it and then at the other two men. 'He wants to see me again . . . he says circumstances have altered.'

Captain Skinner put down his pen, too, and reached up to pull his shirt away from his skin to let some air through. 'What the devil does that mean?'

'I don't know,' Ainslie said, frowning.

Carter stood up. He opened the office door and had a brief conversation with Grey who was outside, then came back. 'They're going to get the locating device ready.'

'I still think it's a mistake.' Ainslie slumped back in his chair and tapped the bridge of his nose with a knuckle. 'If he finds out I . . .'

'It's very small, General . . . really. Just a button under

your collar or behind your belt . . . he'll never notice. As soon as the others leave we can . . .'

'He said circumstances had altered,' Ainslie repeated. 'I don't like that . . . it could mean . . .'

'How did he sound?' Captain Skinner asked, not liking Ainslie's look, either.

When the General looked up, his eyes confirmed it. 'He sounded upset. He sounded . . . he sounded desperate.' Ainslie picked up his pen, began to tap it on the blotter. 'In fact, he sounded like a very very frightened man.'

# Fifteen

Skinner lifted his foot from the pedal. 'Is he asleep?' he asked softly.

Laura peered down at Timmy's face where it rested against her shoulder. 'Yes,' she whispered, wiping the last of the tear streaks from the rounded cheek. Skinner turned on the piano bench and regarded the child on Laura's lap with a sadness that ran through him like a hunger pang.

'I'll carry him up,' he offered.

'No . . . let him be . . . you can take him up when he's really deeply asleep . . .' She raised her head and smiled at him in the faint light from the other room. Skinner had been playing in the dark, patiently lulling the child's distress away with long soothing melodies.

Two full days had passed and still the gunmen hadn't returned. Nor had anyone come to rescue them.

Timmy had been told that his mother was too ill to see him – that he might 'catch' what she had. He'd accepted that story for a while, watching them carry trays of food into the room. But this evening, after dinner, he'd made a charge for the door as Laura had come out and had seen the empty bed. There had been no consoling him, then. Morgan had tried to make up another story but was unable to carry it off, and in the end Skinner had told Timmy the truth. Or, at least, told him his mother was dead, as simply and as quietly as he could. Morgan's grief seemed to blind him to his son's needs. Over the past two days he'd grown silent and withdrawn. He seemed to hate Skinner more and more for what he'd made them do with his wife's body, seemed to hate them all for what had happened, although he focussed his abuse on Hallick. So Timmy was comforted, as usual, by just about everyone except his own father. He didn't seem to expect comfort from that direction anyway.

Skinner got up and went over to the long windows, drawing one of the curtains aside. 'Damn.'

'What is it?' Laura looked up and stiffened as she saw a strange flickering glow surrounding Skinner's silhouette with pastel rainbows. 'Is someone coming . . . are those . . . ?'

'That, my dear and only wide-awake student, is the Aurora Borealis. One of nature's greatest wonders.' With an extravagant gesture he swept the curtains fully back, then went along and opened the other two pairs. The three tall narrow windows shimmered and seemed to melt under the rising and falling waves of light she could now see banding the sky high above the dark horizon.

'The Northern Lights.'

'Exactly. Now appearing nightly for your edification and delight, if not mine.'

'Why not yours?' She couldn't understand the bitterness in his voice. There was frustration riding his spine and she could see his hands clenching and unclenching on either side.

'Because they are showing me where I ought to be instead of where I am.'

'We have enough riddles without you talking in them, David.'

'Oh, I'm sorry . . .' He slumped suddenly and walked back to throw himself into the leather chair next to hers, leaning his head on his hand and pushing his fingers through his hair. 'The Aurora Borealis is triggered by sunspots. My area of specialisation is sun-spots. Or, more precisely, the solar prominences that actually cause those lights out there. Before we left Adabad a rather large group of spots I'd been tracking rotated out of sight and were due to reappear . . . yesterday. And have – as you can see. If I had got back on time I would have been able to put together a project I've been planning for the past eight years.

We had a computer link set up to Jodrell Bank on stand-by, we had a satellite link with the McMath Hulbert Observatory in Michigan, and Pic-du-Midi in France, we had our own . . . oh, it doesn't matter. One of my associates will push my button for me. They'll get it down . . . they'll be getting it down, now, in fact.'

'And you should be there,' she said softly, wishing he was for his sake and glad he wasn't for theirs. Timmy stirred in her arms, settled again with a little snuffle of contentment.

'Mmmm.'

'Tell me.'

'It's all very boring technical stuff . . . Nothing to tell, now. If Jodrell started getting the magnetic field indications I thought they might, there were some ideas I had . . . some new programmes I'd worked out in Adabad. Like a fool I kept them to myself, you see . . .' He laughed without laughing. 'The secretive scientist learns his lesson yet again.'

'Go on,' she prompted. 'I'm not entirely stupid, you know . . . what were you hoping to find?' It seemed to her he needed to say it, to remind himself of what he was outside this house and this situation.

After a while, he began.

As in every science, individual astronomers have special fields of interest, he said. His, from the time he was first interested in the sky, had been the sun.

'It's hardly a major star, and certainly not a big one compared to some, but it's right *there*, right on our doorstep. Bigger or smaller, they are much the same, although in different stages of development. What we learn about it we also learn about them. But, to be perfectly honest, it isn't the logic of that line of argument that makes the sun so fascinating to me.' He smiled to himself. 'It is simply the most incredible, the most exciting, the most beautiful and terrifying thing you've ever seen. We don't look at it directly, of course . . . we'd burn our eyes out in seconds if we did.' He glanced at her. '*Literally*. But we use solar telescopes and spectro-heliographs and other instruments to film it . . . look at some of those films and you're looking at the guts of the universe. We don't actually see the surface of the sun as such . . . we look at the surface of the burning of the sun, the tips of the flames, if you like, head-on for the most part. Because we're looking for and comparing changes, sometimes in the films it seems almost sluggish . . . patterned with what we call granulation . . . a moving tesselation of bright and dark, flowing, flaming, moving . . . flaring occasionally in a kind of incandescent billow as it releases incredible amounts of blazing gases. It is . . . so immense, so dense, that it moves at different speeds around its equator and poles . . . almost as if, even in its immeasurable power, it is too heavy to get itself around . . . a gigantic mass of matter suspended and balanced in one never-ending explosion. Stick a pin into an orange – the earth is the head of the pin and the fruit the sun – that's the size ratio. And it seems *alive* . . . when you look at it . . . *alive.*'

'I'd love to see it,' she whispered.

'I'd love to show it to you,' he said simply. She recognised, in that moment, that he was a natural teacher. She could see the sun as he described it . . . it *did* seem alive. Like Perseus with his helmet and shield, David Skinner also had a gift from the gods.

'Anyway,' he continued. 'Anyway, after a while you even get used to *that*. Then it's the sun-spots that take your attention. What we call a facula . . . just a dot, really . . . grows, expands like a flower . . . with a core, or umbra, and filaments that could be petals, called a penumbra. And sometimes, in an eruptive sun-spot, you get the prominences that cause that aurora out there. Great expanding arches of luminous incandescent gases blown away from the sun itself . . . so high they could swallow the earth in a gulp . . . rising invisibly until they cool, then sluicing back down so gracefully . . .'

He'd pulled off his glasses to show the motion, and the gold rims caught a spark of light from the other room. Sorry . . . I'm waxing a little poetic . . . you really have to

151

see it to . . .' he sighed. 'All right . . . now sun-spots come in pairs,' he went on in a more normal tone. 'The pairs have opposite magnetic polarities, usually appearing above and below the equator but not always. *Sometimes* the second sun-spot isn't on the surface at all . . . sometimes it's deep in the photosphere, detectable only by magnetic variation and close to the very processes that cause the spot in the first place. We call it an "invisible companion". It tracks below and slightly behind its partner. We don't know why some come to the surface and some don't . . . we can't study them except by trace, we can't visually observe how they behave, *see* what it is that makes them different . . . but . . .'

She listened to the soft rise and fall of his voice and tried to follow the path of the 'invisible companion' through the intricate pattern of idea and counter-idea he was weaving more for himself now than for her. Occasionally he would turn his head and the strange glow from the windows would reveal his expression – absorbed, intense, lit also from within. It had always fascinated her to listen to any expert speak on his subject whether she understood it or not. Perhaps it was the power of obsession that was so attractive. In this case, she admitted to herself, it was more. With his glasses no longer hiding his face, she could watch his expression change. Watch the mobile mouth and the sheer blazing intelligence in his eyes, while pretending to follow his words. She did listen enough to nod when a nod was required, murmur when a murmur was required, even ask a question or two. Mostly, however, she just watched. Eventually he ran out of energy, dropped his glasses into his lap, stared down at them.

'You didn't really want to hear all that, did you?' he said ruefully, looked up, and was caught by a soft invisible blow to the chest. She was shining like one of his own stars.

'Yes, I did, or I would have stopped you. It sounds like you were on the verge of finding out something very important.'

He laughed at himself. 'Important to me, perhaps, but hardly to the future of mankind. Since we have another six billion years or so to study the sun before it begins to self-destruct, I'd say there wasn't that much of a rush on.'

'Does that matter? What the "invisible companions" are ... what they mean or do ... you want to *know*, don't you? You've studied it, thought about it, gotten closer and closer to it ... and you want to finish what you started. I can understand *that*, David, even if I can't understand all the numbers and the words. You want to finish what you started ... you must.'

'Must I?'

'*Yes*. It's a great mystery ... a huge mystery, near enough to see but too far away to touch. Hidden – secret – it *is* fascinating ... I wish *I* cared about something so much.' She stopped, realising that she did, and it *was* close enough to touch.

He laughed at himself again. 'Wouldn't you know it – I meet the ultimate perceptive woman and proceed to bore her witless. Story of my life, that.'

'I'm not the ultimate anything!' she burst out. He looked up, startled by the harsh anger in her voice. 'I graduated *cum laude* from Smith, did you know that? Oh, yes, *very* impressive. But with no special talent, no special interest, no special ability in any direction or for any subject. I've had one job after another, but no career, no profession. I think I must be like one of your "invisible companions" ... I'm here, but nobody knows why or what for, especially not me. I'm a brown paper package without anything startling inside ... more brown paper, that's all.'

'That sounds suspiciously like self-pity to me. You were hardly ... what was it? ... a "brown paper person" about Anne and what we had to do the other day.'

'That was easy ... because it had to be done. All the other things I'm expected to do ... aren't so easy. I'm not beautiful but I'm not ugly, not brilliant but not stupid, not witty but not altogether dull ... just adequate. Brown paper, you see?'

'Do you want to be all those things – beautiful, brilliant, witty?'

153

'I should be if I'm going to be the wife of a beautiful, brilliant man with a beautiful, brilliant career in front of him.'

'He must think you are or he wouldn't have asked you to marry him, would he?'

'As long as I don't have two heads I'll do . . . after all, I'm General Marshall Ainslie's daughter. That goes a long way at the Pentagon.'

'That is a terrible thing to say,' his voice was suddenly charged with real anger. 'About him, and about yourself. You have shocked me to my wrinkled little core, Miss Ainslie. I don't think I like having heard that from you.'

'No?' She was angry, too. 'Then perhaps I do have a talent after all, *Professor* Skinner. I can shock astronomers. Do you think there's a market for it?'

There was a sudden click and he looked down. He'd snapped one of the bows off his glasses. 'Damn. *Now* look what you made me do.'

She stared at the two pieces in his hands, her anger gone as quickly as it had come, and as inexplicably. What on earth had she been thinking of, talking like that? She didn't blame him for being cross, she had no right to splatter her lack of self-confidence all over him. It was simply that she could talk to him, it was as easy as talking to Timmy, in a way. He *listened*, his head on one side, his whole attention on you, without ever making you feel stupid.

'I'm sorry,' she apologised in a small voice.

He looked up, his eyes crinkling as he smiled. 'It was a joke, actually. It's been loose for weeks.'

'Oh.' She shifted Timmy, pulled the ever-present binoculars out from where they were jammed into her ribs and handed them to Skinner. 'I'm also sorry about what I was saying,' she whispered. 'I didn't mean it, really . . . I'm just tired, I guess.' She cleared her throat and spoke firmly. 'Larry thinks I'm absolutely beautiful.'

'Of course he does.'

'And he thinks I'll be a wonderful wife, and a real asset

to his career, and that everyone will be absolutely dazzled by my wit, my charm, and my impeccable sense of style.'

'Of course they will.'

Why did she feel like crying? 'And I'll knock their socks off in Washington or London or Paris or wherever he's stationed next, won't I?'

'Not if you don't get some sleep,' he said, thrusting the two parts of his spectacles into his shirt pocket and standing up. 'So, if you'll hand me that Young Prince you've got in your lap, I'll take him upstairs and let you do just that. All right?'

She surrendered the child and followed him out of the room. As they passed under the light at the foot of the stairs she saw, with a sudden rush of tenderness, that his hair was growing thin at the crown of his head, just a little. He was a nice man, a kind man, a good man. He was as patient with her as he was with the child, and probably regarded her in much the same way. It wasn't *his* fault she wished he was carrying *her* to bed. Wished he would come back downstairs after depositing Timmy, and make love to her hungrily and passionately all night long, instead of just saying his usual polite 'sleep well' at her door. She realised she desperately *wanted* this quiet, soft-spoken professor of astronomy. No doubt that would have shocked him as profoundly as it kept shocking her.

After saying good night to a strangely subdued Laura, Skinner returned to the music room, closed the piano, put Berndt's manuscript back on the shelf. As he started out he noticed the binoculars still sitting on the chair and went to retrieve them. A particularly incandescent shimmer from the Aurora caught his eye and on impulse he went over to the window. The curtains of rising and falling light were so intense that he was unable to locate anything except Polaris. Rotating the adjustment, he frowned. A thin dark line bisected the left lens. It was not a crack, but it suddenly occurred to him that Timmy might have thought it was and been afraid to tell him. He smiled ruefully and wound the leather strap around the binoculars, carrying them with

155

him to his room. It seemed likely the retaining ring had slipped or split. He'd fix it and say nothing to the child.

Opening the cabinet of the sink in his bathroom he got out a roll of adhesive tape to fix his spectacles together, then settled himself on the edge of the bath to dismantle the binoculars, putting the pieces carefully onto the closed lid of the toilet. As he opened the lens tube, however, he discovered that the problem was not the retaining ring at all. He gave the binoculars a shake, and a thin curling piece of something shiny and black fell into the palm of his hand.

'Well, well, well, as the three oilmen said,' he murmured, putting the binoculars aside and holding up the strip of celluloid to the light. After a moment, he reassembled the binoculars and used them to examine what was unmistakably a piece of microfilm. Even at full power they were woefully inadequate, but he was able to make out the fact that the microfilm showed a series of lists: names, words and numbers, perhaps dates or amounts or measurements. He wasn't even certain of that – it was impossible to tell more.

Timmy had kept the binoculars on ever since they'd arrived at the house. He had never taken them off, except at night. At his mother's insistence. His murdered mother's insistence. His murdered mother who'd had an eidetic memory which would have been very useful for . . .

'Oh, hell,' Skinner said, his voice resonant within the tiled shell of the bath and shower surround. 'Oh, hell, damn and blast.' She hadn't been murdered for any emotional reason, he'd been wrong to assume that. It had been a professional execution, made to look like Hallick's work – oh, convenient Hallick. Whoever had done it must have thought stopping the eidetic memory would stop information being carried. But Anne Morgan had carefully committed the information to a second method of recording before getting on the plane. This film. Why had she secreted it in the binoculars? Had someone given themselves away? Had she seen or heard something that made

156

her think she might not get to where she was going? Or had it simply been a matter of convenience, a habit of caution wherein a good agent – for agent she must have been – separates volatile components?

He knew *he* hadn't killed her, Timmy hadn't killed her, and it seemed unlikely that Laura had had enough time to kill her before she screamed, although to be fair he had to consider the possibility. That left all the others, including Morgan, and even including Hallick who might have been trying a double bluff against himself. He'd been so *sure* it wasn't Hallick.

After a while he picked up the adhesive tape and fixed his spectacles, then put the binoculars on his bureau to return to Timmy in the morning. He clicked on the electric blanket control and undressed slowly, returning to the bathroom to take a long shower while he considered the alternatives.

In the end, he decided it was probably best to let everyone continue to think Hallick had been responsible. As indeed he might have been. Considering the situation he could hardly open up any other possibilities, it would only drive everyone up the wall, himself included. He'd say nothing, not even to Denning. When they got out of this – if they got out of it – he'd put the entire matter into more capable hands than his own. Especially considering their shaky state at the moment, he thought, looking down. He crawled into bed and lay there looking into the darkness.

It took him a long time to fall asleep.


He was cold.

Clutching the edge of sheet and blanket he rolled slightly to catch the bedcovers around his body, but after a moment realised it made little difference. He was really very cold. Struggling up onto one elbow he squinted at the control box for the electric blanket and saw no light showing. There was a dim line of light showing between the curtains. He looked at his watch. Time to get up anyway.

He knew he'd slept badly, tossing and turning most of

the night. Partly because of the microfilm and what it meant, more because of the conversation he'd had with Laura. No doubt in his agitation he'd knocked the plug for the blanket out of the wall. Muttering, he threw back the covers to get up, then snatched them back again.

The *room* was cold.

They'd had to turn up the central heating now that the big picture window was only a single pane of uncurtained glass, because it seemed to drag the heat out of the main room like a vacuum cleaner. Apparently turning it up wasn't going to be enough – they'd have to put it onto twenty-four-hour operation.

He jumped up, dragged back the curtains, and made a mad dash for the clothes he'd tossed over a chair the night before (maybe it was time he wore those pyjamas he'd bought merely to keep from shocking the servants at the University dormitory where he'd been lodged – even though he hated the damn things). The floor felt cold and he hopped in a kind of awkward dance into underwear, shirt, trousers, socks.

Flinging back the bedroom door he went through the main room and kitchen into the generator room to re-set the central heating timer control. The lamp in the window-less room wouldn't work, either. In the faint light from the kitchen window behind him he could see the generator sitting there like some enormous black toad, malevolent and silent.

Silent.

'Oh, my god,' Skinner whispered, and saw his breath float up before him.

The generator had stopped.

He raced up the stairs and burst into Morgan's room but found only Timmy asleep in the small bed. The double bed was empty. Morgan wasn't in either of the bathrooms, either. As he stood on the balcony looking at the closed doors, hesitating, one of them opened and Morgan came out, buttoning up his shirt. He caught sight of Skinner, flushed, and then closed the door behind him. Sherri's door.

It hardly seemed a time for moral judgements. 'Tom . . . we're in trouble . . . the generator has stopped. Can you start it again?'

Morgan stared at him, open-mouthed. 'You're kidding,' he finally said.

'I wish I were,' Skinner told him. 'Didn't you notice how cold it . . . no, I don't suppose you did.' Morgan scowled and started to say something, but Skinner rushed on. 'I don't know how long it's been off, it feels pretty cold in here but . . . what should we do?'

'Wait a minute, wait a minute.' Morgan was trying to gather his wits. 'I'm civil engineering, not mechanical.'

'But you're an engineer . . . you must know *something* about it.'

'I know the *theory*.'

'Well, that's more than I know. Maybe you'd better take a look. Maybe it's just some simple thing . . .'

They stopped on the way to collect the lantern that hung in the store-room, and Morgan said that maybe it was there because this kind of thing happened often. Encouraged, they entered the silent generator room. The wavering light of the lantern gave an odd perspective to the room, making the bulk of the generator seem even greater.

'That's a hell of a big generator, Skinner,' Morgan said. 'Fifty kilowatts . . . have you any idea of the compression ratios in a diesel that size?'

'Absolutely no idea at all . . . I don't even know what a compression ratio *is*,' Skinner said helplessly. 'Other than what it sounds like. What does it do?'

Morgan started to explain, then said 'Oh, the hell with it. Maybe it's just the fuel line . . . water, sediment, something blocking it. Let's check that out first.'

Skinner set the lantern down on the floor. 'Tell me what to do.'

The fuel line was clear.

By the time they'd finished ascertaining that, Goade, Denning and Laura had appeared, wrapped in blankets, and stood shivering in the doorway. Morgan and Skinner

159

had liberally covered themselves and part of the floor with fuel oil, and looked impressively workmanlike. Unfortunately, like the oil, the impression was only on the surface.

'Well, let's *try* and start it, anyway,' Morgan finally said, looking around the room until his eyes settled on a small engine in one corner. He went over and bent down to inspect it. 'I wish I'd paid more attention in class,' he said regretfully. 'We've got to start this one first.'

'What do you mean?' Skinner asked, coming over to stand beside him with some paper towels he'd got out of the kitchen. He wasn't used to getting his hands dirty and found the sensation decidedly unpleasant.

'This little gasoline engine . . .'

'You mean petrol?'

Morgan looked at him with annoyance. 'Yes, petrol engine. We have to start the petrol engine to start the diesel engine that runs the generator. Trouble is, I don't know much about engines, like I said.'

'Joe does,' Denning offered from the doorway. 'He's always going on about his motorbikes and his car back home.'

'You'd better get him,' Skinner said.

'Now, listen . . .' Morgan protested angrily, but Skinner just stared at him until his eyes fell. 'You'd better get him, Frank,' Tom said grudgingly.

When Denning returned leading a sullen Hallick, Timmy and Sherri came too, completing the group. The child ran to his father.

'Why is it so cold, Daddy?' he asked, tugging at Morgan's sleeve. Morgan was staring at Hallick and shook Timmy off absently.

'We're all cold, Tim, don't bother us now.' His voice hardened when he spoke to Hallick. 'Denning says you know about engines.'

'Some,' Hallick admitted, staring back.

'Start that,' Morgan ordered, pointing to the small gasoline engine in the corner. 'If you can.'

'Why should I?' Hallick demanded.

'Because if we don't get it started we can't re-start the

generator, Joe,' Skinner explained quietly. 'And if we don't start the generator pretty quickly we're all going to freeze to death.'

'Oh.' Hallick looked at Skinner and then smiled, stretching his bruised mouth with a painful wince. 'Okay, Skinnie . . . I wouldn't want the kid to catch cold, would I, hey kid?'

'Make them take those things off you, Joe,' Timmy said, going over and looking up into Hallick's face. He frowned at Denning. 'I think you're mean.'

'Do you?' Denning asked. He reached into his pyjama pocket and pulled out the key. 'You undo them, then.'

'That's nice,' Goade snarled. 'That's *very* nice, making the kid take the cuffs off the guy who . . .'

'Do you know how to do it, Tim?' Skinner interrupted.

'Oh, sure', Timmy said cheerfully. 'I've got some in my toybox back home.' He struggled for a minute, then took the handcuffs from Hallick's wrists. Hallick rubbed the crimson rings where the metal had bitten into his flesh.

'Thanks, kid.'

Timmy walked over and handed the metal circles and key to Skinner. 'You keep them,' he said, firmly. Skinner nodded and put the handcuffs into his trouser pocket. 'Now Joe and me can get this show on the road,' Timmy added marching over to the engine in the corner.

Hallick grinned and followed him, hunkering down to inspect the engine. After about five minutes, he stood up. 'Well, it hasn't run for a while, but it looks okay.'

'It only runs until the diesel starts, then a relay cuts it out,' Morgan told him. 'We'd better disconnect it from the diesel until we're sure it works.'

'You're the expert,' Hallick said sarcastically, and stepped back. When Morgan gave the signal Hallick went over and connected the battery beside the engine to the starter motor and pressed the button. After a couple of tries the engine banged and then chugged into loud and clattering life. Skinner, who had been standing nearby watching everything, hurriedly stepped back with a look of apprehension. 'What's the matter, Skinnie?' Hallick laughed. 'Never been next to a real live engine before? Don't you drive a car or anything?'

'Of course I drive a car,' Skinner shouted over the noise of the engine, annoyed at himself for being startled. 'I get in and turn the key and it goes. If it doesn't I call the man from the garage and he fixes it.'

'Mechanics ain't your bag, that it?'

'My what?' Skinner watched Morgan reconnecting the small engine to the larger one.

'Your bag . . . your thing . . . what you like to do.'

'Oh . . . no . . . not my bag at all. I know a little about electronics . . . but I leave internal combustion to those with an affinity for it.'

'A what?'

Skinner grinned back, a smear of oil on his cheek curving up. 'A bag.'

'Okay . . . hey, okay there, Skinnie,' Hallick approved.

Everyone was smiling, relieved at the healthy and promising sound of the little engine. Morgan turned to Hallick. 'This look okay to you?' he growled.

Hallick went over and looked. 'That's a diesel, right?' Morgan nodded. 'Never worked diesels, just bikes and cars. I guess it's okay. Let it rip.'

It wouldn't start. Everyone stopped smiling.

'Try it again, Tom,' Skinner urged. Morgan did, several times, with no result.

'Shit,' Hallick said succinctly, and kicked the base of the generator.

Timmy had moved over next to Skinner. 'Bad show, Skinnie,' he said, solemnly. 'Damn poor show, if you ask me.'

Morgan glowered at his son, but Skinner nodded. 'I entirely agree with you, Tim. I tell you what . . . while we have another bash at this, why don't you help Laura get some food together? You know where everything is . . . perhaps you could figure out a way to warm some water over the fire in the fireplace. Then we could have a hot drink, at least. What do you think?'

162

'All right,' Tim went over to Goade. 'You do the fire . . . you're good at that. I'll get some water.'

Goade stared down at the small figure that barely reached his waistband, and his big mouth twitched. 'You think that would be a good idea, do you, shorty?'

'It does seem sensible,' Timmy said reasonably. 'We have to . . . to . . .'

'Co-operate?' Laura suggested, and then glanced at Skinner, who smiled encouragingly.

' 'zactly,' Timmy said and went through into the kitchen. Just before they turned back to the generator, Skinner heard the thin little voice say to Laura, 'There's a rat in co-operate, isn't there?'

'Yes,' came her lighter tones. 'And there's an opera. Do you know what an opera is?'

'Sure. Loud singing,' Timmy informed her. '*Very* loud singing.'

They disconnected the gasoline engine and began on the diesel. Using what few tools there were on the workbench, Morgan and Hallick, in an uneasy alliance, took the cover plates off and located the next in-line component, the injector pump. Three minutes after they'd removed it, Morgan cursed and threw the tiny adjustable spanner he'd been using clear across the room. 'How long did you say it takes to freeze to death, Skinner? Couple of hours? Three?'

'What do you mean?' Skinner asked worriedly. He'd helped where he could and his face was a half-mask of smears and dirt. Even one lens of his spectacles, now held together rather precariously with adhesive tape, had a thick oily fingerprint partially obscuring his vision.

'I mean there is no way on God's earth that we can make this generator work again,' Morgan stated flatly. Hallick was staring down at the pieces of the pump in his hands, his face pale behind the bruises. He looked up and Skinner saw the same opinion in his bleak eyes. From the kitchen there came a clatter of cutlery and Laura's and Timmy's voices cheerfully intermingling.

'Why not?'

Morgan leaned against the workbench and folded his arms. 'You said this was Berndt's summer place, didn't you?' Skinner nodded. 'Well, it's winter now. This generator is maybe twenty-five, thirty years old, probably put in when they built the house. There's nine . . .' he swallowed, continued. 'There's eight of us here. We've turned up the central heating and we've filled the time on our hands by taking baths, running the washing machine and dryer for one shirt or a couple of pairs of socks whenever we felt like it. Three meals a day for eight, plus snacks, deep freeze, refrigerator, hair dryer, microwave oven, dishwasher, all the lights most of the time because the days are short, stereo, water pump, toaster, deep-fryer – you name it, we've used it. Half those things weren't even invented thirty years ago. One old man and a couple of servants wouldn't put much of a strain on it, but *we* did, by god we did. We've overloaded it, and as a result we've fractured the shaft of the injector pump and the bearings are completely shot. That's it, and that's all, Professor.'

'Can't we fix it . . . rebuild it . . . substitute something . . .'

'No,' Morgan said.

'Hey,' came Goade's voice from the main room. 'The water's boiling over into the goddamn fire!'

Skinner looked at Hallick, and Hallick shook his head.

Little by little, the house began to die.

# Sixteen

Ainslie was horrified at the change in Doppler. On his previous visit the man had seemed nervous and not particularly well, but no more. Now he was obviously seriously ill. His handsome face was grey and sweat-sheened, his hands shook with a continuous tremor he could no longer conceal, and his eyes were tight with pain.

'My god, Doppler, you need a doctor!' Ainslie exclaimed, coming across the patio as the helicopter that had brought him, blindfolded as before, rose up into the darkness of the desert night.

'Don't concern yourself, General, I have had the doctor,' Doppler said, waving him to a chair. 'It will pass ... it always has.'

They'd had their report from Switzerland on Doppler. He was all he claimed to be, a legal consultant and an arbitrator of some considerable distinction. He served mainly large industrial clients, and had been very successful acting as an intermediary with various unions. The report had stated he'd had a stroke some years before, but had recovered fully and been something of a health fanatic since. It didn't seem to have helped from the look of him, Ainslie thought, sitting down.

'Well?' he asked.

Doppler indicated a manila envelope on the table between them. 'These are the latest pictures of the hostages.'

Ainslie ripped open the envelope and stared at the photographs – Hallick, Skinner and Goade bruised and beaten, Anne Morgan apparently half-conscious and in bed, with her husband looking apprehensive and ill next to her, Denning considerably more lined, Laura holding

Timmy on her lap with lines of fear and tension around her eyes, the boy on the verge of tears.

'What the . . .'

'There was apparently some kind of trouble. Mr Brahms wasn't entirely clear in his explanations . . . an attempt at escape, perhaps. I . . . the men responsible have apparently been removed from guard duty. Replacements will be found, of course, and more carefully monitored. Mr Brahms is awaiting my report on the success of your efforts. I'm sure the next pictures will show an improvement in the condition of the hostages, but it may take several days. I'm sorry, General. Mr Brahms is very angry.'

'*He's* very angry?' Ainslie shouted, tossing the pictures back onto the table. 'My god, Doppler, you can see what's happening . . . they must be desperate to have tried to escape . . . he's a madman, you've got to stop this *now* before one of them gets killed.'

'It *will* stop, as soon as the demands are met. What progress have you made?'

'What's he *doing* to them? You've got to tell us where they are.'

'I'm assured they are perfectly safe and perfectly comfortable. Whatever trouble occurred was started by them, *not* by the guards. Even so the guards will be replaced as soon as I report back. The demands, General . . . let us get on with it and leave the shouting for another time, please.'

Ainslie leaned back in his chair, his face working as he tried to calm himself and forget the expression on his daughter's face. Doppler was right, they had to get on with it.

'The gold has been deposited as I'm sure you know,' Ainslie itemised, gritting his teeth. 'The people from the Embassies have already started to leave, and the concert is being organised.'

'With which conductor?' Doppler asked, leaning forward slightly.

'Sir Charles Groves has agreed . . . fortunately for your Mr Brahms he had to cancel his engagements for the season because of an injury . . .'

'Nothing serious, I hope?' Doppler asked with every indication of concern.

'Right this minute Brahms may be *killing* these people ... how can you care about ...'

'The hostages are perfectly all right. Sir Charles ...'

'Broke his ankle playing football in the garden with his godson,' Ainslie snapped, reaching for the drink that had been waiting for him on the table and gulping half of it. (Where the hell were Captain Skinner and Larry – they should have homed in long ago on the device they'd stuck under his collar.)

'Ah ...' Doppler seemed relieved. 'A remarkable man, Sir Charles. Mr Brahms realises, of course, that the *concert* cannot be hurried, but he would hope that in this case a promise will be ...'

'Your Mr Brahms doesn't have to worry, the concert will go ahead no matter what. That music you sent ... they tell me everyone is ga-ga about it ... they want to know who the composer is ...'

'Sir Charles was impressed?' Doppler said in delight.

'Yeah, Sir Charles was impressed, for what it's worth. Jesus Christ, Doppler, will you listen to *reason* ...'

But Doppler was leaning back in his chair, some of the lines of tension easing from his face. 'How very generous ... how splendid ...'

'Oh, but they said to say there's a problem about copyright or performing rights or something like that ...'

'The papers are on their way ...' Doppler interrupted softly. And in the same, soft voice, continued. 'What about the prisoners?'

'They'll be released as soon as you tell us where you want them.'

'Release will be sufficient ... they will be collected ... just let them go ...' Doppler's voice seemed almost dreamy, but when he opened his eyes they were as sharp as ever. 'And ACRE? What about ACRE, General?'

Ainslie had been waiting for this, dreading it. 'I can do nothing about ACRE.'

There was a sound of a helicopter in the distance,

perhaps more than one. At last, he thought in relief, at last. If we can get this guy someplace we'll beat the goddamn information out of him . . . his rage was rising no matter how much he tried to control it. Doppler heard the engines, too, and glanced up in annoyance.

'We have not finished . . .' He clenched the arms of his chair. 'You must take care of ACRE, General . . . it must be cancelled . . . it *must be* . . . of all the demands *this* is the most . . .'

'I told you at the beginning there was nothing I could do,' Ainslie shouted, seeing the lights of the helicopters out of the corner of his eye. 'I don't know why you think I'm that important . . . I'm not. ACRE is a massive project, thousands of people are concerned . . .'

'Yes!' Doppler said suddenly, his vague voice suddenly tightening with anger. 'Yes . . . thousands of people concerned for their own greed and their own profit while they destroy the land, the life . . .'

'Are you going to sit there and tell me Brahms is prepared to kill human beings for a few birds and bushes?' Ainslie half-screamed in incredulous frustration. 'I've heard of ecology nuts but that is absolutely . . .'

The helicopters had settled, out in the darkness, their lights extinguished and so close together it was possible Doppler still thought it was just the one returning too soon. He was totally concentrated on Ainslie now, his face paling even more and his eyes wide. There was a bead of froth in the corner of his mouth and his hands pounded the arms of his chair. 'Everyone is so concerned with tomorrow and nobody cares about yesterday, do they? Get, get, get . . . take and destroy . . . no respect for the small things, the old things . . . I am sick and I am sickened of mankind, General . . . all of it . . . all of you . . . ACRE must *not* go ahead.'

There was a movement in the darkness around the outer perimeter of the patio and Ainslie knew that Captain Skinner and the others were moving in quietly but steadily, encircling the house to find guards and anyone else who might be there. To find, perhaps, Laura and the others somewhere in that vast white structure that bulked behind him.

'Why not?' he shouted. '*What* is so *evil* about a chance to open up lost land that's going to waste when millions need room to live and . . .'

'Millions . . . millions?' Doppler's face twisted. 'The only millions they're interested in is money, Ainslie, and you know it, don't you? You know it's a sham, the whole thing is a sham . . . exploitation, that's all it is, in the guise of good . . .' More spit had gathered on Doppler's lips and a bit flew out as he gabbled his fury into the night. 'Tell the Norwegians their reports are false . . . tell them the geologists were wrong . . . tell them there is no gold, no oil . . . you all lie so easily about so many things, lie about that. The gold and the oil will wait, they've waited for millions of years. But the people . . . the people . . .'

'*What* people?' Ainslie shouted, his own hands pounding the arms of his own chair. 'There are no people on the North Cape . . . there's nothing there at all . . . snow and ice and reindeer and damn-all else . . .'

Doppler was shaking his head. 'You're wrong . . . wrong . . .'

'I'm *not* wrong,' Ainslie ground out. 'I've been there, flown over it ten times, for Christ's sake . . . it's . . .'

'ACRE must be stopped . . . you will stop ACRE or your daughter and the others . . . will die . . . all d . . . d . . . d . . .' Doppler's face twisted into a rictus of pain, the lips drawing back as he gasped and bent forward, clutching his stomach.

'Skinner!' Ainslie screamed. 'Larry!' He was around the table now, grabbing Doppler as he pitched forward out of his chair, his own rage forgotten, Doppler's rage consumed by the pain that was obviously convulsing him from within. Beads of sweat stood out on the man's finely shaped forehead, trickled down through the distinguished greying temples, dripped off the eagle nose and riveted along the narrow aristocratic jaw. No one is handsome in agony.

169

'Medicine . . . pocket . . . pocket . . .' Doppler gagged, and Ainslie began to slap jacket and trousers, finally found a bottle of thin liquid, no marks or indications of dosage.

'How much . . . how much . . . all of it . . . ?'

Doppler nodded, and he unscrewed the cap awkwardly as he still held the falling man. Captain Skinner suddenly was beside him taking the weight and freeing Ainslie's hands. He lifted the bottle to Doppler's lips, but before he could tilt it Doppler gagged and a flood of crimson gushed out of his mouth, splattering Ainslie's uniform and his own suit.

Doppler coughed and choked, then seemed to relax. Skinner eased him back and the lawyer looked with dying eyes at the three-star general of the United States Army kneeling before him, and smiled.

'Finished too soon . . . tell my son . . . I'm sorry.'

Frantically Ainslie tried to force the bottle to Doppler's lips but weakly Doppler pushed it away, shaking his head. A little more blood trickled down his chin as he choked again. 'Tell my son . . . this was for him . . . and . . . for the Samek . . . not . . . Webb . . . never for Webb . . .'

'Where's my daughter . . . please . . . please . . .' Ainslie begged as Doppler's self-justifying litany went on dribbling out with his blood.

'Safe . . . quite safe . . . in the spring . . .'

'Tell me where she *is*,' Ainslie half-sobbed, clutching Doppler's jacket, shaking him. Doppler moved with the jacket, limp, unresisting. '*Tell me how to get in touch with Brahms!*' he shouted into the face of a man who could not, would not, would never hear him. 'Tell me . . .' he sobbed.

'Ainslie . . . Ainslie . . . he's dead,' Captain Skinner's voice came, hollow with shock.

'He didn't say where they were . . . he didn't say . . .'

'He said they were safe,' the Captain soothed without much conviction. 'Brahms will get in touch with us . . . he still hasn't got what he wants.'

Ainslie looked up, tears streaking his face and not giving damn who saw them. 'No,' he agreed, wiping his cheeks with this hands, leaving smears of Doppler's blood on his skin. He stared at the lawyer's empty body, wishing someone would close the black, blank staring eyes.

'What was all that about gold and oil?' Captain Skinner asked, helping Ainslie to his feet. Ainslie glanced at him, reaching for his handkerchief, dabbed at his face and hands, making the mess worse instead of better.

'Why, Captain,' he said with a faint trace of his former anger. 'You mean to tell me there are actually some secrets you *don't* know?'

# Seventeen

The vast room gleamed.

Already condensation had begun to form on the walls. The glass of the big window was coated with a filigree of frost-fronds, enclosing them in a ghostly world of unmoving translucent growth that thickened as the hours passed. In the kitchen the dead appliances were silent. As no water was now pumped through the pipes the last few drops hung forever frozen in the taps, never to fall. Ice had begun to form in the toilets.

Once they had accepted that the generator was irreparable, desperation and Skinner had driven them. Before the cold had only been their trap, now it could become their executioner. The bedrooms had been denuded of every curtain, blanket, rug and mattress. Laying a base of the mattresses, they had tugged the sofas, dining table and chairs and formed them around the fireplace – now their only source of heat. Skinner pointed out it had been intended merely as a decorative feature, and its heat would be negligible if allowed to escape into the big room. It would rise to hang uselessly and only warm the rafters above. They had to confine it. Over the framework of the furniture they had thrown the curtains, the scatter rugs, what extra blankets they had, propping them up or anchoring them with cushions where necessary until a barely reasonable inner 'room' was created, enclosing the fireplace at one end. The extra advantage cramped space would give them was the sharing of body heat.

Now their voices were muffled and occasional, absorbed in the folds of the makeshift tent. As night fell the light from the fire and the single lantern made the tent glow, and shadows within moved fitfully, slowly. Soon the house was entirely dark around them. Dark, silent, cold.

They had plenty of food and plenty of water – survival in those terms was not a problem. Sherri had sewn Skinner back into his snowsuit so that he could go outside. Rather than open the door time after time he'd gone around the side and broken through the bathroom window in Laura's room. First he pushed through armload after armload of firewood which Goade carried away and stacked against one side of the tent, adding to its insulation. Insulation they would inevitably consume. Skinner didn't tell them how little firewood there was outside, there was no point. Again, the wood had been intended only to provide a decorative fire, not a life-saving one. The last load Skinner had shoved through the window had left the mound of snow, under which Anne Morgan lay, exposed to the wind that had begun to rise around noon. Once the wood was through, Skinner took a pot and began to pass through snow, enough to fill the bathtub. They could melt it as they needed it.

The wind whistled and moaned more loudly now, whining around the corners of the house and plucking at the roof, pushing inquisitive fingers into the windowframes and the crack around the outer door.

Within the tent the light was sufficient for Sherri to see what she was doing, but the warmth was insufficient for her to do it well. Once they had built their shelter, such as it was, clothing was the next priority. Lacking electricity to power the mechanism of the sliding door they had man-handled it open to drag down the thick red velvet curtains. They were using them as wrappings now, but one by one she would cut them up to produce the simplest and warm-est form of clothing they could think of – rough trousers and ponchos. They could not stay in the tent all the time. They had to go to the storeroom for food, the bath for snow to melt. And having enough food created a concom-mitant problem – toilet facilities. There was little room in the tent for privacy. They put a couple of big cooking pots into the entryway, and everyone was expected to dispose of their own waste outside. The snow would cover much.

It would be, Goade observed, a very fragrant spring.

'If we're here to enjoy it,' Denning muttered.

No one could stand upright but no one wanted to, for they were huddled into themselves trying to stop the shivering that Skinner promised them was really their best defence against the chill. But shivering made them feel vulnerable, vulnerability made them feel afraid, and fear made them colder than ever. Within that vicious circle, and within their own circle, the cold was beginning to penetrate their bones.

'What about the oil?' Morgan suddenly said, startling them.

'What about it?' Hallick asked from where he was curled up next to Sherri.

'Why couldn't we burn it? We could fix up some kind of stove, couldn't we?'

'I don't know . . .' Skinner said slowly. He was between Laura and Denning, Timmy against his knees. The firelight glinted on his spectacles as he looked toward Morgan on the other side of Sherri. 'How?'

'All you need is a container and some kind of wick . . . to keep the flame away from the surface of the oil,' Morgan mused.

'There's some big tin cans in the storeroom.' Goade remembered. 'I don't know what's in them, but they're about two or three gallons worth of something. That big enough?' The change in their situation had changed him, too. Gone were the snide remarks and the sullen attitude. He'd worked hard all day, he wanted to survive as much as any of them. Either that or the cold had slowed his blood.

'What shape are they?' Morgan asked thoughtfully.

'Just big tin cans . . . cylinders.'

'That's good . . . that's ideal . . . if you could empty them and cut away part of the front, figure out some kind of support for the wick . . . maybe we could make a stove. A couple of stoves.'

'Wouldn't that set fire to the tent . . . an open flame like that?' Laura asked.

'We don't put them *in* the tent,' Morgan condescended

impatiently. 'We put them at the far end . . . down there opposite the fireplace, make some kind of surround that would reflect the heat into the tent, the way it does from the fireplace. Then we'd have two heat sources – much more efficient.'

'We can do that tomorrow,' Skinner decided. 'Right now I think we should eat something and then get some sleep if we can. If nobody comes tomorrow, we can get on with whatever else we have to do to stay alive.'

Nobody argued with him.

Laura watched as he went out of the tent to get some tins from the store-room. More frightened now than they had ever been since they'd awakened in this strange house, they had accepted his leadership. Not because he was the biggest or the strongest, but because he knew the most. For the moment at any rate, they realised their lives depended on ideas, not muscles. He'd lived in the Arctic, so he must know how to survive in the cold. But she knew, as perhaps the others didn't, how weak the foundation for that line of reasoning actually was, because she'd talked to Skinner about his Arctic assignment. They had talked about so many things during the past days. He'd laughed about it, then. About the silly snowsuit and how pathetic it was in comparison with the 'real thing', the real thing being the skins and furs the Eskimos, for example, used. No artificial fibre could match them. Told her that instead of living *with* the environment, man had simply transported his own ideas of comfort and imposed them, created an artificial little world totally dependent on his own technology. Exactly as Berndt had built this house, in fact. If he'd built a windmill, for example, instead of bringing in a generator, if the heating had been solar heating instead of electric, they would all still be warm. But the house was built during the fifties, when technology was the new god. And this was the result. One small piece of metal had broken, and every-thing had stopped. *Everything*.

After the meal – a stew concocted simply by pouring the contents of a lot of tins into the one pot they could fit into the fireplace – they tried to settle themselves for sleep. Morgan, who said he slept fitfully at best, had a heap of firewood next to him so that he could stoke the fire as required. Goade was so long he had to sleep across the foot of the tent furthest from the fire, but he said nothing, simply rolled himself up in his red curtain and fell asleep. Denning lay parallel with him. Sherri and Hallick were on the opposite side of the tent, and that left Laura with Timmy curled in front of her and Skinner against the outer side of the tent behind her. After a while she suggested that they put the child between them so he'd be warmer, and Skinner agreed.

It seemed insane to pray for the return of the gunmen, but he did. Three days now, and no sign of them. Had something gone wrong with the negotiations? Had the kidnappers been captured? Killed? Were they playing for time, thinking the hostages safe? Or was rescue only hours away?

Perhaps it was only a matter of hours.

Or days, at the most. Days would be all right. Tonight was fine because they were all tired. Tomorrow and tomorrow night would be fine because they'd be busy and would become tired again.

But if they were forced to live confined like this for very long, tempers would fray, arguments and petty hostilities would develop, the claustrophobic tent would become more unbearable because anger and resentment would shrink it even further around them. Yes, they would co-operate at first because they wanted to survive, but they were human and humans wear thin when rubbed together. Controls wear thin, too. And one of them . . . one of them breathing the stuffy, smoky air of the tent as he himself did . . . was a murderer.

There was a woman outside under the snow to prove it.

# Eighteen

Werner Doppler was an extremely irritated young man with the pudgy face of an agitated chipmunk.

'Why have I been arrested?' he demanded, perspiration trickling down his forehead as he turned his head back and forth between Ainslie, Carter and Captain Skinner, 'Why have I been dragged here without . . .'

'You're not under arrest, Mr. Doppler,' Ainslie said. 'But speed and secrecy were vital . . . I'm sorry if you've been upset. I'm afraid you're going to be even more upset, and I'm sorry for that, too. We had no alternative.'

'Interpol has no authority here,' Doppler stated smugly.

'Indeed, that's why you have been handed over to us. Your Embassy knows all about it, they agreed.'

'Did they? Did they? Why should I believe you? I want to see someone from my own . . .'

'Mr Doppler, I'm sorry to have to tell you that your father is dead,' Captain Skinner announced in a flat voice. 'He died the night before last here in Adabad.'

'Dead? My father? Here?' Doppler gasped out the words on a rising tone of incredulity.

'I'm afraid so,' Ainslie told him. 'If you'll come with us we'll take you to him.'

A chastened chipmunk is no more attractive than an angry one, but Ainslie felt sorry for the man. He was obviously shocked, and just as obviously realised that there was more than simple death behind his abrupt and unexplained seizure in a Basle street some twenty hours before by two agents of Interpol. He went with them without further comment, the questions in his eyes left unspoken.

Ainslie had been surprised to find there was a small

morgue in the basement of the Embassy, although he'd never consciously considered the question before. But of course Americans died abroad occasionally, and in countries where local arrangements were not entirely satisfactory; a morgue was probably a necessity. At any rate, the body of Doppler Senior rested, for the moment and probably quite illegally, in the small basement morgue of the American Embassy in Adabad.

Or they thought it did.

For when Captain Skinner drew the sheet back from the face of the dead man, Werner Doppler smiled broadly with almost malicious satisfaction.

'That is *not* my father,' he said. 'And I want to see someone from the Swiss Embassy immediately, please. *Immediately*.'

# Nineteen

They amazed themselves with their own ingenuity.

After emptying the contents of two of the large tins (cooking oil), they cleaned them and cut away a large semi-circle in the upper front with a tin opener. Goade spent a laborious hour working two bedsprings free of one of the mattress bases and they used that as a support for the pieces of blanket from which they braided a pair of wicks. They had to extend the tent to accommodate the stoves; setting them directly on the mattresses was too risky. They took the racks out of the refrigerator and cooker, fastened them together with some lengths of now-useless electrical flex, and covered them with aluminium cooking foil, producing a large triangular stove surround that reflected the heat forward. Like the tent it wasn't beautiful, but it meant warmth. With a heat source at either end, and slightly enlarged, the tent was more comfortable but still cramped.

Still they were without shoes, and any movement outside the tent was limited. At first they wound torn-off strips of blanket and upholstery around their feet, but then Laura remembered the carpeting in the music room. Once again they manhandled the sliding door open and began to pry up the carpeting, only to discover a greater treasure trove beneath: a thick grey felt underlay. Fairly easy to tear or cut, and quite easy to sew. Skinner said it was ideal – felt had actually developed from the loose wool that the old Tartars had stuffed inside their boots. The constant pressure of their feet in the stirrups moulded it together and produced a thick, flexible, absorbent, but easily dried material. They shoved the piano and chairs aside and peeled back the red wool carpet, cutting it free to throw over the top of the tent as a final insulation. The felt made not only boots but also mittens and hoods for when they had to make their brief forays into the snow.

All this activity kept them quite happy for a couple of days.

But no longer.

'Why the hell doesn't somebody come?' Goade kept saying. '*Any*body?'

No one knew.

The deterioration that Skinner had expected began to set in. It was most noticeable in Sherri, who abandoned all pretence of looking after herself except for liberal applications of perfume against the continuous and growing stink of so many people spending so much time in such a small space. She sat cross-legged next to Morgan, her grimy hair hanging around her face like a tattered curtain, stitching and stitching with the dull trussing needles. She rarely spoke, and then only to complain or snap, but the advantage of her withdrawal was that they now all had red velvet suits to wear over the layers of their other clothing. What the suits lacked in style and fit they made up for in increased mobility and warmth. The poncho tops were held at neck and waist by simple drawstrings to contain their body heat, and she had cut one slit on either side through which they could poke their hands when they needed to. Some warmth was necessarily lost through these openings, but sleeves would have taken too long to make. They'd had to get themselves covered as quickly as possible.

Warmth within the tent was no longer a problem. The main room was extremely cold, the outer and upper rooms more frigid still, but the insulation in the walls meant it was still warmer inside the house than outside. Outside the Arctic waited. It was only when they had to go beyond the outer door of the house that they appreciated the squalor and foetid warmth of their den within.

Laura insisted on heating water to wash her hair and Timmy's – to his public indignation and private relief – also insisting that everyone wash at least the exposed parts of themselves once a day.

'No sense making things worse than they need be,' she would say briskly, handing around towels and soap as she set the washing-up pan in the centre of the tent as a communal basin. Skinner would smile to himself at her gentle tyranny and comply meekly, not only because he hated feeling dirty but also because he was aware that the least illness among them could be disastrous. They could live with a stink, but not with running sores that grew from chafed, dirty skinfolds, nor the germs those sores would breed.

Cosy was a word that never occurred to anyone, and Sherri's perfume was not enough.

'Why doesn't anyone *come*?' Goade would say again. '*Any*body?'

Timmy had grown more and more silent, watching his father who never seemed to pay any attention to him. Morgan's self-righteous bombast had long since dissolved into apathy and self-pity. The hunch of his body away from the rest seemed to mime 'why is this happening to *me*?' with unappealing clarity. He and Sherri would usually sit together, and if she spoke at all it was to him. Her whispers would have a pleading quality, she seemed almost a supplicant at the altar of his sullen resentment. Skinner thought back often to the morning when he'd confronted Morgan coming out of her room, and it bothered him. That a man might seek the solace of sex in his grief was understandable, but it seemed a strange manifestation in Morgan. Nevertheless, it was clear that it continued, for they would occasionally disappear together into one of the icy bedrooms and close the door.

Hallick had looked across at Skinner during one of these absences and winked. 'More than one way to keep warm, isn't there?' he'd chuckled. It didn't seem to bother him that Sherri had transferred her affections to Morgan. Because of Timmy's presence Anne's murder was never discussed by the others. They had to talk to Hallick, eat with him, sleep with him, live with him. Skinner had chucked the handcuffs behind the deepfreeze, and nobody had mentioned them again, not even Denning. Hallick seemed grateful for their grudging acceptance and did all he could to make himself agreeable and helpful. Among other things he was teaching Timmy to draw, something for which he himself had a remarkable talent. Pinned around the tent with splinters of wood were various examples of his sketching – Goade and Denning engrossed in their interminable gin rummy tournament. Timmy with his wooden army, Laura and Skinner laughing over a chessboard they'd made and tried to use with hopeless results as they kept forgetting which bits of wood, cork bathmat or drawer pulls they'd designated as pawns or bishops. In the end they'd fallen back on draughts, which they also taught to Timmy. He, in turn, 'taught' Hallick, who kept himself a very slow learner.

Timmy, Skinner decided, was saving their sanity, at least. He'd started giving the child lessons in arithmetic, and Laura had in English. There was plenty of writing material because all the books on the shelves had at least two blank end pages each. Twice Skinner had carried him outside at night to look at the stars and give substance to the ancient astronomical legends for which the boy had an insatiable appetite. Everyone could now virtually recite by heart the tales that Skinner repeated over and over, patiently embellishing and extending them.

Running out of natural firewood gave Goade an outlet for his aggression. He was methodically breaking up the furniture, having found a small axe in the generator room, and informed them that when he'd chopped up all the beds, bureaux, bedside tables and so on, he'd begin on the doorframes, the bookshelves and the teak panelling. It kept him busy, and it kept them warm. Skinner was dreading the day he would remember the Boesendorfer. What bad temper Goade had left after these exercises he expended on Denning over the card games.

They had also begun to pry up the woodblock flooring, which was of very hard wood and burned slowly, so they reserved it for the nights. The fire had to be kept alight, not only for warmth but because they had long since run out of matches. Oddly enough, they still had plenty of cigarettes, because the smoke of the fire seemed to satisfy any craving in that direction. Only Goade kept puffing, a few a day.

With a strange kind of nesting instinct they had all made little corners for themselves in which they kept their few personal possessions, pushing shelves or pockets into the side of the tent. One afternoon, finding a small amethyst brooch of very old-fashioned design on a mattress, Laura had started to hand it to Sherri, but Skinner reached out and claimed it.

'That's mine,' he said softly, pinning it back into his wallet from where it had fallen. Goade looked up from his cards, started to say something, but changed his mind.

'Did it belong to your wife?' Laura asked gently.

'Yes . . . well, it was meant for her but . . .'

'I'm sorry, you don't have to . . .'

He smiled at her. 'It's all right, she died almost fifteen years ago.' Looking down at the brooch where it gleamed against the dark leather he touched it with a fingertip. 'It was my grandmother's, really. I'd had it cleaned and the setting repaired . . . I was going to give it to her for her birthday, but that same week she was killed . . . hit by a car while crossing the street.'

'How dreadful, David.' She had told him about the death of her first fiancé, he knew she understood something of what it had been like, so only nodded in confirmation. 'What was her name?' she asked after a moment.

'Margaret. That was my grandmother's name, too . . . that's what made me think of . . .' he closed the wallet and tucked it into the niche in the tent that held his briefcase. 'It's not worth much . . . I don't know why I still carry it about. Silly, really.' His hand hesitated and then he thrust it into the open mouth of the briefcase. 'I think I found something of yours, too, by the way.' He pulled out several sheets of torn-off endpapers heavily scribbled over with crossed out lines and words, and looked at her until she flushed with embarrassment. 'I suppose you know how

183

good this is,' he said quietly. It was a poem. At first he'd thought it something she'd merely jotted down from memory for one of Timmy's lessons, but after scanning it he'd seen the progression of the poem from page to page. Fascinated despite himself he'd followed her train of thought, picked up the haiku form on which she'd based the structure, saw how she'd polished and developed the thing until it had reached its final form. Like all haiku it was deceptively simple, but she'd built the seventeen syllable form into something more.

> The sun's dull red eye
> burns once through the afternoon
> and blinks. The ice drips.
> The little birch tree
> drops its snow coat, springs upward,
> is naked again.
> Winter's green sky moves
> relentlessly. Our short day
> glaciates, is gone.
> Night waits. Unbroken.
> Your silence does not warm me,
> or the small birch tree.

'It's not finished . . . it's still coming.' She reached out a hand for the pages but he held them fast.

'Easily?'

'No . . . but eventually. My father and Larry think it's a childish habit I haven't grown out of yet.'

'Writing good poetry is hard work.'

'Surely a scientist wouldn't give it house-room?' She kept her voice light but he saw what it meant to her.

'Ah . . . but *I* was born in Wales, remember?' It was one of the thousands of unimportant facts they had exchanged over the long days. 'The Welsh have *two* national sports, rugby and poetry. You should write all the time, never mind what they say. Poetry is far from childish – it's as old an art as astronomy is a science. Older, probably.'

'You almost make it sound respectable,' she laughed. 'I tell you what, one day I'll write a whole book of poetry about stars and dedicate it to you. Would you like that . . . can you imagine something as impossible as that?'

'If I can imagine the centre of the sun then I can imagine a book of your poems,' he told her gravely.

'Oh . . . hot stuff, hey?' She built the wall of laughter a little higher.

He handed her back the torn-off pieces of paper without smiling. 'Only if you feed the flame. Speaking of which, I think we need more wood for that fire.' He left her there with the poem in her hand and too many words in her mouth to speak. Eventually she stuffed the papers into her cosmetic case, remembering she had promised Goade to bring some of the drawers down from the bureaux upstairs. She crawled out of the tent, pushing her feet into her felt boots which were lined up with the rest outside. Skinner was bent over in the rear corner of the main room prying up more of the woodblocks with the kitchen cleaver and she went up the stairs without speaking to him.

As she approached the bureau in the bedroom she caught sight of herself in the full-length mirror beside the door and paused, hardly able to believe it. She began to laugh, softly at first and then more openly. The combination of red velvet poncho, trousers, and the big shapeless felt boots made her look like an animated Death-cap Toadstool, or one of Disney's less successful dwarfs. The more she giggled the funnier she looked to herself, bobbing and swaying about, her hair swinging across her cheeks.

'What's so goddamn funny?' It was Goade, looming in the doorway with a scowl. She looked at him and began to laugh even more. A red toadstool over six feet tall was infinitely funnier than one standing at around five foot four, and chokingly she told him so. His scowl deepened and he came across to jerk the top two drawers out of the bureau – with some difficulty.

'Better than freezing to death,' he muttered, and went out with a drawer under each arm. Her laughter faded and she turned away from the mirror. He was right, of course, there wasn't really anything funny about it at all. She went over to the bureau and started to pull out the next two drawers, then stopped. Goade had had to pull the top drawer quite hard to get it out, and she saw that whatever had been jamming it had fallen down.

It was only a pair of Sherri's tights wound around a small sheaf of letters. As she pulled them free, one of the hand-written sheets fluttered to her feet and she bent down to retrieve it. Irresistibly her eyes were drawn to the first words and then she couldn't free them. It was obviously a love letter, although from the wealth of clinical detail included along with the pretty words, it was more pornographic than romantic. Whoever he was, he remembered every inch of Sherri's body, had enjoyed it repeatedly, and was looking forward to doing so again as soon as possible, with variations. She wasn't shocked by the words – she'd discovered in the last few days she had quite a facility for imagining the same kind of thing from an opposite point of view – but she *was* shocked at herself for reading some-one else's intimate mail. Quickly she folded up the sheet and thrust it into one of the envelopes, practically knotting them within the tights with her eyes closed. Apparently Sherri hadn't missed them. Like some of the cosmetics and nail varnish bottles that were still scattered across the top of the bureau, she obviously hadn't cared enough about them to carry them downstairs. She'd take them down and give them to her anyway, and some of the cosmetics, too. Maybe if she had them there she'd take a little more trouble over her appearance. Tucking a drawer under each arm in imitation of Goade she went out of the room and started down the stairs, but the loose felt boots made negotiating without handholds treacherous, and she slipped. As she dropped one of the drawers to grasp the handrail she let go also of the handful of Sherri's things and they fell over, one of the bottles of nail varnish smashing just beside Skinner and spitting a long pink tongue over the wood blocks. He looked up as she gave the fallen drawer a kick that sent it crashing to the foot of the stairs.

'Did you drop this or throw it?' he asked, gathering up

the unbroken containers and the wodge of letters and tights. 'I said I thought your poem was good, not bad.'

She gathered up the fallen drawer and held it out until he dropped the things into it. 'I don't take criticism very well,' she smiled. 'Anyway, those are just some things of Sherri's I found.'

'Oh.' He peered at her more closely. 'You look cheerful, I must say.'

'Yes. I suggest if you're feeling depressed you should take a look at yourself in one of the full-length mirrors upstairs. It gives one a whole new perspective on things.' He stared after her as she went back to the tent, stopping to stack the drawers beside Goade, who was chopping up the first two with great satisfaction. She kicked off her felt boots and disappeared on her hands and knees into the mouth of the tent. Puzzled, he looked down at himself and then over at Goade. What on earth was she on about – had he spilled soup down the front of himself or what? Perhaps she wasn't as calm and in control as he'd thought, and he realised that frightened him. He didn't think he could stand it if she began to give way. He needed her to be just as she always was, he needed it very badly.

Sherri and Timmy were the only ones in the tent. Laura worked her way over the mattresses and tumbled blankets and put down the things she'd brought from their room. Setting aside the felt boot she was restitching, Sherri looked from the small heap of things to Laura.

'What's this?'

'I thought you might like to . . . freshen up, put on a little make-up. Sort of cheer yourself up a little.'

'What for? I'd only have to take the damn stuff off again, and anyway, who can see me in this hole? Can hardly see myself.' She prodded the rolled tights, then put down her needle to draw out the little sheaf of letters. Slowly she looked through them, smiling and humming to herself, and then suddenly leaned forward and tossed them onto the fire. 'Won't be needing *those* anymore, that's for sure.' She took up her sewing again, then looked at Laura

187

through her mass of tangled hair. 'I suppose you read them, did you? Give you a thrill?'

'I *didn't* read them,' Laura said defensively. 'I don't read other people's letters – ever.' But she felt her cheeks flushing as her body betrayed her. Sherri looked at her for a moment in the light of the fire now blazing up with the letters, and laughed. It wasn't a very nice laugh.

'Oh, I see. Still playing Miss Prim and Proper in the middle of all this? You say you didn't read them, fine, but don't think I believe it. You read them, you imagined the guy who wrote them doing it with me, and it turned you on. You're in the mood, honey, it's all over you like a neon sign and it's pathetic. You've not only fallen for Skinnie, you're in rut for him, and you don't know what to do about it. You can't keep your eyes off him . . . off his crotch, off his hands, off his mouth. I've seen it. Only you want it to be more than your eyes, so you went through my letters looking for lessons on how to get laid. You picked the right teacher but you're aiming at the wrong target. What you see in that cold fish beats me. You want him bad, but he's not interested. Well, I've seen that scene a hundred times, even played it myself. It's the pits. Reading my letters won't do it. The only thing that will do it is shoving your hand down his pants and seeing if he rises to the bait . . . might be worth it at that, sometimes those icy ones can go right up in flames when you least expect it. Go on . . . do it. Do it tonight. I'll watch, but I won't tell, honey. Go on – see if you learned anything from those letters or not.' Sherri's eyes were hot and wild behind the tangled curtain of hair as she goaded Laura, enjoyed seeing her blush, seeing the tears fill her eyes.

We're all turning into animals, Laura thought, horrified. But I won't . . . I mustn't. 'Don't be ridiculous,' she snapped, avoiding Timmy's fascinated gaze. He didn't know what they were talking about except it concerned Skinner and seemed to upset Laura.

'Leave her alone,' he said to Sherri.

'Shut up, you little twerp,' Sherri snapped. 'Play with your goddamned soldiers and shut up.'

Laura was chagrined to find that Sherri had discerned her physical obsession with David so easily, and in her embarrassment flared up at the other woman.

'There's no need to be vicious to the child . . . *he* didn't read your letters.'

Sherri returned to her stitching, her face suddenly wiped smooth of lascivious enjoyment. 'Just as well, isn't it? Might have given *him* ideas.'

'Timmy . . . why don't you help your Daddy in the kitchen?' Laura said in a choked voice. Sherri's moods seemed to go on and off like light bulbs, revealing her one moment, obscuring her the next.

'He'd only say I was in his way. That's all he ever says,' Timmy protested.

'Probably because it's true,' Sherri muttered.

'Go on, Tim,' Laura insisted, and with a sigh Timmy crawled out of the tent. She turned to Sherri. 'I don't care what kind of a life you've led, and I don't care what you think of me. But if I have any feelings for David they're *my* business, not yours, and they're certainly nothing to discuss in front of a child.'

Sherri's hands went still. 'Never wanted anyone before, have you?' she asked quietly. 'Maybe thought you did . . . but not like this, right?'

'I . . .'

'It scares you but you like it, too, because it makes you feel alive, right? Makes you feel real for the first time in your life.'

Laura stared at her for a long time. 'Yes.'

Sherri nodded, went on sewing. 'Shame you'll never get your little professor, honey. Die empty, won't you?'

'I'm not going to die.'

'You're already dead. We all are.' She waved the hand with the needle vaguely. 'Unless you call this living? I don't.'

Laura turned away and began to fold up the blankets, making a bad job of it in her anger, fighting back her tears. What Sherri said was true, she *would* die empty, when all she wanted was to be full of him. In every way, not just physically. Perhaps it would have been easier if it were just that.

'Never mind,' came Sherri's voice from beside her. 'It won't go on hurting forever.'

'What won't?' Morgan asked from the doorway of the tent.

'Her head,' Sherri said easily. 'She's got a headache – she reads too much.'

'Not something *you'll* suffer from, then, is it?' Morgan said in a snide tone, putting down the dishes for the evening meal.

It suddenly occurred to Laura that the tin opener cut through the lid of the tins a lot more easily than anything could cut through the tensions that were building up in this claustrophobic little blanket-shrouded world they'd created for themselves.

When the others eventually came in to eat, the circles of anger seemed to widen, overlap, intensify.

Goade was sulking because Denning had made a high score at cards, and when Hallick bumped his arm and made him spill some of his food he snapped, 'When I was at Fort Bragg we kept killers out of the mess hall.'

Laura looked up from serving Timmy. 'I didn't know you were at Bragg, John. When was that?'

'Huh?' Goade was scraping some gravy back into his bowl. 'Oh . . . couple of years ago. Why . . . your Dad ever stationed there?'

'Once, for about six months, but I thought . . .'

'What?'

'Nothing. It was when I was pretty small, so I don't remember much about it. We moved around a lot when I was small.'

'Army for you,' Goade grumbled, moving away from Hallick. 'But they know how to build a glasshouse all right, and what to keep in it.'

'What's a glasshouse?' Timmy wanted to know.

'A prison,' Skinner explained, scowling at Goade.

'The stockade,' Laura amplified. 'That's what they call it in the Army.'

Sherri giggled suddenly. Everyone looked at her, but she kept whatever amused her to herself and went on eating.

'Good place for cheaters, too,' Goade said malevolently to Denning.

'You ought to know,' Denning countered.

Hallick seemed to be growing smaller and smaller and Timmy looked at him. 'Maybe we could make a stockade for my fort, Joe . . . I don't have one of those.'

'Maybe,' Hallick muttered. 'Maybe tomorrow.'

' 'kay.' Timmy went back to his stew. 'There's pineapple in this,' he suddenly observed, chewing cautiously.

'Yes, I know,' Laura said. 'We've run out of canned potatoes so I made Hawaiian stew this time. Just for a change.'

'It might be a good idea to start organising the food,' Skinner suggested. 'I'll take an inventory tomorrow of what there is and how much, and then we can work out a . . .'

'Why?' Morgan asked.

'Because if we have to be here for a long time it would be better to start cutting down now rather than later.'

'What do you mean, "a long time"?'

'I think we have to face the possibility that no one will come for us,' Skinner stated quietly. 'That we might have to last out until spring . . . we can walk out in spring, when the snow melts and it gets warm enough.'

'Until *spring*?' Morgan choked, putting down his bowl. 'That's months away. Someone will come before then.'

'Yes, probably they will . . . but even so . . .'

They finished the meal in silence, digesting this along with the stew. Neither went down very well.

'I'll help you wash up,' Joe offered, and followed Laura out of the tent with the dirty dishes. After a few soggy disasters trying to bring hot water from the fireplace to the kitchen, Goade had built a second 'stove' next to the sink over which they could heat a bowl of water. Washing was

191

better than drying because at least you got to put your hands in warm water for a few minutes before it started to go cold again.

'I didn't kill her, Laura,' Hallick said in a desperate whisper as they washed up. 'I didn't.'

'There's no point in talking about it, Joe,' she said gently.

'But I want to talk about it. What Goade said . . . the way Morgan looks at me . . . but I *didn't*. I didn't kill that girl in Cleveland, but nobody . . . I didn't do the other thing, either. I don't have to make . . .' He reached out and grabbed her arm, jostling some of the water out of the bowl onto the floor. 'You got to believe me, Laura . . . *some*body's got to believe me . . .'

She looked down at his arm clutching hers and he took it away with a hopeless groan. 'You're scared of me, aren't you?'

'No,' she answered honestly. 'I'm not afraid of you, Joe. But . . . that night when you drank so much brandy . . . you were different, then.'

'I know,' he whispered. 'But . . . not *that* different. I know I got a temper when I drink, but . . .'

She left the kitchen with the dirty water to empty it outside because, like the pipes, the drains were frozen. He followed her through the main room and waited while she poured the water into the snow and then followed her back when she brought a bowl of fresh snow back to be melted in the morning, slapping along behind her in his felt boots like a puppy. After she'd put the bowl on the draining-board and stacked the dishes neatly beside it, he took hold of her arm again. 'Don't hate me like they all hate me, Laura.'

'I'm too scared to waste my energy hating anyone.' Hallick's grip tightened and she stood very still. 'You're hurting me, Joe,' she entreated. 'Please let go.'

His hand tightened again. 'Just tell me you don't hate me . . . that you don't think I . . .'

'Let her alone, Hallick.' Denning was in the kitchen doorway.

Hallick snatched his hand away. 'I wasn't doing anything to her.'

'Not yet,' Denning came toward them. 'Not yet.'

'It's all right,' Laura said quickly. 'We were just talking ...'

'You didn't look very happy about the conversation,' Denning said, still coming forward. The sun was setting and the sky framed by the kitchen window was a faint pink, but there was still sufficient light to see Denning was enraged. 'Can't keep your hands off them, can you, Hallick? Have to touch them, don't you?' He took hold of Hallick's poncho and dragged him away from Laura. 'You filthy little bastard, who do you ...'

'*That's enough!*'

Laura had often heard voices described as whips, but it was the first time she had ever actually felt one lash. And it was coming from Skinner's mouth.

'He was pawing Laura ... he had his hands ...' Denning growled.

'*Let ... him ... go*,' Skinner lashed again, and Denning released Hallick abruptly. 'Go back to the tent and shut up. We have enough problems without this kind of thing.'

'He ...'

'*Do it!* Do what I say or I will cause you both a great deal of pain. I don't want to, but I can and I will, so I suggest you do what I tell you to do, and *now*!'

The sun had winked out and the room was shadowy.

'Who do you think you are?' Denning snapped.

'In this particular place and time I am God. Believe it. You will do what I tell you to do or not only will I hurt you, I will *let you die*. Somebody has to say yea or nay around here, and I am *it*. Get back to the bloody tent before I break your necks. *Move!*'

They went.

Laura stood where she was and watched Skinner slump suddenly against the side of the cabinet. When she went over and touched his shoulder, he was shaking. 'David ...'

'Was he hurting you ... touching you ...?' The whip

193

was gone and his voice was as soft as it had always been with her.

'No . . . he was only . . . begging me to believe he didn't kill Anne.'

'And do you believe him?' .

'I . . . don't know. Do you?'

'I don't know either.'

She felt the hard shape of his shoulder beneath the layers of velvet and shirts. 'Would you have hurt them, David? Really?'

'Oh, yes.' He lifted his head, but she couldn't see his face, only the shape of it in the darkness and the glitter of the spectacles. 'Oh, yes, quite easily, I'm afraid.' He cleared his throat, straightened. 'Quite easily.'

She was afraid to ask him how. She didn't really want to know.

But she believed him.


Laura lay in the dark tent, watching the faint fingers of firelight stroking the undersurface of the blanket roof overhead. All around her the even breathing of the others made a softer echo in the occasional silences of the wind outside. Another storm was building up. David said the wind made people irritable. It was far more difficult lecturing on windy days, he said, something to do with ionisation . . . he talked of so many things in the darkness. And other times he slept deep and still beside her, face-down to obliterate his surroundings. As now. She turned her head and looked at him. In sleep his face was unlined, as innocent as Timmy's, the deep hollows of his eye sockets unmarked by crinkles of laughter or anger. She freed a hand from her blanket and reached out to touch the line of his eyebrow, unable to stop herself. Timmy had curled up next to Hallick tonight, somehow sensing his misery, and there was nothing between David and herself. Nothing and everything.

Restlessly she sat up, hugging her knees. It probably *was* the wind that was making everyone so irritable. Goade and Denning had had another argument over their card game, and Sherri and Morgan had returned from one of their forays to the bedroom obviously angry with one another. She sighed, and in taking a breath noticed a sharp acrid odour. Moving as gently as she could she crawled a little way down the tent and peered at the oil stoves. The oil in one was very low, so low that one of the tails of wick was beginning to dry out, and the wick itself was smouldering slightly. It was Goade's job to check the oil, but he had forgotten after his argument with Denning, apparently. There was no point in waking him, she could turn a valve and fill a tin can as well as he could.

Gathering up the lantern she managed to get over the others and out of the tent, pausing to light the lantern with a twist of paper she ignited in the dying flame of the oil-stove. She slipped into her felt slippers and shuffled through the kitchen to the generator room.

Raising the lantern she advanced into the darkness, intimidated by the massive bulk of the silent generator and the looming curve of the oil tank. The walls of this room weren't insulated and the cold in here was bitter. Goade had wrapped some rag over the tap of the oil tank to prevent his flesh freezing to the metal. She put the lantern down and got on with what she had to do, it was too cold to linger. As she waited for the tin to fill she heard someone shuffle into the room behind her.

'I saw the oil was getting low,' she said over her shoulder. The steps halted.

'It's all right . . . you go on back. No sense in both of us catching pneumonia . . . and it isn't even our job, is it?' she said with a laugh.

She cut off the flow and held the tin under the spigot to catch the last few drops. There was little point in her tidy gesture, however, because when the blow came from behind the tin in her hand flew wide, spreading oil in an arc across the tank, the small petrol engine, and the forward corner of the generator. As she was dragged away from the tank a long smear of oil came with her, leaving a shining snail-track across the gritty concrete floor.

# Twenty

'Who the hell is Axel Berndt?'

Larry Carter stared at Captain Skinner in high frustration, his blonde hair in strings over his forehead and a smudge of ink across one cheekbone. If his loss of perfection gave the Englishman any satisfaction he didn't show it.

'According to Interpol Axel Berndt is the name of the dead man downstairs. And, I would imagine, the real name of the mysterious Mr Brahms. He was running his own show; there was no intermediary.'

'And where is the real Doppler?' Ainslie asked from behind his desk. Captain Skinner knew he had just come from yet another hysterical confrontation with his ex-wife and her pompous husband, and it had not gone well. Ainslie looked about three miles past bone-weary. The press, too, were clamouring for their 'rights' . . . the right to truth, excitement, increased circulation, and someone to blame. The whole story had come out with Berndt's death.

'In a sanitorium in Switzerland, trying to live another hundred years with the help of someone else's glandular secretions. Axel Berndt was one of his major clients, apparently, and asked Doppler for the loan of his passport in order to carry out "secret negotiations". He'd done it several times before.'

'Some negotiations,' Carter muttered, throwing himself onto the sofa.

'The post-mortem report says Berndt had only weeks to live, if that. I guess he knew it.' Ainslie concluded. 'Which leaves us where?'

'Which leaves Laura where, you mean,' Carter corrected him.

'He said they were safe,' Ainslie said. 'He was dying, he *knew* he was dying – but he said they were safe.'

'Then presumably they *are* safe,' Captain Skinner said without conviction, dropping his sheaf of papers onto Ainslie's desk and sitting next to them, swinging one leg.

'Does Doppler – the one in the sanitorium – does he have any ideas?'

'None.'

'The son?'

'None. Doppler's son, I presume you mean.'

'Hey, that's right . . . he said, "tell my son", didn't he?' Ainslie exclaimed, sitting upright. 'Where's *Berndt's* son?'

Captain Skinner slapped at a fly that had settled on his wrist. 'Berndt had no family, he never married. No son listed anywhere in the books.'

'He *said* "my son",' Ainslie insisted. 'I couldn't have made a mistake.'

'You didn't,' the Englishman said. 'Berndt was engaged once, many years ago, to a Norwegian actress. It was, as they say, a Great Love. She died in a train crash. Her name was Eva Boyar.'

'Boyar . . . *Boyar*! That's the name of one of those . . .'

'Yes,' came the tired admission. 'Yes . . . it seems likely that Karl Boyar is Axel Berndt's son. If there's a way of proving it, and I should imagine there is, he stands to inherit something like two hundred million pounds.'

Carter began to laugh, weakly at first, then with growing hysteria. The other two watched him expressionlessly, waiting for it to finish. 'And he went to jail for stealing . . . a few paltry industrial diamonds. Didn't he *know*?'

'According to the boy's maternal grandparents, no, he did not,' Captain Skinner said. 'Berndt had directed them never to reveal it until he gave his permission. Until the boy was "ready", apparently, whatever he meant by that.'

'But he could have . . . with all that money he could have . . .'

'The boy refused to see his family, and Berndt had other scores to settle,' Captain Skinner pointed out. 'He was a very efficient man. Perhaps also a very vengeful man.'

'And now he's a dead man . . . we know where *he* is. Where's my daughter?' Ainslie demanded. 'Where's your brother . . . where are the rest of them?'

'Wherever he put them,' Captain Skinner said. 'Wherever he's been keeping them safe.'

# Twenty-one

She was cold.

She was so cold it hurt to breathe. It was hard to breathe, too, because she was nearly buried in the snow and her body didn't seem willing to make the effort.

Rolling over on her back she felt the snow compact under her, and nearly cried out as the pain in her head and all her joints stabbed deep. Above her the tossing intertwined branches of the birches moved against a wavering curtain of pearlescent colour that flickered, moved and was occasionally obscured by racing cloud shapes. As the wind flowed over her she realised two things simultaneously: there was a lump on the back of her head and the front of her was wet and exposed because her velvet suit was gone. She wore only her two dresses and her light underthings and she was freezing to death. Was meant to be freezing to death.

Agonisingly she forced herself to sit up, swept by nausea and the wind. The glow of the Aurora made her dress change colour as she watched. Where was the house? How far was she, how long had she lain there? After a moment common sense told her she could not be far and could not have been long gone. Whoever had intended the sub-zero cold to kill her hadn't counted on it shocking her to consciousness instead. Looking down she saw she still had the felt boots on. How incongruous they looked with only her bare legs rising from them. Why take off the velvet suit and leave the boots? And then she saw the tracks.

One set coming to where she lay, none going back. Whoever had carried her out had worn boots, too, just as shapeless and just as large. Had dropped her and walked backwards in the same tracks, making it look as if she had wandered out here to wait for death alone.

The cold must have been clearing her head because it all seemed very obvious. It was also killing her a little more with each minute that passed. Already her face and hands were numb, her legs nearly lifeless. She tried to stand up, slipped, fell onto her face again. All right, then, she would crawl, she would drag herself, but she would *not* die just because somebody wanted her to die.

Her body ached, her hands stung as she pulled herself along elbow deep in the snow, her hair lashing her face like tiny ice-glazed whips and her breath flowing from her mouth and nostrils like smoke. Again and again her body sank into the treacherous snow and she began to cry, feeling the warm tears run cold by the time they reached her chin or dripped off her nose. Back, from track to track she crawled, sprawled, dragged and pushed herself. She made faces, David said one made faces to prevent frostbite, but you can't make faces with your hands and knees.

She wasn't going to make it, she *was* going to die. Who would cook the meals, who would correct Timmy's sentences, who would listen to David talking about Satie and sun-spots and Japanese netsuke figures? How terrible, how unfair, how incredibly stupid.

And then there was somebody there, two legs in front of her. Two felt boots and two big legs encased in red velvet. She raised her head, up and up, looking through the frozen strands of hair that clattered against her cheeks, to see Goade smiling down at her.

'Jesus Christ, you're tough,' he grinned.

Had he brought her here, then, was it he who wanted her to die? But why?

She wanted to stand up, to strike at him, to fight – but could only crouch there on all fours in the snow, sobbing in frustration. His face was a large shadow split by the white of his teeth.

And then the face was obliterated as he stripped off his poncho and bent down to put it over her, tugging it over

200

her head and then grunting as he scooped her up into his arms and wedged her against his chest, freeing one hand momentarily to brush the snow from her legs, and then turned to start moving through the heavy snow as quickly as he could, following her tracks and his own.

The branches scissored overhead and the wind tore the words as he gasped them out. 'What the hell were you playing at? You crazy? What did you do . . . go out to the loo and decide to take a walk in the pretty woods? Daft as a brush, you are . . . don't cry . . . you're wet enough already . . .' His gruff angry voice muttered on over her head as she clung to him numbly, astonished, grateful, carried like a child with her legs hanging over his arms.

'I didn't want to die . . .' she managed to say through chattering teeth.

'What?'

'Somebody put me out . . .'

'Don't talk . . . here, look . . . we're back, it's all right . . .' He was pushing through the open door of the house, kicking it shut behind him, shouting. 'Skinnie! Frank! Gimme some blankets or something for heaven's sake . . . hey!'

And then it was all a blur. David's astonished face over her own as he gathered her from Goade's arms. She was being rolled in blankets, rubbed hard all over, carried into the familiar stinking sweaty beautiful warmth.

'I didn't go out . . . somebody took me . . . I was coming back, David . . . I was trying . . . don't be cross . . . I tried so hard . . .'

'Yes, I know . . . It's all right, love . . .' His hands were on her head, touching the huge lump on the crown, and he was so angry, so very angry. Everyone was shouting and moving around the tent, banging into one another and trying to help. Skinner put his face down and she heard his whisper close to her ear as he tucked the blankets around her. 'You're all right now, it's all right . . . just rest . . . quietly, now . . . shh . . . don't talk, my darling . . . quiet . . . be quiet.'

Somebody, Sherri she thought, handed him a bowl of

soup and he made her drink some. Someone was chafing her feet with a towel, roughly. It was Joe, she could see his long hair moving as he bent over them way down there, way way way down there far away about a hundred miles away and receding faster all the time. Goodbye, goodbye. And she slept.

According to Goade he'd awakened and seen the oil-stoves burning out, remembered at last he'd meant to fill them, and had gone out to the generator room to find 'oil slung all over the goddamn place' and Laura missing. After checking the tent and all over the house he'd come to the conclusion that she'd gone to the toilet. He had waited, then knocked on the inner door to the entry with no response. Finally he'd opened it and found her red velvet suit in a heap on the floor and the outer door open. The area beyond the door was churned up for quite a distance but after going to the perimeter of their 'disposal area' he'd discovered her tracks leading into the woods, followed them, found her crawling in the snow and had brought her back. End of story.

'She must have been half-asleep,' Morgan concluded. 'Why take off her trousers *and* poncho to go to the toilet?'

'She said somebody put her out there,' Goade challenged, staring at Hallick. 'Somebody took off her clothes and then put her out there to die.'

'No . . . not me,' Hallick protested.

'You were after her last night in the kitchen . . .' Morgan accused.

'Joe wouldn't hurt Laura . . .' came Timmy's voice from where he was sitting beside Sherri. She was holding him almost absent-mindedly, gazing off into the shadows.

'Joe *likes* to hurt women, Timmy,' Denning stated flatly.

'No . . . no . . .' Timmy pulled away from Sherri's loose grasp and crawled over to put himself almost protectively between Hallick and the others. 'Joe's my friend . . . you're just being mean . . .'

'It's all right, Tim,' Skinner reassured him wearily. 'No one's going to hurt Joe.' He tucked a corner of the blanket

202

more tightly around Laura's shoulders. 'No one's going to hurt anybody. We're all going to settle down and go back to sleep and we can talk about this in the morning. There's no point in saying anything now . . .'

'I'm not sleepy any more,' Timmy argued automatically.

'Even so . . . lie down and try to sleep,' Skinner told him. 'That's what we're *all* going to do.' After some mutters and grumbles, everybody did lie down, but from the sound of their breathing it didn't sound as though any slept. Skinner lay beside Laura, putting himself between her and the others. He wondered if the violence of his rage was being felt by the murderer through the juxtaposed mattresses. He hoped so. He devoutly hoped so.

When the first grey light of day became apparent, Skinner sent everyone out of the tent on various tasks, and then shook Laura gently until she awoke and looked up into his eyes. She seemed all right, but still very sleepy. After a moment, she smiled. 'Hello.'

His response was so unexpected that it took her a moment to comprehend what he was asking. 'Were you raped?' His eyes were darker shadows in his shadowed face, and she felt the tension in him as he waited for her answer.

'No. Nothing like that. Somebody hit me, that's all I remember. I'm sure I could tell if . . . I could tell, couldn't I?' she whispered.

There was a flicker of a smile, even within his anger. 'One would expect so. I'm not a woman but . . . one would expect . . .'

She tried to explain as carefully as she could, but it was all so hazy and blurred now. 'I couldn't sleep. I saw the oil in the stove was low, so I went into the generator room to get some. While I was there somebody came in and I told whoever it was to go back because two of us didn't need to be cold . . . and . . .'

'What?'

'I said it wasn't even our job, was it? So why should we both get cold . . .'

203

'Getting the oil is Goade's job.'

'It wasn't John . . . it wasn't John behind me, David.'

'Who was it?'

'I don't know, I didn't see.'

'How did you know it wasn't Goade, then?'

She thought for a minute, then shook her head. 'I don't know . . .'

He considered this for a while. 'Were you bending over when you were hit?'

'Yes . . . yes, I think so. I'd just turned off the valve . . .'

'Damn.'

'Why?'

'Because you were hit on the crown of the head. If you'd been standing up the person would have to be taller than you . . . but if you were bending down . . .'

'Oh.' She wanted to reach out and touch him but the blankets were tucked so tightly around her . . . she lay still, watching him breathing, blinking now and again, deep in thought. His beard was darker than you'd expect with blue eyes and beige hair, and it seemed another mask behind which he hid.

'David?'

'Hmmm?'

'Was Anne raped?'

His eyes focused on her face. 'No . . . Anne wasn't raped. It was only made to look as though she was.'

'How do you know?'

He flushed deeply and looked away toward the fire. 'I . . . checked. There was no . . . no . . .'

'No semen in her vaginal tract?' she said in a matter of fact voice, and he jerked his eyes away from the fire and back to her face in astonishment. 'That was a very sensible thing to do,' she approved. 'That would prove Joe hadn't done it.' A tiny crease appeared between her eyebrows. 'But why ask me if *I* was raped?'

He simply could not believe that the awful thing he'd done did not seem awful to her at all. It still made him feel sick, but she thought it was sensible. Sensible? What kind of a man did she think he *was*?

'I had to be sure . . . I'm sorry.'

She looked into his face, saw how distressed he was at having to tell her about what he'd done. It seemed a perfectly obvious thing to do, as far as she was concerned . . . unpleasant, perhaps disgusting, but . . . necessary. One has to do necessary things. If a child is bleeding you don't faint, you stop the bleeding. If a dog is in pain beyond enduring you take it to the vet to be put down. If loving someone isn't going to do them any good, you try to stop loving them. None of these things was easy, but neither did they present any alternatives, so in a sense they *were* easy. You get on with them, or you're not worth – what was her father's favourite phrase? – not worth the powder to blow you to hell. It seemed to her this man was worth a great deal of powder.

'You'd better be very nice to me from now on, David Benjamin Skinner.'

'I beg your pardon?'

'I said you'd better be very nice to me, or I'll tell everyone you're a dirty old man,' she threatened compacently.

'What?' he choked, staring at her.

'Well . . . a dirty young man, then.' He didn't seem to know whether to laugh or cry, just kept staring at her in that wide-open vulnerable way, and she couldn't bear it. 'It's all *right* . . . you're . . .'

'You little bastard! You little pervert!' It was Morgan's voice, shrill with outrage. There was a scuffling outside the tent, and a crash. Skinner scrambled to the flap of the tent and disappeared through it. Laura disentangled herself from the blanket and crawled after him, pushing the loose blanket aside to see what was going on.

Morgan and Hallick were rolling about on the floor beside the tent, and it looked like Morgan was trying to strangle Joe. Goade was standing in the kitchen doorway holding Timmy by the shoulders, a look of interest on his face as he watched the two men turn over and over one another, struggling. Denning was at the far end of the room where he had been prying up woodblocks from the floor. Sherri was closer, and her eyes were burning as she seemed to suck in the violence like nourishment for some inner craving. She seemed proud of Morgan as he tightened his hands around Hallick's throat, a cave-woman watching her man display his strength.

'Stop it!' Skinner shouted, going over and taking hold of Morgan's shoulder. 'I said stop it, Tom!' Morgan paid no attention, almost smiling as he looked down into Hallick's purpling face.

'*Dammit!*' Skinner exclaimed, and raising his locked hands over his head he brought them down on the back of Morgan's neck with all his weight behind them. Morgan's arms seemed to melt, and he fell off Hallick onto the floor.

'He had it coming,' Denning called across the room. 'He was after Sherri . . .'

'Wasn't . . .' croaked Hallick. 'Wasn't touching . . . just . . .'

Morgan shook his head and tried to struggle to his feet as Hallick rolled over, coughing.

Skinner stood looking at Morgan for a moment, then shook his head in regret and turned away. 'It seems to me that you should channel your frustrations into something more constructive, Tom . . . helping break up the furniture, for example.'

'Do you know something?' Morgan said to no one in particular. 'I think I've had enough of being told what to do. You act like this is a *class* on survival techniques, Skinner . . . little rules, little lectures, little demonstrations . . . I believe I'm tired of it.' He was on his feet now, and his face was almost lax, as if he wasn't behind it at all but had gone off somewhere to think things over. He took a step toward Skinner and Skinner stepped back.

'Don't,' he warned.

'I think I would enjoy killing you,' Morgan said reflectively.

'Don't,' Skinner repeated, as Morgan reached for him.

It only took a second. There was a heavy thud as Morgan's body landed on the heap of coverless books in the corner. The denuded pages were all that was left after they'd taken the covers for fuel and the end papers for lessons. Skinner straightened up.

'I see you've managed to spill oil all over the floor again,' he said in annoyance. It wasn't the first time the oil had been spilled – the dark blotches on the wood floor and the ever-present stink was as much a part of their existence as the constant tension about Hallick. 'We'd best mop that up before someone slips on it. Bring some of those papers, will you, Tom?'

He turned to face Morgan and Morgan lunged, catching Skinner around the knees and bringing him down with a crack that sent his glasses spinning into the baseboard. Morgan bore down on the man beneath him, grinning with anticipation as he brought his arm back to smash a fist into Skinner's face. But as his knuckles came forward, Skinner squirmed beneath him and caught hold of Morgan's wrist as it grazed his jaw. With a sudden turn he freed himself, sprang to his feet still holding the wrist, lifted a foot and brought it down squarely in Morgan's ribcage before letting go and moving back.

The air wooshed out of Morgan in a howl, and then there was a silence filled only by his gasps as he tried to regain his lost breath. Skinner was still breathing quite evenly and everyone else was so shocked and transfixed they were unable to make a sound. After a while Morgan got up and tried again.

This time he caught hold of Skinner's throat, but Skinner simply brought his own arms up and caught hold of Morgan's, at the same time swinging his feet up and falling backwards. With Skinner's feet in his stomach, Morgan sailed through the air once more, landing against the stack of empty tins by the door. They scattered noisily across the floor.

'I do really think that's enough, you know,' Skinner declared, getting up and brushing off some of the sooty grit that had transferred itself from the floor to his clothes. 'It's a ridiculous waste of time and energy.'

Goade watched him fussily brushing his clothes. 'What's that . . . karate?'

Skinner glanced at him. 'Oh, no. Just judo. I took it up when I was teaching in Japan some years ago. I find karate a bit over-done, all that smashing and yelling and so on.' He walked over to retrieve his glasses and found the other shaft had broken. 'Now that's unfortunate.' He was still examining them when Morgan started toward him from behind.

'No . . . Daddy . . . no . . .!' Timmy ran forward to intercept his father, but Morgan swept him away in his eagerness to get at Skinner. As Timmy banged into the kitchen doorframe he squealed. Skinner whirled around. He saw Timmy falling and he saw Morgan coming. Tossing the two pieces of his spectacles onto the top of the tent, he went toward Morgan.

They collided virtually opposite Laura. She saw that, unlike the calm of a moment before, Skinner's face was now white with anger. His blue eyes were almost black, and his mouth was pulled back in a grimace of rage as he bent to drive himself into Morgan's oncoming attack. The whole of his compact body was a fist, and Morgan simply folded over him like a limp glove. Skinner continued to thrust forward, throwing Morgan back into the floor and coming down on his chest with his knees. Then, methodically, he began to beat Morgan's face with his fists, right, then left, again and again, battering his head from side to side like a metronome.

'David!' Laura shouted, horrified as his fists continued to strike, flecks of blood flying each time Morgan's head jerked from side to side. She realised that it was the sight of Morgan pushing Timmy that had triggered Skinner's temper but, even so, his reactions ran deeper and darker than that last ignoble display of a man abusing his son. She scrambled to her feet in order to get to him, and the cold air of the outer room sluiced her body with ice. Reaching out for support she grabbed the near edge of the tent and tried to steady herself, but it was the edge of the hot foil-covered stove surround that her hand encountered, and she jerked it away, losing her balance. Heavily she fell against the surround. It seared her shoulder even as she heard the makeshift stoves inside tip over. She cried out with the sudden, unexpected pain, and then saw burning oil running out from under the foil to slide flickering toward the heap of coverless books that rose in the corner between the bookshelves and the back wall.

Skinner had stiffened at the sound of her brief, involuntary scream, his right fist frozen in mid-air above the unconscious Morgan. When he turned it was to see Laura on her knees, clutching her shoulder, and beyond her a rising wall of fire as the books and oil combined with the flames.

Goade was already running toward the fire and began to stamp on the nearest books with his felt boots, but almost immediately one of them became saturated with the oil and began to burn, too. He kicked it off impatiently and it fell against the far side of the tent, unnoticed, as everyone raced over except Sherri who'd gone down on her knees beside Morgan and was sobbing and stroking the blood from his face.

'Tommy . . . Tommy . . .' Her thin voice was lost in the shouting as Skinner and Goade tried to slide the red carpet off the top of the tent to smother the flames, and Denning and Hallick raced for the door to start bringing snow from outside.

'Laura . . . get dressed!' Skinner shouted. She ducked as the carpet slid over her head. The two pieces of his spectacles fell near her and she grabbed them up and then crawled back into the tent, jamming them into her bra. She pulled on the red velvet suit frantically as the smoke from the fire started to flood into the tent. Suddenly, right in front of her, the side of the tent began to smoke, char, and then ignited. As she watched, a lick of flame ran up the artificial fibre of one of the blankets like a zipper and the material fell back to show Skinner and Goade beating at the flames that were now soaring high enough to reach the

209

underside of the balcony. The condensation had formed icicles there, and one by one, they fell like daggers down into the flames.

'David . . . David!' she screamed. 'The tent's on fire!' He stared at her through the frame of fire that was widening every second. She began to grab things at random, stuffing them into her poncho as the flames spread.

'Joe!' Skinner called, and as Laura struggled out of the smoke-filled tent she nearly tripped Hallick who was running with an armful of snow, followed by Denning carrying more.

'Put it on the tent!' Skinner directed, but realised immediately that the thing was already beyond them. Thousands of gallons of water surrounded the house, but they could do no more than bring it in handfuls, armfuls at best.

The heap of loose pages was burning fiercely now, and the wind rushing in through the open door began to combine with the updraft from the flames. Burning bits of paper floated up, swirled, and drifted down onto the spilled oil by the kitchen door. It caught almost immediately. Everywhere the oil had spilled, splashed, rivuleted or soaked the fire followed. And wherever it went, it found more on which to feed, as impossible to contain as the mercury from a splintered thermometer.

Laura ran over to where Timmy was cowering against the wall and picked him up. Behind her the tent was now alight in several places as the burning paper settled on the blankets that had been kept dry by the heat encapsulated within the tent. Layer by layer the sheets and blankets began to burn, some melting apart, some smouldering where natural fibres inhibited the flames but did not stop them. Then, from beneath the mound, thick black smoke began to roil and spill heavily across the floor like a flood, rising. The foam padding within the sofas and chairs was alight, and she remembered that this black coiling smoke was deadly. Deadly.

'David . . . that smoke . . .' she called, pointing to the

ugly black whirls and snakes of smoke that were purling across the floor. He whirled around, saw where she pointed, and shouted back.

'Get the boy out . . . go down to the sauna . . . down by the lake . . .'

She didn't want to leave him, and started to shake her head, clutching Timmy against her. He ran across, grabbed her by the arm. 'Get out . . . take him out, dammit . . . there's nothing you can do here . . . and help Sherri get Morgan out, too. Go on . . .'

'No . . . you come, too . . . David, please . . .'

In the far corner a massive chunk of ice that had gradually grown like a crystalline cobweb at the end of a rafter melted free and fell with a crash, and she jumped, falling against him. 'Please, David . . .'

'Get out . . . we won't stay long . . . it's going to go, but we have to save what we can . . .' he explained, pushing her away. More ice fell as the heat in the room grew. The teak panelling behind the books was burning now, and the flames were spreading in the airspace between the panels and the joists to which they were attached. The oil on the floor around them was burning and the heat made them sweat beneath their heavy clothing. 'My bloody fault . . . my fault . . .' he groaned, leaving her and running over to grab Hallick by the arm. She couldn't hear what he was saying, but he was gesturing toward the kitchen, toward the store-room. The flames had a voice, now, crackling and licking and roaring along the shelves of books, the whole tent was a hollow shell of flames that collapsed in on itself, driving the black smoke toward them.

She pushed Timmy toward the open entryway door, and went to help Sherri.

Morgan was coming around, moaning and cursing through his broken mouth.

'We have to get him out . . . that smoke . . . get him up off the floor . . .' she choked at Sherri. Together they helped Morgan to his feet and staggered with him away from the fire that was taking root in a dozen places and sending new shoots and tendrils to flower everywhere. Denning and Hallick pushed past them, heading for the store-room. At the door she turned. Over the rise of Morgan's shoulder she could see Skinner and Goade being driven toward her by the flames. For some reason she couldn't understand Skinner had been trying to get through the sliding door into the music room, but it had been impossible. His velvet poncho was smouldering in several places, as was Goade's.

'Got to . . . got to . . . got to get . . .' Morgan was saying, trying to get back to the tent. Sweat was mixing with the blood on his face, streaking it into a crimson zebra mask.

'No . . . let them die . . . let that bastard die . . .' Sherri screamed, tugging at him. Laura's hand acted without consulting her, and she found herself slapping Sherri's face.

'Go on, get out, get out . . .' she hissed at her. 'You've got what you wanted all along, haven't you?'

She left them to struggle out alone and ran back.

Skinner was almost spellbound, blinking through streaming eyes as the fire ate away the house in front of him. The room that had seemed almost an ice-cavern had been coated only on the surface. Behind the shell of frozen condensation the wood structure had remained dry and took the flames eagerly to itself. Wood well dried by central heating – panelling, joists, struts – was ripe and ready for burning. The black smoke from the foam upholstery was swirling around his thighs, now. Suddenly the big picture window, thick with frost and too quickly heated, buckled and shattered, falling out to join the broken sheets and shards of its companion on the snow in front of the house. Immediately the wind that had been only gaining admittance through the open door at the side flooded in and added its icy breath to the heated air that was cycloning around the big room. The thick oily smoke rose, combined with the white smoke. The room became a haze of grey poisonous vapours. Choking and gagging he turned and ran into Laura who had come up behind him.

'The boots . . . the boots . . .' she kept repeating with what seemed idiotic insistence, waving her arms. He squinted and saw what she meant . . . the line of felt boots lay along the edge of the flaming oil. He nodded and she ran to scoop them up, then came back to him.

'Oil's going to go . . .' Goade shouted. Skinner had grabbed Laura and was dragging her to the door. He looked at Goade who was pointing toward the kitchen. Suddenly he realised what the big man was screaming about. Beyond the kitchen lay the generator room. And in it, the two tanks of diesel oil and petrol.

'Get her out . . .' he said, pushing Laura into Goade's startled embrace. It was necessary to jump the pool of burning oil in the doorway, but he saw that the flames had not yet reached the generator room, and he ran over to slam the heavy door shut. How much time would that buy? Jerking open one of the cabinets he began to pull out what he could . . . plates, pans, cups, cutlery, whatever he touched he took, piling the small items in the large. There was simply no telling how much of the house would burn and how much would survive. He'd sent Hallick and Denning to fill as many boxes as they could with food before the flames got to that end of the house, and wondered if they'd have enough sense to break the window over the deep-freeze and throw tins through it. He thought he'd told Joe to do that. He *thought* he had but he wasn't sure.

If only he could have got to the Boesendorfer.

Why hadn't he started earlier . . . when he realised he was going to *have* to walk out before spring, when he'd added up the food and the mouths and the days and found the tally didn't match?

He couldn't carry any more, he had to go. The heat was building up around him and several of the cabinets he'd grabbed things from were now in flames. If it hadn't been for the wind blowing in the gap where the picture window had been he wouldn't have made it through, but the storm's fitful rise had become a full gale now, and it blew the smoke away as it fanned the flames. He glanced toward the store-room but couldn't see whether Hallick and Denning were still in there or not. The stairs were completely in flames now, and he saw he couldn't make it out of the door. Running around the blazing circle of furniture that had supported the tent he felt flames lick him from both sides as he tried for the window. When he felt the low frame against his legs he climbed over it and took the full force of the wind on his left side. It nearly had him over, and he felt the broken glass of the window cutting his feet through the layers of socks and blanket strips. He had got a few yards beyond the glittering barrier of broken glass when the two tanks in the generator room went within seconds of one another.

It was as if a large flat board had hit him from behind, sending him sprawling on his face into the snow. Smoke spewed out through the window frame and objects began to dot the snow – bits of wood, metal, some in flames, falling and disappearing under the drifts. The big pot he'd been carrying was underneath him. If it hadn't been for the snow it would have smashed his ribs. As it was he thought a few might have gone.

The house was rumbling and roaring behind him now. The explosions had fractured the inner structure, soaked it with oil and petrol, there was no saving it. He could feel the heat on his back, thought it possible his hair was on fire, and his clothes. Rolling over in the snow he found himself facing a house that seemed to be built of flames. Walls of fire, rafters, roof beam, floors, doors, everything was visible and everything was burning. The snow around it was melting, already the glass he'd stepped on was lying on bare ground that glistened and reflected the fire. The line of melting snow seemed to almost have a life of its own, moving toward him, flowing, falling in on itself, the surface black with soot and smut, cracking, splitting to show the white underneath and then that, too, melted.

He felt a hand under his arm and Goade was helping him up, pulling him away.

'Did the others . . . did everyone?' he rasped, his throat raw from the smoke.

'Think so . . . come on . . . let's get the hell out of here.'
The wind was tearing at their clothes and pellets of snow

were beginning to fly and sting their heat-seared faces. Goade took a step and nearly tripped over the potful of cutlery and oddments Skinner had been carrying when he fell. The big man looked down.

'What's the matter . . . couldn't you pull the kitchen sink off the wall?' he asked, sarcastically.

Skinner stared back at him. 'I was too busy putting on my mascara.' He started coughing and clutched his ribs.

'Never mind,' Goade consoled him. 'You haven't got any eyelashes left anyway, you bloody twit.'

# Twenty-two

'Berndt's servants have identified Webb as a man who'd become close to Berndt over the past few months,' Captain Skinner said. 'He's a consummate actor, full of charm and a real manipulator. Looks like he convinced Berndt that this was the way to accomplish what he wanted.'

'To accomplish what Berndt wanted – or Webb?'

'What do you think?'

'And Webb is with the hostages now?'

'Yes.'

'And what *he* wants is that information?'

Captain Skinner nodded. 'From what we know of Webb it's probable that the entire financial deal we've been investigating was his work. He was one of ours once. Until he decided what we paid wasn't worth what we asked him to do for it. So he set up business on his own. God knows he knew how. Old contacts must have warned him the net was closing.'

'What happens when he gets the information?'

The Captain shrugged. 'I suppose it depends on the situation, doesn't it? He went with them to get it, but if he gets it he'll still expect to get away with it. Remember, he thinks *we* think he's just one of the hostages like the rest. I imagine that if Berndt's part of the deal had gone through he would somehow have managed to slip away from the rest once they were turned loose. If not, he'd just walk away and leave the guards to do what they threatened to do. Kill them. Either way he gets out of it alive, all evidence against him gone and, presumably, with three million dollars in gold on tap when he feels safe enough to draw it out of that Swiss account.'

'You think that was for him, too?'

'It certainly wasn't for Berndt.'

'The people from the Embassies . . . what about them?'

'Could be red herrings . . . could be he wanted them replaced with people he could use later on. Who knows?' He lit another of his cigarettes and sat down in Ainslie's chair behind the desk. 'You still haven't told me about the gold and the oil.'

Ainslie shrugged. 'Geologists' reports turned up gold and oil at the North Cape. The Norwegians wanted to set up operations quietly before all the vultures descended. They also wanted ACRE – seemed like a good idea to combine them. That's all, nothing more. The whole thing is five – maybe eight years away yet. I still don't honestly understand why he wanted it stopped *now*.'

'He was dying.'

Ainslie grimaced. 'We're *all* dying. Some are just dying faster than others, that's all.'

Captain Skinner watched him through the cigarette smoke. Ainslie had started falling apart when Doppler – or Berndt – had died, and he'd gone on falling apart ever since. With the line broken, he seemed to be convinced that his daughter was lost to him forever. He kept blaming himself for arguing with a sick man, cutting short the time in which they could have made him talk and reveal where Laura and David and the others were being held. It did no good to tell him that dozens of agents were following Berndt's lines back, tracing contacts, looking through everything from receipts to wastebaskets, searching for the links that might lead to how, and where, the hostages had been taken. Now that they had a starting point, they would eventually get to the end of it.

Ainslie said that 'eventually' was enough time to die in. And he was right, of course.

Captain Skinner leaned forward onto the desk and looked at the last set of pictures they'd brought back from the house in the desert. Idly, pointlessly, he began to move them around the desk top, trying not to see the hopelessness in his brother's eyes.

# Twenty-three

Maybe it was a mistake, Skinner was thinking, standing at the entrance of the sauna and looking through the trees at the skeleton of the house before shutting the door. Maybe we all should have just taken deep breaths of that black smoke. It would have been quicker.

The rocks in the pit glowed dully, revealing the shapes that lay around it in dim outline. He dumped the tins on the floor, and Goade raised himself on one elbow and squinted over at them.

'That the last?' he croaked. They were all hoarse with the smoke they'd inhaled – those who could talk at all.

'I saw a few more lying under the trees,' Skinner spoke with difficulty. 'We can get them tomorrow.'

Goade fell back onto the slat bench, and watched as Skinner began to hammer at one of the tins with a rock. With everything he'd gathered up from the kitchen the one thing he hadn't brought was a tin-opener. That had been in the tent. 'You bring any wood?'

'Outside.' It was amazing to find, under the snow that had fallen since the fire, quite a lot of wood that hadn't burned at all. The house was gutted, a total wreck. Even the Boesendorfer was gone – and with it the steel wires he'd intended to use to make snowshoes. The felt boots would have been warm enough if he could have kept them dry. He finally succeeded in bashing in the top of the tin and held it out to Sherri who turned her head away.

He and Goade had found Morgan this morning, under the wall next to his wife. He'd gone back to drag her body away from the fire and had been there when the tanks exploded. Skinner hoped he'd been unconscious as he froze to death beside her. He hadn't been burned at all. Neither of them had been.

He held the tin out to the child who was huddled next to Hallick.

'Not hungry, Skinnie,' Timmy whispered. 'You eat it.'

'I had some,' Skinner lied. 'I think it's peaches. You like peaches, don't you?'

Timmy took the dripping tin and began to pick out the contents gingerly. After a moment's chewing he said, 'I think it's pineapple.'

'You like pineapple, too,' Skinner grated and began to cough.

'Not so much,' Timmy said. 'Laura can have it when she wakes up.'

Skinner took the tin and put it down under the bench, then went over to where Laura lay on the bench opposite, reaching down and touching her forehead. She was definitely feverish, it was more than the glow from the sauna fire he felt. Her exposure, followed by the smoke she'd inhaled – he supposed it was inevitable.

'She bad, Skinnie?' came Hallick's croak. He'd still been in the store-room when the tanks blew up, but had been crouching at the far end of the deep freeze. The blast had driven the freezer into him and crushed his arm and chest against the shelves. He had managed to get out of the window at the back, but was in a bad way. They'd splinted the arm – it was all they could do – but two of the fractures were compound and they didn't have any kind of antiseptic. Denning was near to him, asleep and breathing with some difficulty. Age and smoke were a bad combination, too.

'Not good . . . but not too bad,' Skinner replied.

'She's a tough one,' Goade said gruffly. 'She'll be okay.'

Skinner looked at him but didn't speak, just settled himself beside Laura, leaning back against the bench. It was quiet in the small room, and warm. Whatever other virtues the sauna lacked, it didn't lack that. It had been possible to drag embers from the house and get a fire going in the pit before night-fall, once the main fury of the flames

219

had abated. The hardest part had been keeping the embers alive in the wind until they got them here. The storm had gone on all night, and it had probably been the snowfall as much as anything that finally put an end to the conflagration. The flames had been out by the morning, only their memory kept alive under the stones in the pit.

He knew that the next day or the day after he'd try to walk out. He also knew it was virtually hopeless. But if he and Goade brought enough wood down, and located as many tins as they could, the others could stay alive for quite a while in the sauna. And if he could figure out a way to break off and bend the smaller branches of the birch trees he might still fashion some snow-shoes. Wearing Morgan's velvet suit and maybe Denning's as well as his own, taking a little food with him on a sledge . . . maybe. Maybe. He just had to keep going south, the stars would guide him. Everything else had changed, but they hadn't.

He began to cough again. They were all coughing so nobody had paid much attention to his, but he knew some fluid had begun to collect deep in his lungs that he couldn't seem to bring up. He lay down and turned on his side to cough again, dozed off, woke, dozed again, woke again.

The room was dark, except for the glow of the fire. He'd better get in some wood so it would last through the night. Wearily he dragged himself to his feet, picked up one of the last sticks and thrust it into the stone pit until it began to burn, then went through the outer room and opened the door. A swirl of moisture surrounded him. Mist? A white-out, that was it – they'd had them at the Pole. The hanging impenetrable fog that would descend without warning over everything, obscuring even the nearest objects. Perhaps it would have lifted by morning.

He stepped out and felt for the heap of charred wood he'd dumped by the wall of the little hut. As his fingers touched it he stiffened, then relaxed. Now he was hearing things, on top of everything else.

He began to pick up the lengths of wood, scrabbling blindly in the snow, when it came again. He straightened and peered into the fog, holding up his little torch. Then he began to laugh at himself.

'Is that you, Santa?' he called out, hoarsely. Jingle bells, jingle bells, jingle all the way. He laughed again, coughed, leaned against the wall. Skinner, he told himself, you are well and truly finished. Now you're hearing bells. Next it will be elves.

But the bells went on, no matter how hard he shook his head. He stepped away from the wall and held his torch up, spluttering and flickering in the mist. There was a movement in the whiteness . . . a swirl of something darker – a shape.

Suddenly, impossibly, he was facing a reindeer.

There was no mistaking the long face, the big dark eyes on either side of the narrow head, and certainly no mistaking the antlers. It stood there, staring into the glow of his torch with a wild and antic eye, tossing its head and making the bell under its throat jingle again. It couldn't be Rudolf, he decided, because its nose was wet and black.

'Now, let me guess,' he conjectured, shuffling forward and expecting the animal to disappear into the haze of his imagination. 'Dasher? Dancer? Prancer? Vixen?' He began to laugh again as the animal backed off a step or two in the face of his advance. 'Donder? Cupid?'

A voice spoke not far from him and he turned, expecting the jolly shape of Santa and finding instead something even more grotesque.

The reindeer shied as Skinner's laughter escalated to helpless hysteria, and the bell under its throat gave a cheerful *glissade* of notes. Skinner was laughing so hard he was weeping, still holding the torch up, rocking back and forth in the snow.

He laughed and cried for quite a while before he collapsed.

# Twenty-four

'Captain Skinner?' It was the co-pilot, leaning over the back of the next row of seats, speaking as softly as he could. 'There's a message, sir. I think . . . you'd better come up front and take it yourself.'

Glancing across the aisle at the dozing figures of Ainslie and Carter, Captain Skinner nodded and got up to follow the officer up to the Flight Deck. He was gone quite a while, and when he came back his face was pale. Ainslie had woken and watched him approach with a sinking sensation in the pit of his stomach.

'Have they found them?'

Captain Skinner sat on the arm of the chair across from Ainslie and felt in his pocket for his cigarettes, taking his time about lighting up. Finally he looked into Ainslie's face. 'When the Finnish Police got to the house it was a burned-out wreck. There were two bodies there – the Morgans. They were down in a sauna by the lake. There was no sign of the rest of them. There were some tracks leading to the lake, but it had started to snow by the time they arrived and . . .'

Ainslie buried his face in his hands. 'Gone again . . . my God, gone again . . .'

'How long before we get there?' Carter asked gruffly across Ainslie's shoulders, his face taut with disappointment.

'Another six hours or so . . . we'll refuel in London and then go straight across. We'll have to change to a chopper at Helsinki – Ivalo isn't built to take a jet of this size.'

'Ivalo . . . where's that? Oh, never mind . . .' Carter turned away before Captain Skinner could speak. After a moment the Englishman sat back down in his own seat, and reached over to pick up the pack of photographs.

Well, David . . . you sent the message and I didn't get it in time. I'm sorry. He turned the picture of Skinner on its side once again, then righted it and stared into the face that stared back at him. Above it, in the wall, lay the answer they'd had on the desk in Adabad for days. Somehow David had ascertained their exact location and with painstaking care had embedded tiny fragments of glass along the lines of the woodgrains in the teak panelling of the wall. When the flashbulb went off, they reflected its light. So tiny, so irregular that the kidnappers had not noticed and neither had he – until he'd turned the picture sideways and read the stars. Or had them read by a Morse expert.

*A. Berndt. Lat 67 N Lon. 27.5 E.*

Forgive me, David.

They had been kitted up with parkas and boots, and when the helicopter finally settled on the edge of the lake, they stepped out into a swirling haze of snow. Beyond the wind of the whirling blades, however, the snow flakes fell slowly, drifting down fat with moisture and clumping to their shoulders and hoods like cake icing. Struggling through the knee-high drifts, they approached the blackened fingers of wood and chimney that pointed accusingly at the low grey sky. Several men were moving about in the ruins which were being rapidly obscured by the snow. Ainslie wiped the melting flakes from his eyelashes. It had seemed bitterly cold in Helsinki, but here the air was slightly warmer, although still uncomfortable to breathe.

A hooded figure turned as they approached, and came to meet them. He introduced himself as Inspector Leem and he was not a happy man. Gesturing with his pipe he told them as much as they knew. It wasn't a long speech.

'And down there . . . that's the sauna hut?' Captain Skinner asked, looking over his shoulder. 'Where you found Morgan and his wife?'

'Yes,' Leem said. His English was slow but excellent.

'The wife had been dead a long time. It seems they moved there after the fire . . . we found a few tins and so on. But they have apparently been taken away again . . . or tried to walk out on their own. We have helicopters searching, but the snow . . . it is difficult, the visibility. . . .'

'We noticed, coming across,' Carter said. 'How far could they get in this?' He glanced up as yet another search helicopter swept over them, heading toward the flat of the lake ice.

'They have not . . . cold-weather clothing, you understand? The bodies in the sauna wore only light clothing. The stones in the sauna are cold . . . they have gone some time before, I think. Some time.'

'And you don't hold out much hope?' Ainslie asked.

Leem looked at him and shook his head. 'I am sorry.'

'Damn . . . damn!' Ainslie beat his hands against his sides and walked away from the others toward the house, slowed, stopped, gazed unseeingly at the mess of blackened wood and stone.

Another helicopter snarled over, circled the house and set off in another direction. Captain Skinner saw Leem's face draw together in a frown as he looked past them toward the lake, and he turned to see what had caused the policeman's reaction. Two more figures were struggling through the snow from a helicopter that had just landed. One in the same regulation gear the other policemen wore, and one so different that he blinked his eyes several times to make sure he was seeing what he thought he saw.

The second man was very tall, and his thigh-length white cape was embroidered with bright bands of red and blue. He wore it over a jacket drawn in at the waist by a wide leather belt. His boots were knee-high, seemingly of soft leather bound round the legs with more embroidered bands. On his head was a tall hat ending in what looked like jester's points, from which several brightly embroidered streamers fell down over the back of his neck. When the pair of them drew closer he saw the big man had high cheekbones that underlined light blue eyes. His face was scored by deep

224

wrinkles – a man who lived outdoors and watched the sky.

Leem went forward to talk to the newcomers, and shouted for one of the men searching the ruins. When this man had joined the group there was a brief interchange, and then, incredibly, Leem began to pound the strangely-dressed giant on the arms. The man was laughing and nodding, and gesturing away to the north.

Carter and Captain Skinner hurried over, and Leem turned with a triumphant grin. 'They have them . . . they are all right . . . they are all right!' Carter stopped, looked incredulously at the group and then at Captain Skinner, who felt a smile rising throughout his body. Then Carter ran back for Ainslie, shouting.

'This man is named Aslak,' Leem explained. 'He is a Lapp . . . fortunately one of my men speaks some Lappish . . . he came to investigate the smoke from the fire because he knew it was on Berndt's property, and Berndt has been a great friend of the Lapps for many years. Aslak in particular, apparently – or he wouldn't have come. It takes a lot to make a Lapp leave the reindeer herd when they're on the move because they do not drive them, you see, only follow. And reindeer are the way and wealth of a Lapp.'

'But . . . why is he . . . here now?' ,

'Twice a year the reindeer cross Berndt's land and all the north,' said Leem as if it were something every school-boy knew. Probably every Finnish schoolboy did, but it was news to Captain Skinner. Ainslie and Carter came up as Leem spoke.

'Is she . . . are they . . .'

Leem turned and smiled. 'He says he has a child, two women, four men. Come . . . he says the women are ill, and one of the men is injured, badly. We'll have to get them to Inari as fast as possible . . . there's a good hospital there.'

Aslak went with them in the first helicopter, and through the interpreter he tried to explain what had happened. Ainslie kept questioning him about the women until he was sure about Laura, and after that he was quiet, staring

225

out at the snow that streaked the plexiglas dome of the helicopter. Captain Skinner knew his brother was safe, too – Aslak spoke of the 'spectacles' one wore. In the heat of the helicopter they were all sweating and steaming, but from Aslak's heavy clothing and boots there came only the scent of open spaces and – although it seemed odd – dried grass. Leem finally explained that the Lapps insulate their feet against the sub-zero weather with a special grass they gather and dry during the summer. 'It's better than anything else . . . none of the new fibres can match it . . . like so many things, old is still best when it suits the way of life.'

Ainslie's head turned at that. 'You said the Lapps cross the land here twice a year. How far do they go?'

'Oh – hundreds of miles, some families. From the Norwegian coast right across Finland to Russia . . . they've been given the freedom of the borders by all the governments. They follow the natural trails of the reindeer.'

'And how far north do they go . . . as far as the North Cape?'

'Oh, yes, certainly. All through there. Why?'

'What if the North Cape were developed?'

'Developed? You mean . . . industry, cities . . . ?'

'Something like that, yes. What would that do to the Lapps?'

Leem puffed on his pipe for a minute. 'Eventually – destroy many of them. The routes would be disrupted, you see . . . and the reindeer feed only on the moss that grows . . .' He puffed a while longer, looking at Aslak's profile outlined against the plexiglass. 'Mind you . . . it is happening gradually even now, the children are being educated and are leaving the wandering life to come south. Many families are settling . . . they are a very independent people but in the end . . . well . . . it happens everywhere today, I think. The old ways go.'

'You said Berndt was a friend to the Lapps,' Captain Skinner recalled as the helicopter began to descend toward the snow field below. A great straggling herd of reindeer sprawled in a moving skein across the whiteness, constantly

226

turned back by men dressed in clothes as bright as Aslak's, and by the smaller fast-moving shapes of dogs. Several large tents dotted the snow, almost like the tepees of the American indians, but lower and fatter.

'Yes,' Leem said, raising himself slightly to look down. 'Through his representatives, of course. Apparently his mother had been of Lapp descent. He insisted they should be allowed to choose to settle rather than be forced to abandon a way of life that has been theirs for . . . oh, many centuries. Beyond history, really. He was a modern man, an industrialist himself as you know, but he said or wrote once that the Lapps should have "the dignity of time" to make their peace with progress. He was a good man . . . but a strange one. You knew him?'

'No . . .' Captain Skinner's eyes met Ainslie's across the cockpit. 'I think I would have liked to . . . in different circumstances.'

'So with many people . . . but . . . he hid,' Leem said. 'Hid from our world. Hated it, some say.'

'Yes,' Ainslie agreed. 'Yes – he hated it.'


The Lapps had put the surviving hostages in their largest tent. They were all around the fire that burned in the centre, covered by layers of rugs and skins. Ainslie and Carter were first in, scanned the faces, and rushed over to Laura. David Skinner, and a young Lapp woman, were trying to get her to drink something. He looked over his shoulder and then handed the cup to the girl.

'David . . . my God . . . are you all right?' Captain Skinner staggered over the thick layers of matting to his brother's side and took hold of his arms.

David smiled at his brother wearily. 'As you see, Edward . . . quite all right.' He glanced over at the two men who were next to Laura, watched for a moment, then turned back to the Captain. 'How are you?'

'How am I?' Captain Skinner asked, and then started to grin. 'Getting along, thanks.'

'Good,' Skinner murmured. 'Good.' He looked again

227

toward Laura, then settled himself on the skins cross-legged, rubbing his beard with both hands as if it irritated him. 'They'll have to get her to a hospital . . . I think she has pneumonia. Hallick . . . that's Hallick there . . . has a fractured arm and crushed ribs. And Goade has a sprained ankle but that's not so urgent, of course. Let me see . . . what else? Ummm . . . the boy, Timmy, he'll need looking after because his parents are both dead . . . and the woman over there has become rather . . .'

'David . . .' Captain Skinner interrupted.

'What?' Skinner was still looking around the tent, checking his brood, or so it seemed to his brother.

'It's all over now. You can stop worrying . . . it's all finished.'

Skinner's eyes were again on Laura, who was now propped up in Carter's arms and being patted all over by Ainslie, who seemed to think some bits of her might have dropped off somewhere. 'Yes . . . well . . . I suppose it is, at that. It's been . . . difficult, Edward. Damned difficult, you know.'

'Difficult,' Captain Skinner echoed drily. 'I would imagine so.' He, too, looked around the tent. 'Would you excuse me a moment . . . there's something I have to do.'

Ainslie couldn't stop touching his daughter, couldn't believe she was alive, here, whole, his again. 'Don't worry, sweetheart . . . we'll get you home, it will be all right . . . oh, baby, I'm sorry we . . .' He was interrupted by the sound of Edward Skinner's voice pitched unnaturally into official tones.

'Alan Joseph Webb, I arrest you in the name of the Queen for offences against the Official Secrets Act. I must warn you that . . .'

Ainslie turned as the Captain's voice continued. Turned, froze, stared. The Captain was arresting Denning.

'Oh . . . and for the murder of Anne Morgan, Edward,' Professor Skinner put in from across the fire, the light reflecting in the lenses of his glasses. He started to reach up to take them off, seemed to think better of it, and dropped his hand into his lap again. 'I'm afraid he killed Anne Morgan.'

Goade glanced across the tent at Skinner in surprise. 'When did you come to that conclusion, Skinnie?' he asked in an unmistakable English accent.

'Just now. If Edward is arresting him for espionage, then it must have been he who . . .'

He was interrupted by a thin, keening laugh that raised the hairs on everyone's neck. Sherri, from where she lay, facing the wall of the tent. 'And everybody blamed Joe . . .' she trailed off in a sob. 'Even Tommy . . .'

'No!' Denning exclaimed.

'No . . .' Laura gasped, opening her eyes. She struggled to sit up in Larry's embrace and everyone turned to look at her. It was only a brief distraction, but Denning caught at it. Throwing back the robes that covered him, he made a lunge at the Lapp girl who'd moved away to allow Ainslie and Carter to talk to Laura. He encircled her throat with one arm and with his free hand ripped the broad bone-handled knife from her belt. Then he pushed her at Captain Skinner who was crouching on his heels and poorly balanced. The two of them fell back into the fire, knocking over the pot of stew that was simmering there. The brown liquid flowed thickly over the fire and instantly the tent was filled with steam and a smell of burning meat.

'Don't worry . . . he won't get far,' came Goade's calm voice through the steam and the shouting.

Captain Skinner struggled up, beating at his parka. The Lapp girl was so astonished she didn't even notice her own sleeve was on fire until Skinner began slapping at it.

'You obviously didn't read that dossier I sent you,' Captain Skinner rebuked Goade. 'He's qualified on both light planes and helicopters. Who do you think must have flown you out of Adabad in Berndt's private plane?'

Laura's protest had sent her into a racking fit of coughing. She kept trying to speak, but could not. She saw the same anger growing in David's face that had been there when Timmy had been knocked down by his father. She knew this time it was for her, she knew exactly what he was going to do, but couldn't call out to stop him.

Larry Carter and Skinner were out of the tent within seconds of one another, and she turned to her father. 'Stop him ... Daddy ... he'll be hurt ... he can't ...'

'Larry can take care of himself, kitten, don't worry,' he reassured soothingly, but she shook her head, tried to speak, and started to cough again. When the spasm had passed she was too weak to talk and he eased her back onto the pile of hides, wiping her mouth with his handkerchief, then wiping her eyes as she began to sob, helplessly. 'You told me *he* was Webb,' Ainslie accused over his shoulder, nodding toward Goade.

Captain Skinner paused at the mouth of the tent, looked at Goade, grinned, and looked at Ainslie.

'I said "the man in the picture" – Denning and Goade were together in that photograph.'

'You *said* that he was ...'

'I lied,' Captain Skinner admitted cheerfully, and went out.

'He's a dreadful liar,' Goade added, rolling over onto his elbow and trying to get up. 'The only one worse than him was Cross. They made quite a team.'

When Captain Skinner emerged from the tent and stood up, he noticed several things at once. The snow had stopped, and it felt marginally warmer. No one was near the helicopters except the police. There was no sign of Carter, or of David. The Lapps were going about their usual camp chores calmly, and one of the women smiled at him.

Leem started toward him with a questioning look on his face, and began shouting something about the ambulance helicopters being held up temporarily because of the weather.

Then he saw some of the Lapp men running toward the reindeer herd with angry shouts, waving their arms. A figure was dashing between the brown and creamy-beige backs of the animals, and antlered heads were tossing wildly. From behind the round shoulders of the farthest

230

tent, he suddenly saw two more figures – Carter and David, struggling through the snow toward the herd. And then he saw nothing – because a wall of white abruptly swept down and swallowed herd, running men, tents, helicopters and himself.

It was almost like going deaf and blind together.

The shouts of the men and the barking dogs became faint and muffled, and even the people who had been near him seconds before, speaking or clattering cooking pots and harnesses, were silenced. Only the tinkle of the bells from the herd pierced the whiteness with any clarity. He could see only the faint loom of the tent next to him, the one further along was no more than a darkening of the mist. Someone crashed into him from behind. It was Leem. Then Ainslie appeared in the mouth of the tent and stared around him as he stood up.

'White-out,' he observed with professional interest. 'What's its elevation?' he asked Leem.

'About a thousand metres,' the policeman told him. Ainslie looked at Captain Skinner.

'All he has to do is go straight up . . . we can't even take a shot at him once he . . .'

Leem looked puzzled and Captain Skinner explained quickly about Webb.

'I will warn my men.' Leem whirled and was lost in the mist after three steps.

'Where . . .' Ainslie started to ask, and Captain Skinner gestured toward the faint sounds of shouts, barks, and bells.

'Over there,' he indicated. 'Somewhere over there.'

When the mist came down on them, Skinner automatically grabbed Carter's sleeve. 'Stand still,' he directed, but Carter struggled on a few more steps before stopping.

'He'll get away!' he shouted, trying to pull his arm free. Skinner held on tight.

'He can't see any better than we can,' he pointed out. 'Forget your eyes, use your ears.'

Carter stared at this man he'd only seen in photographs

231

up to now. Skinner was bigger than he looked in the pictures – about five ten, and much more solidly built than he would have expected an egg-head to be, somehow. He was wearing the bulky clothes the Lapps had given him, but he still had the wire-rimmed spectacles on. The effect of this badge of aestheticism was somehow marred, however, by the fact that on one side it was held together by grimy adhesive tape, and on the other with a thin winding of reindeer hide. And there was something about the face behind those spectacles, too. It seemed to Larry Carter that professors of astronomy didn't usually wear expressions like that.

He decided that he did not like Professor David Benjamin Skinner at all.

And wondered why.

'He'll be trying to get back to the helicopters,' Skinner calculated. 'If we stand here there's every chance he'll pass quite near us.'

'And there's every chance he won't,' Carter snapped. 'Stand here if you want . . . I'm going after him.'

'That would be foolish,' Skinner said. 'Really.'

Carter gave him a disgusted look and stalked off into the mist toward the sound of the bells.

Skinner stayed where he was, pulling his hood back and tilting his head to one side. He was not interested in the bells, or the barking dogs, or the shouts of the angry Lapps. He was interested in only two sounds – laboured breathing, and the crunch of snow underfoot. After a while he summoned up images of Denning as he had been in the house – eating, playing cards, putting wood on the fire. Denning was left-handed. He began to move to his right, taking a step, stopping, listening, taking another step. Inside his sleeves his hands were drawn up into fists, because one other image kept blurring the rest – Denning, something heavy in his left hand, striking down Laura from behind then carrying her outside and leaving her in the snow. He may have been moving slowly, but his rage was racing unchecked through every muscle in his body. Denning had tried to kill Laura.

He was going to kill Denning.

A figure loomed up out of the mist not four feet from him. His hand started toward the wide leather belt the Lapps had given him along with the rest of the outfit. In it, because no Lapp would have considered him dressed without one, was a duplicate of the broad-bladed knife that Denning had taken from the girl. But the figure was not Denning, it was Aslak, the tall Lapp who'd found them at Berndt's place.

'Skinna?' Aslak said, coming forward.

Skinner could see that Aslak was furious. He started pouring out a flood of Lappish, waving toward the sound of the bells and the barking, but the only thing Skinner could pick out of the rush of words was 'Poro'. Aslak was angry because the deer were being disturbed and many of the does were heavy with calves due in the spring. Two of Aslak's children had been to school in Inari and actually spoke a little English. It was through them that they had been able to communicate, although more had been done in mime than anything else.

Aslak paused in his anger and looked more closely at Skinner. Then he asked a question, not a single word of which Skinner could understand. Just as Skinner opened his mouth to speak – although what he intended to say he never did know – there came the sudden sound of shots, in the direction of the herd. Aslak's eyes widened, and he turned toward the sound with his thick white cape swirling around him. Skinner turned, too, and listened. There was a great silence everywhere, and then, through his feet rather than his ears, he sensed it. The shots had made the herd panic . . . it was not a rumble or a roar, just a growing vibration through the snow that came easily through the soft leather of their boots.

'Poro,' Aslak said in a horrified whisper. Suddenly he began to yell, running forward into the mist, waving his arms. The barking of the dogs began again, closer now, and the shouts of the Lapps were more frantic, as they tried to halt or turn the invisible herd away from the tents that lay directly in their path. Looking around him wildly, Skinner tried to see the herd, but there was only the growing crescendo of the bells, and then, beneath that, the hoarse panting grunts of the deer as they ran.

One minute he was alone in the mist, the next surrounded by a mass of heaving jostling animals, their thick tongues out and their nostrils billowing more white into the mist. They were not running fast, but there were so many of them that he was knocked first one way and then another, buffeted by their creamy flanks and thrusting heads. One buck's antlers caught momentarily in the sleeve of his thick embroidered coat, then ripped free as the animal tossed its head. He felt cold air penetrate the gash but couldn't tell whether the sharp prongs of the antler had reached his flesh or not. He felt his balance going as the heavy bodies thronged and charged around him. They did not try to run over him, but separated as they reached him, flowing around him like warm water over a rock. The big splayed hooves threw up gouts of snow that struck him in the face again and again.

He began to yell and shout as Aslak had done, and the deer gave him a wider berth, some hesitating and being pushed aside by others who kept on, creating eddies and whirls in the mass. Wild they might be, but their long co-existence with the Lapps had taught them that a man did not yell without reason. Their memory of the shots was dimming, their panic abating, but not enough. Not nearly enough. They still poured past him, toward the tents. If there were so many here, right beside him, how far did they stretch on either side? He'd had only a glimpse of the herd from the sledge on which Aslak had brought them to the camp. Five hundred? Six hundred? How were they running . . . wide or long? He kept shouting at them and waving his arms, and then saw, through a swirl in the mist, someone else caught up in the stampede. Denning.

He was not more than a few yards away. He could see him because the motion of the animals was tearing the mist apart. Denning was running with the herd, using their mass as cover in order to get closer to the helicopters. It couldn't have been Denning who fired the shots, he had no gun.

Had Carter been wearing a gun? He couldn't remember. It was more likely to have been one of the Finnish police.

Skinner began to run, too, following Denning as best he could, trying to work diagonally over toward him between the thrusting bodies of the reindeer. Denning was almost directly ahead of him now, running not like an old man but a young one, staggering now and again but keeping upright. Skinner was nearly close enough to reach out and touch him when one of the larger deer caught Denning in the legs and he went down. Skinner tried to leap over him in turn, but fell half across him, and went sprawling. He rolled over, his arms up over his head to protect himself from the stampeding hooves.

Denning still had the knife in his hand. As he saw Skinner and registered his identity, he raised his arm, the knife blade out. It caught one of the passing deer along the ribs. With a hoarse scream it wheeled, blood staining the creamy fur along its body. The antlered head tossed and its steaming breath flowed like smoke. The herd was thinning, they were being given more space. Skinner got to his feet and reached for the knife in his belt. The injured reindeer was eyeing Denning with a mixture of pain, fear, and outrage. It pawed the snow with its big front hooves, gouging fresh gashes in the churned-up surface. Denning began to crawl away from the tossing antlers. The blood from the slash ran down the animal's ribs and began to drop in crimson splashes on the white snow beneath. Denning kept looking from the deer to Skinner, trying to slide away and regain his feet at the same time.

A dog raced up, one of the thick-furred Samoyeds, barking and making charges at the reindeer. With a final toss of its antlers, the deer turned and ran into the curtains of mist, the dog at its heels.

They were alone.

Skinner took an even tighter grip on the thick handle of the knife and started toward Denning.

'I don't know who you really are, but I know what you did,' he croaked.

Denning had got to his feet and held his own knife out

235

in front of him, the blade toward Skinner's belly. 'I didn't kill her,' he said, all trace of age gone from his voice. The eyes above his beard were desperate, but not careless. He was gauging Skinner's threat: his distance, what strength he had left, and his anger.

Skinner paid no attention to his words. They were no more than he expected, an attempt to distract, a bid for time. He kept on coming.

Instead of waiting for it, Denning suddenly darted toward him, making a wide sweep with his knife. Skinner dodged to one side and hit Denning on the shoulder with his left hand, speeding his forward motion sufficiently to make him over-balance. Denning went down on one knee into the snow, but turned quickly enough to ward off the downward slash of Skinner's blade. He caught hold of Skinner's wrist and used it to pull himself up, bringing his knife up with him. The blade hit the edge of the wide belt around Skinner's waist and then skidded off to cut a long slit in the thick wool above.

Cold air flooded in, and he felt a deeper line of cold where the tip of the blade had razored into his skin. Denning's left hand still held his wrist with a steel grip, keeping the knife out of harm's reach.

He kicked out with one foot while flailing at Denning's knife hand with his left forearm. His boot caught Denning in the thigh, too low, too low. And then his hand found Denning's wrist and locked around it. They stood at arm's length in the snow, facing one another, trying to force one another to drop their respective knives, their muscles straining until their arms began to shake.

Then Skinner threw himself backward onto the snow, bringing his legs up together into Denning's stomach and, using them as a fulcrum, he threw Denning over his head and away. Denning's grip broke, and he had to let go, too. Skinner rolled over quickly, bringing his knees up under him and pressing his left hand into the snow. Before Denning could do the same Skinner had launched himself upright, and in two steps was over Denning. He brought his foot down on Denning's arm, meaning to break it. The snow wasn't hard enough, and the arm simply sank deep into the slush. He reached down and made a grab for Denning's knife, but Denning reached up and took hold of him before he could grasp it. Denning was trying to push his foot off the knife-arm.

Skinner kicked him in the face.

The toe of the boot was too soft to do much damage, but Denning's head jerked back under the impact, and Skinner had to follow through or fall. He stepped over Denning, pivoted on his forward foot, lost his balance, fell anyway. He felt the ribs that had been cracked in the explosion give further, and the pain was intense. The cold air was searing his raw throat every time he breathed in. Denning, too, was breathless with the effort, but he was rising, getting to his feet, swaying.

Skinner rolled away, over and over, until he had sufficient distance to give him time to get to his feet. Denning had transferred the knife to his left hand so he must have done some damage to his right arm after all.

Skinner took a deep breath, ignoring the pain in throat and chest. Denning squinted through the mist, heaving and gasping, his right arm numb from the elbow down. Something in Skinner's face seemed to tell him the end had come. His shoulders slumped.

'All right . . .' he gasped, straightening slightly. 'I give up.'

'I don't,' Skinner told him, and raised his knife.

Taking a step back, Denning stared at him in disbelief. Then another step back, as Skinner continued to come for him.

'I said . . . I give up . . . you can't . . .' He was backing more quickly, now, his face blank except for his fear in the face of Skinner's inexorable, steady, seemingly deaf advance. 'No . . . Skinnie . . .' He stumbled on the churned surface of the snow, lurched, regained his balance, still backing away. 'Look . . .' he glanced behind him. The mist was thinning slightly, he thought he could see figures for a moment, coming toward them. Then they were gone again. 'I know it's hopeless now . . . look . . . look . . . I'll . . .' Frantically he let go of his knife, tossed it aside into the snow with a wide gesture of surrender.

'That was silly,' Skinner observed in a conversational tone.

'For god's sake, Skinnie . . .' Denning's voice was shrill with fear.

'Let's not bring outsiders into this.' Skinner leapt for Denning's throat. Denning threw up his arms and turned aside as Skinner's knife slashed past his face. They went down in a sprawl and Denning began windmilling his arms, trying to beat, hit, gouge, hurt Skinner in any way he could. One blow was lucky and Skinner's knife spun away across the surface of the snow, whirling and turning, the dull blade catching an occasional gleam from the sun that was burning through the mist from above. With a snarl of rage Skinner brought his knee up and managed to press it into Denning's stomach, leaning his whole weight behind it. Slowly the air was driven from Denning in a thin, bubbling stream. His pleas were lost in the flow and his eyes stared into Skinner's white and mindless fury. Then Skinner put his hands around Denning's throat, smiled, and began to squeeze.

Denning's body convulsed and he tried to break loose, his fingers scrabbling at the front of Skinner's slashed jacket.

'You shouldn't have left her out there,' Skinner rasped. 'She'd done nothing to you . . . nothing . . . nothing. . . .'

'Didn't . . . didn't . . . asleep . . . took my pills . . . you *saw* me take them . . . asleep . . .' Denning's voice was becoming a mere gurgle as his eyes began to bulge in his empurpling face.

Skinner stopped the pressure. He didn't lessen it . . . just stopped, momentarily, staring down. Denning's eyes were rolling back, his legs had ceased to drum against the snow, his face was like a bruise.

And then, suddenly, it was no longer Skinner's decision. A rope dropped over his shoulders in a perfect circle, lodged in the bends of his elbows. It began to tighten and drag . . . his fingers slipped from Denning's throat, and he was jerked back into the snow while others ran up. The world became a forest of other men's legs and boots. Somebody knelt beside him, loops of rope held lightly in one hand. Aslak. He looked down at Skinner lying breathless and bound in the snow. Behind the skewed spectacles Skinner's eyes were slowly coming into focus again as reality entered the place where his anger had ruled.

'No, Skinna,' Aslak said, shaking his head and reaching out to loosen the lasso from around Skinner's arms and chest. 'No . . .'

Skinner closed his eyes. When he opened them again, he saw his brother's face looking down at him with a strange and worried expression. 'David . . .'

'Did I kill him?' Skinner asked, lying limp and hollow on the cold snow.

'Nearly . . . but he's coming around,' his brother assured him.

Skinner lay looking up at the thinning mist. 'Thank god. I don't think he did it after all.'

The helicopters had arrived to take the injured back to the hospital at Inari. Ainslie stood between the two Skinner brothers watching the police load Laura's stretcher. She had fallen into a coma shortly after Skinner and Larry had run out of the tent in pursuit of the fleeing Denning. Larry moved beside the stretcher, obscuring her from view. After helping position the stretcher he climbed in after it, settling himself proprietorily next to her.

David Skinner was seated on top of one of the Lapp sledges which was already loaded and waiting to make the night's run. He sat very still, his head down. The brief spell of late afternoon sun was ending and more clouds were racing toward them from the north. He looked over at Laura's father, then raised his head.

'Well,' he said, briskly, pushing his hands deep into the pockets of yet another borrowed jacket. 'She'll be all right now, won't she?'

'Larry will take care of her,' Ainslie allowed distantly. 'He's a good boy.' He glanced over at the man on the sledge. 'They're engaged, you know.'

'Yes,' Skinner said, softly. 'Yes, I know that.'

'Goade' limped over. They knew now his real name was Mike Halloran and he was one of Captain Skinner's agents. 'At last,' he announced to Captain Skinner, and the Captain nodded before turning to Ainslie.

'I'm sorry about all the tall tales, General, but not having that list meant we had no way of knowing who at your Embassy was involved in the fraud and who wasn't. You see, we were *hoping* Webb would make a move to stop the courier . . . but we didn't expect the one he made. Cross had indicated that the evidence in his lists would get just about everyone *except* Webb. We might have got someone to talk under pressure, but he would have been long gone by then. It was *my* people who were holding the real Goade in Adabad. We chose him because Mike here looked enough like him to use his passport. When Cross died on us we didn't have time to re-arrange things. The fact that the courier was on the plane had already been dropped into the network to filter back to Cross. We intended to trap Webb if and when he came out into the open. We can hold him on the murder charge, now, of course, while we go through the whole bloody exercise again . . .'

David Skinner had taken off his glasses and was unwinding the grimy adhesive tape from them slowly and carefully. 'I take it you think he killed Mrs Morgan because she had all your information stored in her memory?'

'What memory?' Captain Skinner asked curiously.

'Goade' smiled sadly. 'Anne Morgan wasn't carrying any information for us, Skinnie. *Tom* was the courier.'

Skinner looked up from what he was doing, his hands stilled. 'Oh.' He resumed unwinding the adhesive tape. 'And he knew who Webb was?'

'No. Neither did I. We decided *you* were Webb, actually.'

Skinner stared at him. 'I beg your pardon?'

The big man grinned. 'Nobody had seen Webb for a long time. You're both about the same height, and we never figured he'd literally tie himself up to someone else the way he did with Hallick. But it was a damn good cover, all right, and easy enough with the connections he had. His tame rat at the Embassy simply appropriated Denning's passport and papers and told the old guy to take a pew while he got the wheels in motion with the Adabad police. The *real* Denning has been sitting by the pool in a fancy hotel in Adabad enjoying himself on expenses – *he* wasn't in a hurry to go back. Naturally, we figured Webb would operate on his own – and you were on your own. We figured Webb had killed the real David Skinner and taken his place. I knew Edward, but I'd never met you, had I? Didn't know you'd even be on the plane. Can't say I much liked the idea of having to tell Edward his brother was dead . . . anyway, that's why I kept acting like such a bastard. That way I drew attention to me and away from Tom, which was the most important thing. And I thought if I kept nagging at you, maybe you'd do or say something to give yourself away. I was so *sure* you were Webb at that point.' When Skinner continued to stare in amazement, 'Goade' went on trying to explain. 'Well, Skinnie . . . you were so damn *interested* in everything, weren't you? Kept prowling around, poking and prying. When Anne was killed I wasn't so sure anymore, but Morgan, he was convinced you were, then. He pretended he thought it was Hallick . . . but all the time he was just waiting for a chance to get his hands on you. When Laura got attacked I knew damn well it wasn't you . . . he couldn't see that she was the *last* person you'd use. He thought it was just a distraction, and he blamed himself for Anne's death, because it was him who mentioned her funny memory. That made him go a little crazy . . . he wanted an excuse to kill you, any excuse. When he took his chance . . . well . . . things went wrong.'

Skinner nodded and went on unwinding the tape. 'It

seems to me a great deal went wrong,' he commented mildly, and then his voice sharpened. 'In fact, your beautiful plan went wrong all down the line, didn't it? It seems to me you'd have been better off using a bloody carrier pigeon to send the thing, Edward. Then perhaps Timmy wouldn't be an orphan, would he?'

'David . . .' Captain Skinner began in an apologetic voice, but stopped when his brother held out something to him.

'I believe this is what you're so worried about, isn't it?' Skinner said in a thin, bitter voice. He handed over the curling strip of microfilm that he'd wrapped around the bow of his spectacles and concealed with adhesive tape. Some of the sticky white gum still adhered to it. 'You haven't asked me for my opinion, Edward, but I think you're in a dirty business. I think you should get out of it and open a nice little accounting consultancy somewhere. Look after your wife and children. Stop playing games.'

Captain Skinner took the microfilm and nodded. 'You're probably right, David. You usually are. But at least this particular game is finished, and we've got what we need to stop it for good.'

Skinner put the pieces of the spectacles into his pocket and looked at the diminishing dot of the helicopter as it flew south.

'Yes,' he said. 'Everything's finished now.'

# Twenty-five

'Unfortunately, you can't prove it, kitten,' Ainslie argued, staring out at the snow falling past the window. 'Although Denning – Webb – whatever his name is, still insists he didn't kill Anne Morgan and didn't try to kill you.'

Laura stirred in the bed, tried a deep breath against the pressure in her chest, settled for less. 'Of course he didn't. He didn't have any reason to kill me, but she did.'

'Yeah, maybe.'

'She *did* . . . Daddy, *Sherri* killed Anne Morgan and then tried to kill me. Earlier that afternoon I found some letters of hers and gave them back to her. She was sure I'd read them, but I hadn't . . . not to see who they were from, anyway. I'm sure now they must have been from Tom Morgan. She thought I realised that, and realised she must have killed Anne. I kept trying to think what I'd seen or heard or felt when she came up behind me in the generator room that made me sure it wasn't the Sergeant. It was what I'd *smelled* – her perfume. You don't tend to re- member smells consciously, do you? And then, when she started laughing as the Captain was arresting Denning . . . well . . .'

'But why . . . *why* should she kill Anne Morgan?'

'Oh, *Daddy*. She'd obviously been having an affair with Tom – I'm sure if you tried you could find people in Adabad who knew that. She had a physical hold on him, he *wanted* her – but he didn't love her. He loved his wife. Perhaps Anne found out about it, I don't know. But I think they were leaving Adabad to make a fresh start. His feelings for Sherri were only physical, but Sherri was in love with him. I think she followed them and intended to use those letters to blackmail him into coming back to her. She was desperate.' Laura looked down at the blankets and swallowed. 'If you love someone and they don't love you – it's terrible. The pain is terrible. I think she decided that with Hallick there as an automatic suspect she'd get rid of Anne and then she wouldn't *need* to blackmail Tom – he'd come to her and love her. It never occurred to him that Sherri might have killed Anne . . . he was so caught up in those other things you said were going on. He slept with her because she was there . . . because she kept taunting him with Hallick right from the start. I guess he thought his private life had nothing to do with being an agent.'

He turned from the window and frowned. The oxygen tent had been taken away that morning and he wanted to tell himself she was looking better, but she wasn't. There was a dullness in her eyes he'd still found no way to remove.

'You seem to have accumulated a lot of insight into other people's emotions lately, kitten,' he observed gently. 'But it still isn't proof.'

She sighed, pleated the edge of the sheet between her fingers. 'I know. But the letters *were* there . . .'

'Yes,' he admitted. 'I asked Skinnie and he says he remembers you bringing some letters downstairs.'

'And did you tell him what I think . . . about Sherri?'

Ainslie drew up a chair and sat down. 'Yes, I told him that, too. He seems to agree with you.'

'Well, then . . .'

'But it still isn't *proof*, kitten. And even if it were . . . they couldn't bring her to trial. Not the way she is. Maybe never.' He remembered the last time he'd seen Sherri, just before they'd transferred Laura down to Oslo so he could continue the ACRE talks. Staring, silent, lost and beyond rescue forever – Sherri Lasky was a hostage to another kind of fortune now.

'When he went back for Anne's body . . . she knew she'd done it all for nothing. He cared more about a dead wife than he did about a living woman. After that she didn't care what happened to her,' Laura whispered.

244

'I guess so, kitten. Your Skinnie says it's logical.'

'He would. But he's not "my" Skinnie, and his name is David.'

Ainslie started to chuckle and didn't see the look on her face. 'He's quite a man, your . . . that David Skinner. I wish you could have seen him at the Press Conference. Everybody screaming and yelling questions and demanding lurid details . . . and he just sat there, calm as hell, answering them all in that careful way he has, never getting thrown by any of it. Almost like it had happened to someone else, not him.'

'How is he?' she asked, too casually.

'Oh . . . fine, fine. Seems kind of sad but I guess he's just pooped. From what the others tell me he pretty much kept you all alive up there, one way or another. That right?'

'Yes, that's right.' She imagined David at the Press Conference as her father described it. And saw him, too, moving through the rooms of the isolated house, sleeping beside her in the tent, talking in the shadows, laughing, telling Timmy stories, playing Chopin, holding her close in the cold and the dark, after Goade had brought her back . . . 'That's right, he did.'

'He's offered to adopt the boy, did Larry tell you?'

She stared at him. 'No . . . he didn't.'

'Oh? Funny. Anyway, Timmy's going to live with Morgan's brother . . . he and his wife flew over yesterday. They're nice people, you'll like them. They'll be coming to see you soon, Timmy too.'

'And David?' The sheet was pleated all along the edge, now, as her fingers worried at it.

'Hmmm? Oh . . . no . . . although I see his flowers got here.' He glanced over at the mass of white roses Skinner had ordered that morning from the hotel florist. 'No . . . Larry got them on to the lunchtime flight . . . I gather Skinnie's late for term, and there's some experiments he's involved in. Anyway, honey, I expect he just wants to forget the whole thing. He said you'd probably want to forget it, too . . .' he trailed off, watching her profile as she turned

245

away to look at the window and the snow. 'You *have* tried to forget it, haven't you, sweetheart?'

No, she thought. 'Yes,' she said.

'Good. Besides, as soon as you're well there's the wedding to plan . . . all that stuff. You'll enjoy that.' He stood up abruptly. 'Well, Larry will be along any minute. I have to go over to Helsinki this afternoon.'

'Why?' She looked at him and he grinned.

'Because Joe Hallick *now* has to be extradited from Finland and he wants me to argue for him. One good thing, I understand after all this fuss they're looking into his case again. Everybody loves a hero . . . maybe they'll turn up some new evidence, who knows?' He watched her for a minute, then cleared his throat. 'Anyway, I'll be back by tonight. Oh . . .' he fished inside his overcoat as he lifted it from the back of the chair. 'Skinnie *did* give me this and asked if I'd bring it to you, so he's got better manners than you thought, hey?' He smiled down as he handed her the long, rather lumpy hotel envelope. 'I like him, you know. Kind of an odd bird . . . but I like him.'

'Not so odd, Daddy. Just not . . . not very obvious about things. He's the kind of man you discover a little at a time.'

'Whatever *that* means,' he laughed and left her with a wave from the door.

'Dear Laura (the letter said)
One night at the house you told me you were a "brown paper person" – meaning you thought yourself innocuous. I disagreed, if you remember, and I was right. Through all that's happened you've proved you're a very special woman indeed – you have strength, compassion, humour, warmth. But you give so much away to others, you don't keep enough for yourself. Be selfish, please – otherwise you'll find that when you most want to reach out you won't be strong enough to do it. I know how terrible such a moment can be, believe me. Find your *own* way, don't let them tell you who you are. There's not a vestige of brown paper anywhere about you, Laura. You're everything a man would be proud to love, and I'm sure Larry realises that. I hope you will be very happy.

Yours sincerely,
David B. Skinner'

It was a very neatly typed letter from Professor Skinner. She supposed he'd used a machine at the hotel. But, across the bottom, written hurriedly as if afraid of changing his mind, there was a message from someone else. The pen had dug into the paper, and the words leaned against one another for support, pushed out into the light, exposed.

'*Please accept this. I could not bear any other woman to wear it.*'

Slowly she unwrapped the small tissue-wrapped object that had made a lump in the corner of the envelope. She had saved it from the fire for him, and now he'd sent it back. She was still staring at it when Larry arrived, bounding in with a rush and a kiss and good news.

'Hey . . . guess what? My promotion's come through! Those lunkheads at the Pentagon finally took your father's advice and gave me a new assignment. We, my lovely girl, are going to *Washington* after the wedding . . . can you believe it? It's starting, honey . . . we're on our way.'

She could believe it. Looking up at his handsome face and the new bars on his shoulder, she could well believe it.

He started raving about the parties and the people and the opportunities, only slowing down when he noticed she was staring at something in the palm of her hand instead of giving the expected shrieks of joy and enthusiasm. 'What's that?'

'A wedding present from Professor Skinner.'

'Oh? Funny kind of wedding present if you ask me.' He glanced at her face and shrugged. 'Well . . . I mean . . . it's nice, I guess, but sort of old-fashioned, isn't it? That's not going to be your style, babe . . . when we get to Washington I'm going to pick you out the classiest wardrobe you ever saw. We'll be meeting important people . . . I want my wife to knock their eyes out. Absolutely. They'll all want to meet *you*, all right.'

She closed her hand over the amethyst brooch and dutifully asked about the new assignment.

# Twenty-six

The taxi pulled up at the kerb of the small sidestreet in the small town.

Laura leaned forward to pay the fare, then stepped out and watched the cab disappear into the night. There were no lights on in any of the houses, and no sign of life anywhere in the street except a lone cat washing a paw atop a low brick wall. It blinked at her, curious.

Taking a firmer grip on her suitcase she walked over and undid the gate. The housekeeper had said he would be late, but surely not as late as this? Perhaps she hadn't left the message on his desk after all – she hadn't sounded very bright on the telephone, and the line had been bad.

Laura was weary. She'd discovered that finding your own way can be very hard work.

She went up the two brick steps and started to knock on the door, then hesitated. Very faintly, from around the side of the house, she could hear music. A piano, played very carefully, so as not to disturb the neighbours. Only she and the cat could hear it. She went back down the brick steps and crossed the uneven lawn, soft and damp underfoot in the unexpected warmth of a January thaw. Halfway along the side of the house a set of french windows was very slightly ajar, a thin edge of curtain teased out by the midnight breeze. The cat followed her across the patio, watching her every move with large yellow eyes. She put her suitcase down.

It was dark in the room beyond, but the moon overhead gave enough light for her to see. His back was to her and his shirt collar was just visible above the frayed edge of an ancient brown cardigan. He needed a haircut.

She pushed the window open quietly, stepped to the end of the keyboard and waited. The movement broke his concentration and he turned his head, his eyes widening. He was thinner than she remembered, and looked pale. Or perhaps that was just because the beard was gone now. She smiled but said nothing. After the most minute of hesitations he continued to play, eventually smiling back at her over his spectacles.

Coming around the piano she stopped to touch his shoulder lightly, felt the flex of his muscles beneath her fingertips, then moved on into the room. There wasn't much furniture in it, apart from the piano. She selected a small chair and carried it across, setting it down firmly to face him.

And then, because she remembered David Benjamin Skinner never started the next thing until he'd finished the last, she listened patiently to the closing phrases of the Chopin nocturne she'd asked him to play so often on the Boesendorfer. This piano wasn't nearly so grand, but somehow the music sounded better here.

His fingers continued to find each note with precision, although his eyes never left her face. And when the piano was silent, when at last their shadows moved together in the dark room, whispering, murmuring, merging – she was given her first lesson in astronomy.

We are on a small and lonely planet circling through space. Around us are the great stars: Polaris, Arcturus, Antares, Vega, Rigel, Deneb, Altair . . .

They may *appear* as cold as ice, but their light only reaches us through the endless fall of night because they are burning . . . burning . . . burning.

*Perseus:* Northern Hemisphere. Ascension 3hr. 20m.
North declination plus 45° Algol (β Persei) Mag.
2. Mirfak Mag. 1.9, and others.

### Perseus

Perseus, they made much of him
winging home from destiny,
and ran to see.
He slid from the broad back
twisted the sweaty bridle free
and slapped the beast to the stable,
then sent the star-eyed woman away
to be robed in white
and returned to his table.
Helmet to a corner, shield upon the floor,
he called out for wine and meat –
fell, laughing, into a chair.
'Enough of snakes and dragons –
tell me
what's happened since last I was here?'

Taken from *Constellations* by Laura Ainslie Skinner.

## Jack M. Bickham
## The Excalibur Disaster £1.50

Transwestern Flight 161 is a new Excalibur jet, *en route* from
St Louis to New York. The 199 passengers will never step from
the plane alive.

The crash is a mystery. The cause – pilot error? systems failure?
– lies hidden in a smoky heap of metal and bodies at Kennedy
Airport. One of those bodies was Jason Baines, head of
Hempstead Aviation, makers of the Excalibur. The horrible truth
begins to dawn on investigator Jace Mattingly. There are other
Excaliburs flying, and in each one a tiny, undetected flaw . . .

## Linda Palmer
## Runaway! £1.25

For three children, whose lives have been spent in misery and fear,
escape is the only answer. Escape across the vast American
continent, to the tinsel-wrapped daydream of Hollywood. Snared in
a sordid web of drugs, vice and murder, their hopes are dashed, the
icing on the Hollywood cake turns to dust and ashes – until
Jake Bloomberg comes to the rescue and fulfils his own dreams . . .

'Filled with a gallery of wonderful characters who will come back
to haunt you' SIDNEY SHELDON

## Arthur La Bern
## The Last Cruise 95p

Captain Mallet's ship, *The Sun Queen*, embarks on her final cruise
from Southampton to New York, Cape Town, and her lonely grave
n a Tokyo breaker's yard. For the wealthy passengers it was the
voyage of a lifetime: Parminter, American ambassador with a
neurotic wife and two troublemaking teenage children,
Tewkesbury, the boorish self-made tycoon, Françoise Corbeille,
arrogant and beautiful singing starlet, the mysterious Purcell, a
magician with extra tricks up his sleeve . . .

## Robin Cook
## **Sphinx** £1.25

Beautiful Egyptologist Erica Baron is mesmerized by a centuries-old
statue in a Cairo antique shop, believing she has found the key
to a dazzling hoard of untapped treasure. But there are others, more
ruthless and corrupt than herself, determined to get there first,
whatever the cost. Lost in a deadly web of intrigue and murder,
Erica races to unlock the secrets of a pharaoh's tomb and plumb
the curse that has kept it intact since time began . . .

## Ted Willis
## **The Lions of Judah** £1.25

The year is 1939 and war looms. The Nazis, at the peak of their
power, hound the Jews with vicious malevolence. Kurt Reiss is
Jewish, and determined to fight for his people – whatever the cost.
When he is captured, after an assassination attempt on Goering, he
knows his hour has come. But he is wrong. Instead, he is offered
a deal he dare not refuse, and where the penalty for failure is
unthinkable in its consequences . . .

'Willis is a born storyteller' DAILY MAIL

## Alan Scholefield
## **Point of Honour** 95p

It was the perfect subject for a book: Captain Geoffrey Baines
Turner VC killed in action on the bloodstained French coast – and
who better than his son to write the story of one man's Dunkirk?
David Turner begins his research and uncovers a vipers' nest of
half-truths, malicious rumour and blackmail. His father, revered by
some as a hero, is branded rapist and murderer by others . . .

'Completely believable' DAILY TELEGRAPH

## Garson Kanin
## Moviola £1.50

The Hollywood novel that tells it all.

Meet 92-year-old B. J. Farber, rich and cantankerous, a movie
mogul about to sell his legendary studios. This is his story – the
scandals, heartbreaks, passions and mysteries – Fatty Arbuckle's
sex disgrace, Chaplin the comic genius, Garbo's tragic romance,
the discovery of Monroe and her mysterious death, the trials and
backroom feuds behind some of the greatest films ever made.

'More film stars' real secrets than there are footprints in the cement
of Hollywood Boulevard' DAILY MAIL

## Emma Cave
## The Blood Bond £1

Eleven years ago, three people sealed a terrible secret in blood.
Now, they meet again in London – Esther, the apparently cool
career girl, a slave to sexual passion ; Brian, the frivolous Chelsea
idler who courts violence by night ; Charles, the smooth social
charmer with the pale eyes . . . Terror mounts as the past exerts its
fearful spell and the games of a summer night merge into a bloody
day of reckoning.

'Entirely original, entirely enjoyable . . . Emma Cave has mastered
the secret of horror story writing'
AUBERON WAUGH, EVENING STANDARD

## Matthew Vaughan
## Major Stepton's War £1.25

Gervase Stepton, a major in the Confederate army, has seen the
brutality and experienced the agony that makes a soldier the
killing machine he is. Serving under General Lee and the legendary
Stonewall Jackson, he fights at the blood-soaked battle of Bull Run.
Captured, Stepton suffers savage torture at Fort Delaware. Sure as
hell he'll kill the Yankee bastards who slaughtered his family back
home in Virginia. A tale of vengeance wreaked from the whorehouses
of Richmond to the battlefields of Manassas and Malvern.

## Leslie Thomas
### That Old Gang of Mine £1.25

Meet ODDS – the Ocean Drive Delinquent Society – a band of geriatric drop-outs chasing excitement and danger in their twilight years in the Florida sun. There's Ari the Greek, K-K-K-K-Katy the dancing queen, Molly Mandy who supplies the gang's arms cache (and one and only bullet), and ex-hood Sidewalk Joe.

Hot on their heels comes the baffled Salvatore, local police captain, and bumbling private eye Zaharran. Never was organized crime so disorganized.

'Hilarious' DAILY MIRROR

## David Fraser
### Blitz £1.50

An epic novel of a city and its people, pushed to the very brink of endurance . . . Saturday 7 September 1940 : the first day of an ordeal which reduces London to ruins and its people to despair. *Blitz* recreates the first shattering eleven days of this holocaust ; tells of three families, their lives torn apart ; of an American war correspondent burdened with the task of reporting the living nightmare ; of the courage, self-sacrifice and hope shared by all, when every day brings a thousand tragedies . . .

## Patrick Alexander
### Show Me a Hero £1.25

Into the 1980s, a tyranny of the Left rules Britain with Saracen troop carriers, while propaganda cloaks the corpses. Backs to the wall, the Resistance plans Operation Volcano, while up at the sharp end of every strike is the man they call the Falcon – a Robin Hood with an Uzi machine-gun and nerves of steel. One of nature's heroes, temporarily useful, ultimately expendable . . .

'Probably very near the truth' YORKSHIRE POST

## Colin Dexter
## **Service of all the Dead** £1.25

*Churchwarden murdered during service*, the headlines screamed. Inspector Morse found there was more to it than that. After the second death the case was closed; everyone agreed that the murderer had gone on to commit suicide.

Everyone, that is, except Morse. He sensed that unrest still reigned over the Oxford parish of St Frideswide. He found new evidence and discrepancies; and then, another body . . .

'He pulls off his tricks with confidence and cunning GUARDIAN

## Earl Thompson
## **Caldo Largo** £1.50

Johnny Hand is in love with life, freedom and the unbridled pleasures of sex. In the brawling world of seagoing men, every woman in every bed in every port is a challenge — from Lupe, who shrugged off her marriage vows as easily as her dress, to Cehlo, the teenybopper temptress . . . A novel that swells with life and explodes with action — the deadly perils of Cuban gun-running, the scorching love nests of Mexico . . .

'Earl Thompson is an exceptional writer — full of power, able to expose a whole world, to create people who blaze off the page' COSMOPOLITAN